WHEN TO LET GO

JO COX

1

Adie strode across the Market Square, dodging a kebab that lay in the road like a splatted pigeon, and grunted at Josh to steer a wide berth. It would be a casualty of Saturday night, which had rapidly become Sunday morning when they'd missed the last train out of London and headed back into the bars. After eventually attempting to sleep on a bench at the station for so long they each had slats imprinted on their faces, they'd boarded the first one just after seven and now made their way through the deserted streets of their home town looking like a pair of zombies the morning after Halloween.

"I'm hungry." Josh slowed and shot The Anchor a longing sideways glance. Given it was the only pub with early opening and fried breakfasts, the implication was clear. "How long ago did we eat those chips? It has to be at least five hours, right?"

Adie ignored him at first. She wanted sleep and then a run, but knew she'd buckle as her belly grumbled in sympathy, the lure of a full English too great. "Ugh, fine." She slapped his shoulder and then tugged the sleeve of his polo shirt. "You're paying, though. I blew my budget last night."

"Deal."

She pushed through the double doors and her stomach gave a violent lurch with the smell of beer-stained wood and grease. It hadn't yet received the message that they were only here to eat and she didn't plan to drink any more. As Josh ordered at the bar, she sunk into their favourite booth and rested her head on her arms, hoping not to spew.

It had been a while since they'd gone so hard on a night out, but for some reason the answer to weekend boredom was always dancing on tables or, to be more precise, watching other people dance on tables. They'd both given up that game years ago and were now only one slip-up away from becoming the types who sat at the bar and shook their heads with the fond memories of a mis-spent youth.

How it had ended up quite so messy, then, was unclear. Adie was sure she'd stuck to her usual plan and withdrawn enough cash for a few rounds, her debit card still safely tucked up at home so there was no temptation of spending more. Since she'd bought the house last year, it'd been necessary to budget. Josh was the most likely culprit, given he still lived at home with his mum and had no such concerns. He turned thirty in eighteen months and lamented that fact every damn day, but never did a thing to change it.

"I got you a healthy OJ." He slid a glass across the table, leaving a streak of condensation.

Adie grunted, not bothering to lift her head. "Thanks." She yawned, stretching as she sat up and rubbed her fingers into her eyes. "What are you doing later?" When there was no reply because he was too busy flicking through his phone, she pinged a beer mat and it hit him square between the eyes. "Oi."

"Hang on, I'm chatting to that girl from last night."

Adie slumped forward again, wondering if it was wise to comment. "How's Emma?"

"She's fine. Stressed about this whole rent thing, but okay besides that."

Emma was the Chair of Kaleidoscope, the LGBTQ youth group where Josh volunteered, and Adie knew there was more to their relationship than friendship. All she ever heard was Emma this, and Emma that, but she didn't want to push it. Josh was adamant they were just friends, and it wasn't for her to argue.

"No luck finding a new venue?"

He dropped his phone on the table and curled back in the seat with his arms folded. "None. I've said I'll do some fundraising so we can afford to pay for a hall, but I don't have a clue where to start. It was a massive mistake."

"No, it wasn't." She shook her head and tried not to roll her eyes. He was on such a downer and she couldn't work out why. "Need a hand?"

"I need about twenty, and if they had brains attached, that'd also be useful."

"I'm pretty sure I still have a brain after last night. If you come over this evening once I've slept and feel more human, I'll see if I can engage it."

Their fry ups arrived suspiciously fast, which most likely meant they were not as freshly cooked as the sign advertised, but right now neither of them cared. Adie banged a healthy dollop of tomato ketchup on the side of her plate and swigged the orange juice, then made light work of a sausage.

"Emma said she'd help too." Josh slathered his toast in

butter, then set it on a side plate and scratched his short-cropped curls. "But I don't want it to seem like I'm totally incompetent."

"No, only a bit incompetent." So that she could come to the rescue, no doubt. "What's the problem with making it collaborative? You should get a little committee together, not do it by yourself."

"I have no intention of doing it by myself."

"No, I gathered that from the way you snapped my hand off."

He shrugged. "It makes sense. You're better with money than I am. Being the daughter of two accountants has to have some perks."

Being an accountant's daughter had nothing to do with it, there just wasn't anyone at home willing to treat her like a hotel guest. She didn't have much choice but to look after herself. "Alright, so you have me on your committee. Let's ask Emma too, and some of the others."

"No. I told you, I want to do it myself. Well, by myself with your help. Besides," he mumbled. "Emma's busy with her new boyfriend."

Which of course Josh had no interest in because Emma was just a friend. Adie picked at her mushrooms, then set her fork on the edge of the plate. "What's the new guy like?"

"I dunno, seems alright. Looks a bit like you, actually."

"Lucky Emma."

"Yeah, if you're into man buns, tattoos, and Doc Martens."

Adie peered at her outfit. He'd hit the nail on the head there, and Emma's boyfriend must be a real catch. "I have only one objection, and that is the term man bun." She pinned back a loose strand of hair and smiled at him. "So what about this girl from last night? Are you meeting up?"

He shrugged again as he took a bite of toast, spreading crumbs over his lap. "No idea."

Underwhelmed with his enthusiasm, she returned to her food. He'd been like this all night, swinging from excitement to malaise faster than the DJ changed the music. She'd probe further later because it wasn't usually this extreme, but right now she was crashing fast and needed her bed.

Leaving half a fried egg and a tomato, she pushed away the plate and wiped her fingers on a napkin, then knocked back the last of her orange. "Do you mind if I leave?" She was already sliding out of the seat and patting her pocket to check the house keys were still there. "You can text me when you're on your way over later."

"Yeah, go." He wafted a hand and managed some approximation of a smile. "I'll try to cheer up by then."

"You don't need to cheer up for my sake, I've spent almost a decade staring at your miserable bloody face." He needed to do something for his own sake, though, before it ended up set in a permanent frown.

Adie gave him a big wet kiss on the cheek and then scratched her chin. How anyone could kiss stubble on a regular basis was a mystery. Then she dug her hands in her pockets and made a beeline for bed, her mind whirring with ideas. Fixing any of Josh's deeper issues might be a job for a skilled professional, but the surface ones were a piece of cake.

* * *

She woke at three when her neighbour mowed his lawn, the sound of whirring blades cutting through her brain faster than the grass. Rolling onto the bare floorboards, she pressed her cheek to the cool wood. If anyone saw her right now, they'd think she'd lost her mind, but her days of coping with these hangovers were long gone.

The phone vibrated on her bedside table and she groaned as she reached to slide it off, kneeling and reading the message from Josh that he was on his way. He'd hit another wave of positivity and drawn up a list of potential money spinners for them to go over, which was good because she'd forgotten hers in the intervening six hours, not that it'd be tough to come up with more.

After tapping out a quick reply, she lobbed her phone at the duvet and crawled to the bathroom, cursing that the place was still a building site as she snagged her knee on a rough piece of wood. She'd had the best intentions of renovating it, but life got in the way and time passed in the blink.

Giving up on the run and going straight for a shower, she emerged to find Josh standing in the entrance hall clutching the door and breathing hard. "Fuck, this thing's a workout on its own," he yelled up the stairs. "Who needs the gym, I'll just open and close your front door a few times."

"You know what would be a great workout?" She brushed through her hair and left it to fall over her shoulders, splattering her tank top with water. "Decorating."

It wasn't the first time she'd tried to enlist Josh's help, but in his defence, it was a bigger job than either of them could handle. She needed a new kitchen, bathroom, and carpets; a lick of paint was the least of this house's problems.

"If you want to trade for help with fundraising, you can forget it. You need professional help in more ways than one."

"Funny, I was thinking the same about you earlier," Adie muttered as she joined him in the living room, collapsing onto the sofa and resting her feet on the arm. She knew it wasn't fair given what a rough trot the past couple of years had been, but it was hard to remain sympathetic when he never wanted to share. At least, never wanted to share what was really bothering him. "I've got a few numbers, so I'll sort it. For now, what are these grand ideas to raise money?"

He pulled a sheet of paper from his pocket and unfolded it as he perched on the edge of the armchair. "Number one is a drag night." He looked up for approval, and Adie nodded. It wasn't a dreadful idea. "Number two is a pub quiz." Better, given it'd take less organising. "Then I have a note here that says T-shirts. Think it was about selling them." He squinted at the sheet and then re-folded it.

Adie frowned, unsure how to say this without sounding dismissive. In the end, she couldn't. "Is that it?" She shuffled into a seated position and crossed her legs, rubbing a hand across her brow. "They're all great, but maybe you should also think of ways to get recurring donations, since you need rent every single month. We can set up a quiz in The Anchor easy enough and make a couple of hundred quid, but it's only a temporary fix."

What they needed was a few benefactors willing to give monthly or annually to keep it going, and then to top up with other events. If Josh enlisted help, other people could run quiz nights and sponsored whatevers as and when, whilst he focussed on the regular income required to keep the club viable long term.

Josh tapped his trainer on the floorboards. "Alright then, smarty pants. Tell me where we find someone to do that."

"I don't know, but it can't be that hard. It's not like you need thousands, it's only hiring a hall once a week. A handful of people all donating a relatively small amount would cover it, surely? Do you have the figures so we know what our target is?"

He paused for a few moments, which she knew meant he was considering bluffing. "No, but I can get them."

"Good. Once you have, let's go ahead with the pub quiz for fun and use it as a template for others, then put some work into those regular donors. That stall you're running at the fair in a couple of weeks will be a good place to start, so just get chatting with people." She pulled out her phone to make notes, massaging her temple with her free hand. This hangover would require painkillers in a minute, and she wanted to wrap things up so they could vegetate. "I'll pop in and see my dad this week, too. He knows everyone, it's about time that paid dividends."

He had his golf club membership, even though he hated golf, was on the committee for the local fair, and chaired the local chamber of commerce. If anyone had the power to introduce them to people who could keep the youth group afloat, it was Robert. Now all she had to do was figure out how to sweet talk him.

"You really think your dad is the best person to ask for help with this? He's not exactly good with the gay."

Adie laughed. "Good with the gay?" She lobbed her phone onto the sofa cushion and thought for a second. It was abundantly clear he'd rather his daughter wasn't, but as problems went, it wouldn't be insurmountable. "I think he'll help, there may just be limits. I can't see him coming out in open support—pardon the pun—but if I slip him a cheque to sign and ask for a few contacts, I'll get them."

"Alright, if you say so."

"I say so. You leave it with me. Dealing with Dad is just like playing one of my mum's board games. It's all about strategy and letting him think he's won."

2

It was Tuesday before Adie found time to test that theory, Monday lunchtime and half the evening having ended up a write-off owing to work calls. She darted out of the office at one o'clock before anyone could catch her and strode through the maze of old Victorian buildings converted into offices, across the Market Square, and past the bank to her dad's accountancy firm.

"Hi, is Robert in?" She leant against the front desk and picked up a business card declaring him director, overlord, and master.

"I'm sorry but Mr Green is on holiday this week." The receptionist typed something, her acrylics rattling across the keyboard. "Can I make you an appointment, or is there someone else who can help?"

Typical. Adie slotted the card back in its holder, then ran her hand over the polished oak and considered what to do. A call, perhaps, but he might not answer if he was sunning himself with his girlfriend. "No, it's fine. Thank you."

She was about to leave when another woman, older this time and in an immaculate navy trouser suit, stuck her head around one of the doors that lead off reception. "Are you sure I can't be of any assistance? I'm covering while he's away."

"It was a personal call, rather than business. I'm his daughter." Adie instinctively reached out a hand, and a small smile crept across her lips when she was met with a tight grip. She'd always liked a firm handshake on any woman who had to deal with her dad.

"Adrienne, is that right?"

"Adie. No one calls me that unless I'm in trouble, which is probably why my dad was using it."

"Jenny." She laughed and stepped back into the office; her voice muffled as she spoke again. "Have you eaten? I was about to take a break."

Adie glanced at the clock on the wall behind Jenny's desk. She'd skipped breakfast to run and ended up scoffing her sandwiches by eleven, so would be happy to eat again if there was time before her next call. "Suppose you could persuade me, but I haven't got all that long."

Jenny pushed out a chrome chair and patted the blue fabric backrest. "Take a seat. Food will be here in a minute." She rounded the desk and sat, crossing her legs and picking a wisp of fluff from her trousers. "I'm glad we've finally met. I was starting to think this accomplished daughter Robert's always talking about was a figment of his imagination."

Adie laughed as she slumped down with her hands stuffed in her pockets. She'd never manage Jenny's level of poise and didn't plan to try. "I think the accomplished bit probably is. What's he said?"

"Let's see. You're a recruitment consultant, doing very well, bought your own house last year." Jenny sucked her teeth, tapping a finger on the armrest as she thought. "Runner, board game aficionado, and you drive a clapped-out old car he thinks you should replace because it's a death trap."

"Wow. Yep, that just about covers it all off."

The doing well part was debatable, though. At twenty-nine she was still in the job she'd taken seven years ago, expecting it to be a stop gap. With commission she was making reasonable money, and she liked the people, but she hadn't yet decided what she wanted to do with her life. If anyone ever managed that, these days.

There was a knock on the doorframe and the receptionist stuck her head through. "Sorry to interrupt. Are you having the usual today?"

"Yes, thanks. And whatever Adie wants."

She seemed to clock who it was now and smiled. "Ham and cheese, the same as your dad?"

"That'll do." Adie returned her smile and she went off, re-emerging a few moments later with two small parcels wrapped in tinfoil, stuck together with a label bearing the delivery company's logo. "This is a bit of a treat. I always make my own lunch because it's cheaper. For some reason, it never tastes as good."

Jenny unwrapped her sandwich and left it open on the desk, then smiled as she watched Adie demolish hers. "Was there anything in particular you wanted from Robert or was it just a social call?"

"I came to see if he'd sponsor my friend's youth group, but I'll catch up with him when he gets back."

"You're a philanthropist, too? I'll add that to my list."

"Hardly." Adie swallowed and wiped her mouth with the back of her hand. "But the friend in question is having a major crisis of confidence right now, and left to his own devices will probably put them in more debt."

"Whereas you're careful with money. I can tell." Jenny

pointed to the sandwich, indicating she was referring to the earlier comment about lunch, and regarded Adie with amusement. It was unclear what was so funny about not wasting cash on over-priced bread and ham, though.

"Been saving to do up my house. It's a wreck of epic proportions." She licked her fingers clean and slid her phone from a pocket. "In fact, that's just reminded me I need to ring some contractors after this." It was another task she'd resolved to complete on Sunday and not yet had time for, which explained how a year had passed with no action. She tapped out a reminder to herself, knowing that without an alarm blaring it'd be out of her head again before she'd finished her sandwich. Finding any enthusiasm was proving difficult. "Sorry. Rude of me, but I'll forget."

Jenny finally took a bite of her lunch and rubbed her fingers to dislodge the flour left by her sourdough. She clasped her hands together when she'd finished, like a cartoon villain with a plan percolating. "I'm wondering whether we might be able to help each other." She paused, inclining her head. "I'm having a housewarming on Saturday; we've just moved into the farmhouse out by the hill. Do you know it?"

Adie nodded as she ripped off another chunk of bread. Everyone knew that place. It'd been on the market for ages because it was huge, overpriced, and needed so much work. "Yeah, the one with all the stables?" And the swimming pool, annex, and several acres of land. "That's a hell of a project. Are you trying to make me feel bad for taking so long over my own house? If so, it's working."

Jenny laughed. "No. My daughter is a plumber by trade but enjoys trying her hand at all sorts, and she's moved up from London with us. While she gets herself established, she's started the renovations—"

"And let me guess, perhaps if I came to your house-warming on Saturday we could accidentally meet, and I could hire her?" It didn't take much to work out where this was going. Adie set her sandwich on the desk, leaning forward conspiratorially.

"See, you are as astute as I presumed. I promise she's very good, and in return you can bring your friend. I've invited half the town, I'm sure he'll find some sponsors."

Adie considered for a second but had yet to find a flaw in Jenny's plan. She'd far rather hire someone on recommendation, even if it was a biased one, and working with a woman appealed. Having to ring around a tonne of contractors who'd all talk down to her didn't generate any feelings of joy, and she was even getting some contacts for Josh into the bargain. "I think we have a deal, so long as I can trust your daughter." She smiled, hoping Jenny cottoned on that it was a joke. "I have my doubts because you seem a little shady."

"Oh, I am. I wouldn't be working for your dad otherwise."

After spending the rest of lunch filling in Jenny on all the reasons why the youth group needed to stay open, Adie returned to work and prepared to hold firm on leaving the office at a reasonable hour. Tuesdays were her night to cook and catch up with her mum, and she'd stay late for anything but that.

She arrived at six and grabbed a bag of groceries from the boot before letting herself into the house. The scent of freshly cut flowers hit her nostrils as she took off her shoes and padded through the living room. For years Liz hadn't bothered with them, but just recently Adie had noticed vases popping up all over the house again whenever she came to visit. She smiled, reaching out to feel the waxy petals of the freesias on the sideboard next to her primary school photo.

"Mum!" There was no reply, so she left her dinner ingredients on the kitchen work surface and stepped out through the conservatory. It stood to reason Liz would have been in the garden since she finished work. "Bloody hell, you can't lift that thing on your own," Adie called, alarmed to find her trying to shift a railway sleeper single handed.

"Don't fuss, I'm strong as an ox." Liz grunted as she hauled it into place, sweat glistening on her cheeks and a mottled red complexion filling her chest. "I'm almost there."

Adie could only watch as she reached the end of the lawn and the sleeper thumped to the ground. Her mum stood back and banged her hands together, then put them on her hips. She may be strong, but she never usually had a problem accepting a little help.

"You're a force of nature, do you know that?"

Liz gave a dismissive wave and threw her gloves at a stack of plastic plant pots. Then she brushed back a limp strand of dark hair, now grey around the temples, and slotted it into a ponytail. "It's a bit of landscaping in a suburban back garden, not the Chelsea Flower Show."

"Have you applied for that yet?" Adie winced as a sharp slap landed on her shoulder. It wasn't such a ridiculous idea, though. "I'm serious."

"I know you are. Far too so, sometimes."

"You don't know the half of it."

Liz let out an amused grumble. "I dare say."

They ambled back down the lawn, stopping every few paces to deadhead or remove a weed from the borders that flanked the long, thin strip of garden, and Adie caught up with her mum's adventures as a supervisor at the local garden centre. It was a far cry from her earlier career as an accountant, but after stopping working in Robert's firm when they divorced, she'd decided on a temporary change in direction which had so far lasted four years.

"I've taken on a bit of bookkeeping," Liz dropped in as they made it back to the patio. She drummed her fingers on the iron table and looked out over the lawn. "Not sure how I feel about it."

"Thinking of switching back?"

"No, it was more a favour. That lady I've become pally with at work asked if I could help her husband. He's run into a few problems with his new business."

Adie smiled at the mention of a 'pal'. It'd been a long time since her mum had described anything close to a friend, and this was a step in the right direction. "Nice of you."

"It shouldn't be complicated." She let out a loud huff and looked down at her watch. "Anyway, I'll go shower while you get the food started, shall I? What's on the menu this evening?"

"Gran's sweet potato curry."

Liz laughed. "Which of her many curry recipes? Now Monica, she's the real force of nature." She pointed her finger, still grinning. "Have you heard from her?"

"Not since she left for Canada."

She'd be back, though. You never knew when, or how, or why, but she'd inevitably find her way home. Her own house had long-term tenants, allowing her the freedom to travel, but she kept one foot firmly planted in Adie's spare bedroom.

"Oh well, I'll watch out for her broomstick coming in to

land at Heathrow," Liz whispered as she stepped into the conservatory. It was only in jest. She got on well with her former mother-in-law, even if she'd given up trying to understand her lifestyle choices or how she'd managed to produce such conservative offspring. "How about your dad? Has he been in touch lately?"

It was rare for her to enquire, usually she banned his name from general discussion, and Adie stalled for a second. "Um, sort of. He's texted about dinner, but I've been busy. Did call into the office for a favour earlier. He was away."

"And he didn't tell you?"

"In his defence, I hadn't given him an opportunity. I did meet this new woman he's got working for him, though."

"Robert's hired a woman?" Liz leant sideways against the kitchen door frame as Adie rustled about in her bag of shopping, setting out her supplies on the chopping board. "Let me guess, she's your age and blonde."

"No, actually, she's your age. Clearly very smart, poised, accomplished..." She trailed off, remembering the details from her impromptu lunch date with Jenny. There hadn't been time to give it much more thought earlier. "I think she'll give him a run for his money."

"I like the sound of her already."

She wasn't the only one. Adie's smile deepened at the thought of Robert trying to get anything past Jenny. "She's just moved up here. I didn't get much info out of her, but her family has bought the old Proctor farmhouse."

Liz folded her arms. "Ah, so she has something your dad wants after all."

"What do you mean?"

"The house. Lord, he used to drive me up the wall with that. All the things he'd do with it. I'm sure it's why he held on for so long; there was no chance of affording it after the divorce."

"You think he hired her because of her house?"

"Oh, no, but if this woman has a bit of money, perhaps the influential friends to go with it, your dad is about to become her new best friend. Mark my words."

Adie nodded. Robert could try, but he'd have to fight her for that privilege.

3

They approached Jenny's house on Saturday morning via a narrow dirt track, and Adie slowed to a crawl so as not to further damage her paintwork. It was already faded and chipped; less vintage red convertible and more clapped out old rust-bucket. Once they'd parked on the drive, she stepped out and straightened her T-shirt, slamming the door behind herself and then flinching as the wing mirror rattled. She really needed to get it looked at but had a feeling the garage would tell her the entire car belonged on a scrap heap. They'd had a lot of good times, though, and she wasn't ready to give up yet.

She rounded the bonnet and held out Josh's arms, so he stood like a scarecrow. "Right, let's do a spot check. If we want donations from these people, we need to make a good impression."

"I'm wearing my best shirt." He frowned as he peered down at himself, the sky-blue cotton billowing in the breeze. "Even ironed it."

Adie laughed. Josh was such a mummy's boy, which was equally sweet and infuriating. She might have teased him if she hadn't left in a rush wearing an old pair of ripped jeans. Perhaps they could both use a bit of help from Josh's mum. "Do you remember the rules?"

"Yes. No flirting, don't drink too much, and start a conversation before outright asking for money."

She knew what would happen if she wasn't specific. There was likely to be free alcohol on offer, and after their last similar encounter they'd lost three days. With every passing year, it added on twelve more hours of hangover recovery time, so eventually a night out was going to require a week's annual leave.

Giving a little nod of approval, she let his arms drop. "Good. Here's the plan. I'll introduce you to Jenny, but don't worry too much because she's already fully on board. I have to chat with this daughter of hers, but it won't take long. Once I'm done, I'll sack her off and help. Okay?"

Josh's frown betrayed a lack of confidence and it was unclear whether he'd followed all of that, but he nodded regardless. "Yeah."

They crunched over the driveway and down the side of the house where the ground switched from gravel to paving slabs and then a freshly mown lawn. The garden was long and thin like Liz's, but rough and unkempt, enclosed on two of its three edges by thick evergreens. On the third was a stone wall with an inset gate, leading to another patio area with two red brick buildings.

Adie glanced from face to face as people stood around sipping from plastic champagne flutes or bottles of imported lager but couldn't see Jenny until a hand landed on her shoulder and she spun around. "Holy shit!" Her heart almost exploded out of her chest. "Hello." She took a deep breath and expelled it through the side of her mouth.

"I was about to say thanks for the invite, but now I'm reconsidering."

Jenny laughed, flicking away a wedge of auburn hair. It'd been tied back on Tuesday, but today it fell over her shoulders. She was dressed more casually, too, in a pair of beige chinos and a loose blouse. "Sorry, I didn't mean to frighten you. I'm so glad you came; I was worried perhaps you mightn't."

"Well I did consider it carefully, but then one of my kitchen taps almost snapped off and I decided to make the sacrifice."

"Oh, yes. A tremendous sacrifice." Jenny nodded, her face now serious. "I'll see if we can find you a drink to soften the blow." She let out a quick laugh and smiled at Josh. "I take it this is your friend?"

Josh fidgeted with the bottom of his shirt, then wiped his hand on his jeans and held it out. "Nice to meet you." Give him a seventeen-year-old in crisis or a computer that needed fixing and he was calm, compassionate, and confident, but Jenny was causing sweat patches to form under his arms. "Your house is lovely."

Adie gave his shoulder a playful punch. "Relax, she won't eat you."

Jenny was laughing again and waved someone over, which gave Josh a chance to sort himself out. He took a deep breath and managed a cheeky smile, finding it amusing to kick dirt over Adie's Doc Martens. He knew it was the way to get his own back, but she didn't have time for annoyance before needing to switch on the charm again.

"This is Morgan." Jenny wrapped an arm across the woman's shoulder, beaming with pride. "I thought perhaps the two of you could chat, sweetheart."

She turned her head to what was presumably her

daughter, acting as if this was off the cuff, and Adie had to straighten her frown. This was the plumber? Morgan had a sodding flower pinned in her hair, not that she would admit she'd succumbed to stereotypes and imagined a rotund woman with a builder's bum. The reality was some way off that. She had soft red hair tipped with blonde which lay in a gentle wave over her shoulders, and a deep v-neck T-shirt with short sleeves that hinted at a tattoo on the top of her arm.

Morgan smiled as they shook hands, then lingered to swipe a bug from Adie's shoulder. "Am I being set up on a play date?"

"Not at all. Adie here needs some work done on her house and I've just been telling her what a wonderful job you do."

"In that case, would you like a drink? I can offer you cider, lager or wine."

Adie was now the one fiddling with her T-shirt, trying to work out where that tattoo went. She thrust her hands into her pockets to keep them still. "Nothing that isn't alcoholic?" The raised eyebrows in response implied it was necessary, and she laughed. "Okay, I'd love a lager."

"Come with me to grab one?"

They left Josh with Jenny and wandered into the kitchen. Inside, the house was in better condition than expected. There were oak units around the edge, topped with solid granite worktops, and in the middle of the room was a rectangular wooden table with eight chairs.

Adie leant back against it. "So, your mum was telling me you want to get set up around here. Do you still have clients in London?"

Morgan pulled open the doors of a large American style fridge and set two bottles on the table. "Yeah, I head down there to do jobs a couple of days a week right now, but I'd like to branch out on my own." Her biceps bulged as she twisted the cap off a lager, and it clanged over the surface. "I work with my brother and he thinks he's my boss, but it's supposed to be a partnership. I do all the heavy lifting while he charms the customers, and I'm a bit sick of it."

"I can imagine that. Is your job physical? Looks like it might be."

"Sometimes, but I also lift weights. Or at least, I used to. Any recommendations for a local gym?"

"Sorry, I only run. Never set foot inside a gym, but my friend would know. I'll grab him again later."

Morgan passed over a bottle then swept her hair into a ponytail, tying it with the band around her wrist. "Thanks. In return, perhaps I can help you with your house."

"Yes, great. Want to come and quote?"

"You don't know I'm any good yet." Morgan raised her eyebrows as she took a sip of lager.

"Alright," Adie conceded, trying to play along with her and not give away that this was a complete conspiracy. She seemed to be doing a poor job of that so far. "Can you show me pictures of something you've done?"

Morgan pushed off the work surface with a small smile and led her back into the garden. They turned left, through the gate in the wall to another area of patio. In front of them were the two red brick buildings, crawling in ivy. "I can do better than pictures. Keep in mind it's a mess, though. I only started last weekend."

She shoved through the door of the larger building and Adie squinted to adjust, almost tripping on a hammer in the hallway. There was a pine door to their right and another straight ahead. They went through the first, into a high-ceilinged room covered in dust sheets. Opposite them was a tall window with a stunning view across the countryside, and Adie's mouth dropped open.

Morgan laughed, cocking her head. "Yeah, I had that reaction too. I'm tempted to rent this place once it's finished for that alone. It certainly beats the flat share I just left."

"If you don't, I will." Adie crept forward, digging her hands into her pockets again as she stared out across rolling fields. "This is incredible. Can you get out there?" She turned and thumbed at the window.

"Of course."

"No. I mean, is there easy access? It looks like a great place to run. I stick to the pavements most days, but only through laziness."

"All this countryside, and you run on the dirty streets?"

"Like I say, lazy. I go in the morning before work and it's easy."

She took in the rest of the room. There was a small kitchen area at one end, and at the other a set of stairs leading to a gallery bedroom. Beyond the balustrade was a double bed surrounded by cardboard boxes and suitcases. It looked like Morgan was living in the annex as well as renovating it.

"Suppose I should show you what I'm doing in here." Morgan wandered back into the hallway, flicking a light switch so a bulb buzzed overhead. "That is what you wanted, after all." She pushed open the door and tugged a cord to illuminate the space, and they both clung onto the doorframe as they peered inside the bathroom. "What do you think?"

There was no floor covering, but it did have a new white suite and gleaming chrome taps. The seals all looked neat, which was the limit of Adie's assessment. "Nice. I mean, I wouldn't know a well fitted bathroom from a poke in the eye, but this looks good." She nodded as she stepped inside and turned on the cold water. "Yep. Works."

"I'm glad it meets with your approval. Do you need to see any more? I can show you the shower I refurbished in the pool house, or is it all academic if you don't know what you're looking at?"

She didn't need to see anything but would quite enjoy a nose, having never been in a house with its own swimming pool before. "Suppose we should, this might be a fluke."

Morgan smiled again, biting the edge of her lip, and turned off the lights. Then she led them to the other building, pulling a key from her jeans and unlocking the door. They trod carefully across a decked area, past a pool covered with a blue sheet, to another door at the back. It housed a shower and, so long as it functioned, looked fine.

There was a hint of amusement in Morgan's voice as she gestured to the unit on the wall. "Do you need me to run it for you?"

"I'll take your word for it this time. Nice... hose?" Adie squinted, trying to work out how you complimented plumbing work. "Head? Unit?"

"You too could have a nice hose if you employ me to fit your bathroom. What is it you need?"

"Everything. How far would you go for a client?"

Morgan spluttered, and Adie's head dropped into her hands as she realised what she'd said. "I'm so sorry. That came out all wrong."

"I like to get to know someone before I answer questions like that."

Adie peeked through her fingers. She was more often embarrassing herself in front of strangers she'd never have to see again. This was a new hell. "What I meant was, I know you're a plumber so am I right to presume you wouldn't decorate or anything?" She let her hands fall away, sticking them back in her pockets. It was the only place she could guarantee they wouldn't fidget. "What would you do, and what would I need someone else for?"

"I decorate for family and friends but it's not something I offer as a service. Why don't you let me look at it and I'll see what I can do?"

"Great. Gran will be thrilled."

Morgan clicked off the light and closed the shower room, then they wandered out onto the patio. "Best not waste any time then. Wouldn't want to upset a pensioner."

"Don't ever let her hear you say that. She won't even claim an OAP discount, she's adamant she's still in her fifties."

"And how old is she?"

"Seventy-two." Adie laughed and pulled the phone from her pocket as they reached the gate. "Shall we swap numbers, and you can call me when you're free? Any lunchtime or evening is fine, I'll work around you." She was unsure if she was about to overstep and scratched the phone on her neck. "Um, I'd be happy to show you some places, too. Only if you're interested. In getting to know the area, that is."

She cursed under her breath for what was almost a second miscommunication in as many minutes. She really was only trying to be friendly, and not just for Jenny or Josh's sake. It was rare to meet anyone around town whom she hadn't been at school with and looked vaguely sane.

Morgan smiled and took the phone, tapping in her number and handing it back. "That'd be nice." She waved at Josh with her other hand on Adie's shoulder. "Is that your friend?"

"Yeah, how did you guess?"

"I didn't, you came in together. I'm assuming the fact he's sweating so much has something to do with whatever Mum had to trade to get you here. How on earth did you meet and make the mistake of revealing you needed a plumber?"

Adie pursed her lips, rumbled and debating coming clean. "I have no idea what you're talking about."

4

Playing dumb only worked for so long, and within minutes Adie had spilled her guts. Not only that, but she'd gone into an unnecessary level of detail about how the youth group was run until Morgan grasped her hands and smiled to stop her. She found the entire thing funny, luckily, and was still plotting how to wind up her mum later as she wandered off to collect empties.

"I got a donation." Josh held up a cheque for ten pounds as Adie made her way across the lawn.

She pinched it and stared at the figure. "That's great. Twenty minutes of hall space paid for, then. Any other bites?"

"Well, I've only really spoken with two people, you weren't gone long..."

He peered over her shoulder and the sharp turn to follow his gaze caused something to pop in her neck. She grimaced and rubbed it, frowning as he watched Morgan bundle empty bottles into her arms. "What?"

"She's cute. I thought it earlier but couldn't say in front of her mum."

"Do you want me to find out if she's single for you?"

"Maybe, but we're not twelve. I can't exactly send my mate over because she'll think I'm completely lame."

"Right, we should save that for the actual date." Adie laughed and dodged out of the way as he swiped at her, his eyes still fixed on Morgan. He was breaking one of the key rules, though, and they needed to focus. Heading over there to try out his chat up lines was not on the agenda. "Hate to tell you, but your libido is not one of my primary concerns today. Shall we try to make headway with these sponsors? I recognise a few people here, so I'll go and make conversation."

"Whilst I get a drink?"

"No." Also against the rules. "Absolutely not. I need your help."

Josh groaned and wrapped Adie in a loose headlock. "Thought you would say that. Come on then."

They did far better as a duo, chatting to people they already vaguely knew, and an hour later had secured a handful of regular donations. All Josh had to do was follow up using the email addresses he'd been given and come up with a plan for taking them. It turned out getting a few quid out of people who were half-cut on free drinks was like shooting fish in a barrel.

"How did you get on?" Jenny whispered, sidling up to Adie as she grabbed her discarded bottle of beer from earlier. It was unclear why, given it wasn't exactly a covert operation and they were the only ones in the kitchen.

"Success on all scores." She moved to the patio door, watching as Josh tried to make conversation with Morgan while she refreshed people's drinks. She was nodding politely but hadn't stopped what she was doing, which was a bad sign.

"Why are you looking so pained?" Jenny glanced over Adie's shoulder, trying to sneak a peek. "Oh, don't worry. You're safe."

"Safe?"

"Yes. Nothing's going to happen with your friend, don't worry."

Adie frowned. What was Jenny trying to imply? "You know Josh and I are actually just friends, don't you? There's nothing more between us. I'm not... I don't see him that way."

It was Jenny's turn to look utterly perplexed. "What?" With a slight shake of her head she turned, searching for answers in Adie's face. "I meant my daughter. I saw the way your eyes popped out of your head earlier."

Adie let out a burst of laughter, blushing wildly. She hadn't expected that and had no idea how to respond. "Are you serious?"

"Deadly. What's the matter?"

There were so many possible answers to that question. For one, she'd only known Jenny for less than a week. Even if it were a lifetime, this exchange felt inappropriate. "She's your daughter. It's... weird."

"Don't be so ridiculous, I've gotten on well with all of Morgan's girlfriends. Well, bar the last one, but the less said about that, the better."

Adie stuttered, now trying to work out why this had thrown her so much. Perhaps it was that her parents would never be so open about her sexuality as to discuss it with virtual strangers. In her mum's case it was because she didn't technically know, they'd never had a conversation where she'd officially come out, and with her dad things were complicated. If you could call hating everything about the idea complicated.

"I'm not sure how Morgan would feel about us discussing her like this."

Jenny put her hands on her hips, her expression quizzical again. "Why? I've only told you she's single and attracted to women. Neither of those facts is a secret."

"Okay," Adie conceded. "You know her better than I do." She held up her hands, splashing lager onto her thumb and licking it off. "But for the record, my eyes did not pop out of my head. I was just a little surprised, I'd expected someone less..."

"Attractive?"

"Right, I hadn't expected to be so attracted." With a slight shake of her head, she realised the mistake. "Attractive. I hadn't expected her to be so attractive."

Jenny smirked. "Oh, good. I'm glad we cleared that up."

"Don't look at me like that, you lead me into a trap. She's gorgeous, but we barely know each other, and—" Adie stopped, realising she was about to spill far more information than Jenny needed to know. She was so damned easy to talk to, though, when she wasn't giggling away. "What's so funny?"

"Nothing, I just like you." She shrugged, letting out a brief sigh and then another burst of laughter. "You're not at all what I imagined from getting to know your dad."

That had to be the nicest compliment Adie had ever received, and she couldn't resist smiling. "I have to ask, why on earth are you working for him?" She still hadn't been able to fathom it. They were the biggest firm in town, but even so it was hard to understand how Jenny survived. "You didn't want to keep working in London and commute?"

"Oh, no. I needed something close so I can be here to sort out the house. I've plans for the place, and those stables. Eventually, I intend to give up the day job and... well, let's just say a change of pace is what I'm after."

She tapped a finger to her nose and then looked out over the gardens again, while Adie reached for her phone. Expecting it to be vibrating furiously with SOS texts from Josh, she prepared to tell him he could get stuffed, but paused when she realised it was her gran. Never mind, the same sentiment applied. She wanted to stay for a few days and was fishing for a lift from the train station.

"Sorry, Jenny, but I might need to shoot off. Family duties." As tempting as it was to suggest Monica find a hotel this time, Adie knew she never would. "Thank you so much for today. I'd love to chat more about your plans for the house, though, if you ever fancy lunch again."

"I can do better than lunch, why don't you come for dinner some time?"

Adie laughed, tapping out a reply to say she was on her way. "Sure, I'd like that."

* * *

After kicking Josh out of the car by The Anchor, Adie spun off towards the train station in search of her gran. She found her on a bench, legs crossed towards the young man with whom she shared a cigarette. He was laughing hysterically over something, slapping his thigh and banging a foot on the ground, and they'd barely noticed her approach.

"Have you made a friend, Granny?" Adie tilted her head and offered out an arm. "Come on, let's get you home." She laughed and stepped back, grabbing two cases from the floor.

Monica blew smoke and it curled over her lip. "Believe it or not, this is my granddaughter."

"And taxi driver, hotel provider, and general dogs' body. If we're making introductions, let's do it properly."

"So dramatic."

Monica shook the lad's hand and thanked him for the cigarette, then followed Adie across the car park, her heels clipping on the tarmac. She wrapped the green headscarf from her neck so that it covered her hair and slid onto the passenger seat, inclining her face to the sun.

Adie wedged her bags into the tiny boot, giving the door a sharp tug to contain them, and hopped in on the driver side. "Pub or home?"

"Need you even ask. After eight hours on a plane I require a gin and tonic."

As if she hadn't already started somewhere over the Atlantic. They set off in the direction of town and discarded the car on a side street. It'd be safe there until morning if necessary and it wouldn't hurt her to carry home her luggage.

When they stepped into the pub Monica beamed, spotting Josh in an instant and reaching out her arms to pull him into a bear hug. Adie left them to catch up while she went to use the bathroom and returned to find her pulling the phone from her pocket, turning the screen to Josh.

He leant back, grabbing it from her. "Monica, are you on Tinder?"

Adie sunk her head into her hand. She'd thought this was a passing phase. It wasn't Tinder, but she knew her gran had joined a dating app for the over fifties. In her case, the way over fifties, although that wasn't what the profile said.

"No, not Tinder. I have chatted to a chap a few times this week, though. Roy. He wants to meet up now I'm in the country, but I haven't yet decided. We'll see." Monica snatched back the phone and then shook Adie's shoulder.

"And what about you? Any pretty young things on the scene?"

She slumped against the bar, knowing it wouldn't be long before this became the topic of conversation. It was saying something when hearing about any bloke called Roy seemed the better option. "Let's not go there. It's the same answer every time, and I already know what you'll say."

"Then why haven't you done anything about it? You're twenty-nine-years old, you can't continue this lifestyle forever."

"Why not, you do?"

Monica laughed, signalling to the bartender. "I pursue whatever takes my fancy, whereas you pursue only what is easy. There is a world of difference."

Adie grumbled and ordered a pint, then a gin for her gran. So much for Josh ending up drunk and sabotaging their mission being the biggest thing she had to worry about today. "I'm perfectly happy." The bartender delivered their drinks, and she took a large gulp. "Thanks for your concern."

"And how's your father? I'll pop to see him tomorrow, hopefully catch him when that woman's not around."

"No, you won't. He's away."

Adie had texted him after visiting the office on Tuesday and he wasn't back until next Friday. They'd agreed to meet then, but for now Monica would have to wait.

"Oh." She let out a brief sigh and took a sip of her drink. "He never tells me anything." After a shrug she seemed to forget all about it. "Tell me what's going on with you, then."

Adie took a deep breath, trying to think. "Not a lot. I may have found someone to work on the house, though. Are you still alright to lend me a bit towards it?"

"When was it ever a loan? I'm sure I owe you rent for all

the times I stay." Monica gave a dismissive wave and pulled out a bar stool. "Besides, you'll inherit it one day, anyway. Do you need me to be there when he comes to quote?"

"Uh, no. It's fine, I'll deal with it." The phone vibrated in Adie's pocket and she pulled it out. There was a message from Morgan, asking if she was free tomorrow. "In fact, that's them now. They want to come in the morning."

"You've found a contractor who wants to quote on a Sunday? They are above board, aren't they?"

Adie scoffed, dismissing her gran's question, and tapped out a reply to Morgan with her address. "If I say eleven will you be out?" She peered up from the screen. "Or should I make it later?"

The last thing she needed was a pensioner on heat making insinuations or poking her nose in again. If she found out the male contractor was a young female one, they'd never hear the end of it. Jenny was one thing, but Monica was quite another, and the introduction could wait until later.

"Yes, I suppose I could go and see Liz instead." She prodded Adie's arm. "Are you listening to me?"

"What's that?" Adie read the message from Morgan confirming their appointment and tucked the phone back into her pocket. Then she spotted someone from work over by the pool table and they waved. Seeing a chance to escape and breathe for a minute, she grabbed her drink and started walking backwards. "Sorry, I'll be back in a minute."

"Hang on, I haven't finished with you yet. We need to talk about the car next."

Adie dug a finger in her ear and shrugged. There'd be plenty of time for that as well.

5

Another Sunday, another splitting headache. Adie brushed her teeth for a third time, trying to erase the taste of Jägermeister, and then pinged some painkillers into her palm. She needed to stop trying to keep pace with Josh and Monica because they wiped the floor with her every time, and each hangover was worse than the last. At some point she'd wake up looking like a mummified corpse.

She jiggled the bathroom tap until it spurted some water, which she cupped in her palm to swallow the tablets. They had twenty minutes to kick in before Morgan arrived, and she stood back to survey herself in the mirrored cabinet. She looked like shit but couldn't do much about it now, although a spritz of her good perfume wouldn't hurt. After a liberal dousing, she went downstairs in search of breakfast.

When the doorbell didn't ring, because it had never worked, she heard the rap of knuckles on the front door and dropped her plate into the kitchen sink. Toast smothered in butter was another part of her plan to look human, but that hadn't worked either. She took a gulp of tea and jogged over the floorboards, heaving the door open as it stuck and then shuddered.

Morgan had arrived in a blue van emblazoned with a 'Cartwright Plumbers' logo wearing a matching polo. Accompanied with a pair of navy cargo shorts, it was a markedly different look from the one she'd sported at the party. "Thought I'd give you the full works, what do you think?" She held out her arms, clutching an iPad in one hand. "Am I everything you imagined?"

Adie laughed as she led her through to the kitchen and leant against the cooker. "Absolutely. Are you sure you're okay to be here on a Sunday? It could have waited."

"Wouldn't have offered if I wasn't."

Morgan smiled, running the kitchen tap and then opening the cupboard under the sink to inspect. She measured, prodded, and surveyed, making notes on her tablet, and then gestured upstairs. They took care on the steps, the handrail falling off the wall, and Adie tried to look apologetic as she showed her the bathroom.

"Don't say anything, I know it's awful. I really did intend to do the place up sooner, but before I knew it over a year had passed and it was still... well, like this."

Morgan squeezed her forearm as she stepped past. "You don't need to apologise. I wouldn't have any work to do if it was perfect."

"All the same, I wouldn't want you to think I'm a slob." Adie tidied the various pots and potions Monica had left strewn across the windowsill when she got up earlier, bundling them back into her bag. "My gran arrived yesterday, most of this is her crap. It takes a lot of work to fool the world into thinking you're twenty years younger than you are."

"Honestly, it's fine. I've seen far worse, believe me."

Morgan leant against the sink and her eyes widened as it moved. "Shit, sorry. I'm here to fix the place, not break it." She stepped away, tucking the iPad into one of the many pockets in her shorts. "So, what do you want? Cheap and cheerful? Luxury rolled top baths and gold fittings?"

"That's a good question. It depends on cost, but perhaps somewhere between the two?"

They wandered out of the bathroom and back downstairs so they could have a proper chat in a less confined space. Adie pulled out a chair at the kitchen table and offered her a tea. She flicked on the kettle and pulled out a couple of mugs, slamming the cupboard door and praying it didn't crumble to a million pieces.

"Most of this looks easy, it's just a lick of paint and a few new carpets, but the kitchen and bathroom will be the biggest expenses." Morgan leant back in her chair, frowning momentarily as she peered through to the living room.

"I'm guessing since you're here on official business I don't yet qualify for the family and friends service." Adie drained the last milk from the carton, cursing her gran for using it all on her cereal, and lobbed it in the recycling bin. "Not that I expected any sort of preferential treatment."

She set a mug in front of Morgan, who cupped it in her palms and blew over the top. "I'll quote for refitting the kitchen and bathroom, but if you play your cards right, you might get some help with the rest. I haven't decided yet, I'm waiting to see if we become friends." She took a cautious sip and then set it down, a coy smile emerging. "I seem to recall you offering to show me around yesterday. Does that still stand, or was it another thing my mum coerced you into?"

Adie laughed, rubbing a hand over her brow as she replayed the conversation with Jenny, still not having quite gotten over it. "I promise that had nothing to do with your mum." She folded her arms and pressed a hand into her cheek as she considered what there was to show her. "Let's see, we could start with the park. That'll take all of five minutes. Then I suppose I could take you to the super-market and the pub. Oh, and there's a fair in two weeks. Comes into town once a year, highlight of the social calendar."

Besides the stalls, of which Josh's was one, there was a charity football match and then fairground rides in the field. It would be filled with kids drinking cans of cider as the night wore on, but it was a must if Morgan wanted the true experience.

"Quaint. How about we cut a deal? I'll come and help you paint the living room in exchange for a tour of the fair."

Adie chewed her top lip, considering whether to invite Morgan to the football match too. Better still, ask her to play. She'd tried on several occasions to get out of it but given both her boss and her dad were sponsoring the event it'd been a lost cause. Having another woman and someone under thirty on the team would make it slightly more bear-able. "How do you feel about football?"

"I have very few strong feelings. Why?"

"Because I have lots of them and they're mostly negative right now. There's a charity match as well as a fair. Do you fancy a run out in my dad's team? He's playing, but he's shite and won't last five minutes."

"Oh, thanks. You've got high expectations of me, then?" Morgan laughed, and when she spotted Adie making a flus-tered attempt to redeem herself held up a hand to stop her. "I may live to regret this given I haven't played since school, but sure." She took another sip of her tea, mumbling over the top of the mug. "You'd better not underestimate me, though."

There was no chance of that. If she was anything like her mum, she'd have them all in their place by the half time whistle. "Do you have a preferred position?" Adie sucked on her top lip again, but this time it was to keep from laughing. "On the field, of course."

"What else could you mean?" Morgan shrugged and smiled, then drummed her fingers on the table. "No, put me wherever you like. I'm sure I'll find a way to make it work." There was a grunt of laughter and then she pulled out the tablet again. She swiped across the screen and popped out a little flip stand on the back of the case, propping it on the table. "Now, I'm sure I was here for a reason. Shall I show you what I'm thinking of for your kitchen?"

Adie scraped out the chair next to her so she could see, setting her mug on a coaster. "I like modern." She pointed to the picture of an oak effect door with chrome handles. "Something like that."

"Not the white ones? In a small room like this, light colours can give the illusion of space. A bit like mirrors."

She shook her head, already picturing Josh staining them with coffee. "No, they'd get dirty." Then she scrolled down with her index finger and pointed to a dark marble effect worktop. "That looks good, too."

"Fair enough. Are you always so easy to please?"

"Guess we're about to find out, but my tastes are pretty simple."

"I shouldn't show you this eight-jet whirlpool bath then?" Morgan grabbed the iPad and clutched it to her chest but then spun it around. "Nice, right? Imagine relaxing in this after a hard day."

Adie took hold of the screen and scrolled down to the price, her eyes widening as she handed it back. "Yeah, it might be hard to relax when I'm bankrupt. Besides, I don't really take baths." She went to pick up her tea but then stopped and put out a hand as she corrected herself. "To be clear, I do wash. I just prefer a shower."

Although right now she was certain Morgan might question that. Despite having showered and put on clean clothes, she still smelt like a brewery. She had a little sniff on her T-shirt, trying to remain inconspicuous, but the laughter implied a lack of success.

Morgan leant across, taking a deep breath as she hooked her hand over the back of Adie's chair. "Yeah, you do stink a bit." She laughed, slapping a shoulder as she moved her arm away. "Only joking, you smell great."

Adie felt a warm blush on her cheeks and tried to pass it off as the weather. She stood and stumbled, putting out a hand to the wall as she pushed the chair back and went to open the kitchen window. "So, um." She grunted as she strained to reach over the sink and undo the latch. "Bathrooms. I need a bath for Gran, but I'd rather spend more on a decent shower. Besides that, standard white is fine. Plain tiles, too, I'm not fussed on anything fancy."

Morgan waited until she'd returned and then held up the device again. "Any preference on taps, or..."

"No, I'll take your advice. I've decided to trust you know what you're doing and hope you have as much taste as I think."

An amused smile accompanied the slow nod in response, and Morgan replaced the tablet with her tea mug. "Fair enough. So far, I've learned you're easy to please and way too trusting. Interesting."

Adie frowned, trying to work out if that was good or bad, but it was hard to tell. She wouldn't have called herself trusting, it was just that picking a bathroom wasn't a life or death moment. Someone who did this every day was far more qualified to know what worked or didn't.

"You wouldn't let a professional pick for you, then?"

Morgan inclined her head. "I think I'd want more of a say. I'm not criticising, you've made my job easy." She took a sip before hitching up a knee and resting the mug on top. "What would you take your time over choosing?"

"A wife," Adie deadpanned. After watching her parents' marriage implode, it'd take a lot to go there, and she'd want it to be for keeps. She shrugged, breaking eye contact, and went back to her tea. "Well, you did ask."

"I would hope everyone thinks long and hard before picking a wife, yes."

The amused smile was back, and Adie had started to look out for it. There was a reserved, playful quality about Morgan, whose nature she couldn't quite discern. She wanted to know more, whilst being simultaneously terrified about where her fascination might lead.

"Oh," Adie exclaimed, jumping up again. "I meant to give you something. I got you a leaflet for the gym Josh uses. There's a referral code on there so you get a discount."

She pulled it from under a magnet on the fridge and slid it across the table, then hooked her thumbs through her belt loops while Morgan read the front.

"Thanks, that's great. After you left yesterday, I went for a walk and found a gate that leads straight onto a bridleway. Feel free to come by any time you want to run out there, Mum won't mind you going through the garden."

Adie noted that she'd only said Mum and there'd been no word about Jenny's husband but didn't like to ask. Instead, they talked about the kitchen a while longer, and as the morning turned into afternoon, she tried to wrap up their meeting. Monica would be home at some point, and she wasn't keen for them to meet until the work was scheduled and Morgan could no longer be scared away.

"Thanks for coming." Adie stood and stretched, then wandered through the living room. "I appreciate it, and I'll keep an eye open for your quote. Out of interest, how soon would you be able to start?"

Morgan yanked open the front door, letting out a laugh and running a hand over the edge. "I'm booked out this week but if you get back to me quick enough, I can tell my brother not to make any appointments from next Monday. He'll have to deal with it."

She jumped into her van, slipping on a pair of sunglasses. As she pulled away, Adie waved with one hand as she dug out her phone with the other. There were four missed calls from her mum, but she'd had it on silent. Feeling a surge of panic, she fumbled the phone to her ear with a hand gripping the door for support, and prayed she was okay.

6

Fifteen minutes later Adie strode along a grass verge, making a beeline for the supermarket carpark. She dripped with sweat having run most of the mile from home but could now see her mum's little red Volkswagen on the far side by the bottle recycling bins and jogged over, mouthing an apology to the van driver who'd had to stop for her. She knocked on the window and Liz jumped, clicking open the door.

"Are you okay?" Adie frowned, noting the streaks of tears down her mum's cheeks.

"Sorry."

"What are you apologising for?"

"I'm such an idiot." Liz clenched her fist and banged it on the steering wheel. "I only left the car for two seconds while I took my trolley back and someone had my handbag away. Now I can't get petrol, and my house keys were in there..." She trailed off and sniffed into the back of her hand.

"We can sort all of that, so long as you're alright. I've got a key, and we'll have your cards cancelled."

"I've already phoned to do that."

Adie crouched, one hand holding open the door and the other on her mum's knee. "Good. I can pay for petrol, then we'll go to my place for a bit. Gran should be home soon. We'll make some lunch." She'd decided to spend the morning out shopping so they could visit Liz together in the evening and have dinner, so it'd just bring things forward a touch. "She's looking forward to seeing you. A catch up on her adventures will take your mind off things."

Liz gave a weak nod and then sighed as if resigned to the loss. It could happen to anyone, and she needn't beat herself up, but getting her to believe that wouldn't be easy. "Can you drive?" She held out a shaking hand. "Not sure I'm safe."

Adie hauled herself up on the chassis and stood back while Liz shuffled off the seat, brushing biscuit crumbs from her lap. There was an open packet on top of the armrest, and she reached back through to grab it. Once she was in the passenger side Adie slid the seat back and turned the key, noting there was still a quarter of a tank. Things weren't as dire as she'd made out, but Liz was always cautious, and it wouldn't help to argue it could wait.

She pulled out of the space and drove into the petrol station, filling the tank, and bought her mum a can of drink while she paid. A bit of sugar would help with the shock, not that she hadn't already had the same idea and sat munching another custard cream.

"How was your day up until this happened?" Adie revved the engine and turned onto the road, looking an extra time as they reached the edge of the forecourt. She was always more careful in a car that didn't have bits hanging off and waited for the worst of the traffic to clear before surging onto the roundabout.

The packet of biscuits rustled as Liz slotted it in the side pocket. "I did a little weeding, then I was supposed to meet some work friends later. Not sure I will now though."

"I'm sure if you told them what happened they'd understand why you're shaken."

"I've not got any money. It's fine. The pub isn't really my scene, and I'll see them all tomorrow." As if that was the point. She'd see them all at work, but not socially. It was Liz all over, though. She was confident in her ability with numbers and plants but struggled with friends. It's why she'd have offered to do this bookkeeping—it was a safe position for her to adopt.

"I can lend you the money if you still want to go. Will your mate be there?"

"Expect so."

"Perhaps Gran could go with you for moral support."

"Can you imagine?" Liz laughed, resting an elbow on the door. She stared out the window, amused by the image for longer than it warranted. "Monica would terrify them," she muttered.

"True," Adie conceded, unable to argue on that point. She was worried, after thinking her mum had turned a corner. Everything had escalated during the divorce, taking something that had been an undercurrent in all their lives and turning it into a tidal flood, but it had at least spurred her into getting help. Counselling and a change of direction both seemed to have been beneficial, but then she'd get into these maudlin moods and shut herself off for a while.

When they reached the house, Liz got out and took a bag of frozen food from the boot, cursing under her breath as she went to look for her handbag and remembered it was gone. "Have you space for this?" She held up the carrier, then let it hang and peered at the contents. "It'll melt if we leave it in the car, and that would just about top off my day. No ice cream."

Adie took the shopping as she opened the front door and stepped aside to let her mum pass. "I'll make some."

"The state of this place." At least she was moaning about something else now and not focussing on being robbed. She grimaced as she stepped into the lounge and then stood in the middle of the kitchen while the food was put away. "It's such a mess still."

Adie grunted as she wedged a bag of frozen peas on top of a pizza. "You'll be pleased to hear I had someone out to quote for a new kitchen and bathroom this morning. I'm taking action."

"Good grief." Liz stared through the patio doors, no doubt considering what she'd do with the garden if she got her hands on it. She'd gifted a plant of some description that still sat looking rather sad on the patio, but besides that it was barren. "Don't tell me you might buy some furniture next."

"What do you mean? I have furniture."

"You have the minimum of everything, this hardly feels like a home. Perhaps once it's all finished, we could put up some pictures, too. You can't have bare walls."

It'd worked fine for the past year, but she wouldn't argue. Again, she'd had the best intentions but wasn't all that interested. This was just the place she slept, washed, and ate. On occasion Josh and Monica did the same, but it wasn't somewhere anyone spent a great deal of time.

"I guess, if it'd make you happy." Adie slotted the last tub of ice cream into the freezer and shut the door, hanging the tote bag off a chair.

As Liz turned, her expression was quizzical. "The question is whether it would make you happy. You can't enjoy living like this."

"I don't really notice it. Well, until I go to cook, and the cupboard door falls off. I did almost lose a nail the other week after a partial collapse."

She wiggled her toe, wincing with the memory, and flicked on the kettle while her mum pulled out a chair. Then the phone vibrated in her pocket and she tugged it out, a faint smile emerging as she read the message from Morgan.

"What are you grinning at?" Liz enquired, her eyes narrowing.

"Nothing, I've just had the price through from my plumber. Well, plumber and general fixer upper. Do you want to see what I'm going for?" She opened the PDF and glanced at the figure, sure she must have had a discount because it seemed far too cheap, and then scrolled to the units. "What do you think?"

"It's a bit bland."

"You're a hard woman to please, do you know that?" Adie scoffed, tapping out a message to accept the quote and asking Morgan to invoice the deposit before her mind got as far as picturing all that money leaving her account. Even with a discount, it was more than she'd ever spent in her life. She had a reply almost immediately asking if a skip could be delivered the following Tuesday. "It'll be a million times better than what I have, and the person who's doing it has even said they might help me decorate. With any luck, in a few weeks you won't recognise the place."

"Here's hoping."

When Adie looked up from the phone after a flurry of discussion with Morgan, Liz was staring out the window over the sink, stirring a teaspoon around her mug so that it made an annoying tinkling noise. Her expression had turned blank, and Adie's stomach clenched. She'd lightened up but was now lost in thought, no doubt berating herself over the handbag again. They'd be reliving this for weeks like they always did when something went wrong, and she willed back the woman who'd been laughing and joking on Tuesday evening.

Monica erupted through the front door at just the right moment, snapping Liz from her stupor. She dropped her teaspoon in the sink and carried her mug to the table, managing a tight smile.

"Please tell me you've hired the plumber," Monica called, as she stopped to take off her shoes. There was a loud clout as she discarded them. "I'm poised to send you vast sums of money in the name of a hot bath."

"Yeah, thirty grand should cover it," Adie yelled back. She winked at Liz, then leant against the work surface and cradled her tea.

"On your bike."

Monica appeared in the doorway, fluffing her hair and adjusting her scarf. She lobbed a pair of sunglasses on the table and took a deep breath, then looked from one to the other as if she expected someone to speak.

"I've been robbed." Liz's delivery was matter of fact, but she'd know it didn't take much to get her going.

"You've what?"

Monica was indignant, pulling out a chair and taking a grasp of her hands. Adie smiled, knowing her mum would get all the support she needed, and perhaps a little more besides. She could already picture her gran, offering to hunt them down like dogs or go into the supermarket to demand

CCTV footage. She'd go way over the top, of course, but it'd do the trick.

The phone vibrated with another message from Morgan and she turned the device in her hand. She'd planned to run today and could do to decompress. Perhaps now was a good time to try out that countryside route and get some real fresh air. "If you two are happy catching up, do you mind if I run and we keep our plans for dinner later?"

She tapped the phone on her palm, now wondering if she'd look like a weirdo stalker turning up there again. Morgan had said to go through any time, though, and even texted a photo of where to find the gate. If that wasn't a genuine open invitation, she didn't know what was.

"No, you go, love." Liz smiled and Monica rubbed the back of her hand. Then she tutted and slumped backwards. "I was about to say I'd treat you for helping me out, but I can't."

"I'll treat *you* then."

"My daughter, buying us dinner?"

Adie shrugged. Perhaps she had been a little tight with the purse strings, but now she knew how much the kitchen and bathroom would cost, she could loosen them off to buy her mum a meal in the pub. "Yeah, no big deal. I might have a bit of spare money now the house is sorted."

Monica raised her chin and smiled. "Oh good, time to start saving for a new car."

"Really?" When had life become a series of big purchases to save for? "That can wait, I'm taking a break and throwing caution to the wind for a while."

"My dear girl, you and I need a conversation about living vicariously if you think buying dinner in town constitutes that."

Adie laughed but didn't want to get dragged into that discussion with her mum in earshot. She gave one last thought to running on the roads or trying out the trail, but by the time she was halfway up the stairs knew exactly where she was heading.

7

As the car door slammed shut a clatter reverberated around the grounds. It was silent besides the chirp of crickets and Adie winced, hoping she hadn't disturbed anyone. Morgan had said the gate was past the annex and down the side of the pool house, so she walked across the patio, stealing a brief glance into the kitchen to find it unoccupied. There were a few boxes of empty wine bottles next to the door but, besides that, no signs of life.

When she reached the red brick buildings, Morgan sat on a deckchair with a pair of aviators turned to the sun. She was in gym shorts and a loose white vest, revealing the full extent of the intricate rose tattoo that curved over the top of her arm and across her shoulder. It glistened with sunscreen and she slapped away a fly before lifting the glasses.

Adie shuffled on the slab, tugging on her running shorts to adjust them. "Sorry, I just came to use the gate. Is that okay?"

"And I was just plucking up the courage to go and use that gym you recommended." Morgan stood and dropped her sunglasses on the chair, wearing a warm smile which made her eyes crinkle at the corners. "Of course it's fine. I said you could come through any time, there's no need to look so worried." She raised a hand to shield her face as she squinted. "Do you fancy some company? I haven't exercised in a fortnight but I'm struggling to motivate myself, and a run might be better practise for this football match."

Adie sized her up, trying to work out if she was about to have her ass kicked. "You're more than welcome to join me." She frowned, watching the athletic looking stretches, and shook out her legs. "So long as I won't slow you down."

"Don't be silly, it'll be the other way around. Well, I presume so. Guess we'll have to find out, won't we?" She raised her eyebrows a touch before striding off down the side of the pool house.

Adie followed, noting the spring in her step and the definition of her calf muscles as she pushed open the gate and rolled her shoulders, cricking her neck from one side to the other. "Are you setting the pace, or am I?"

Morgan tapped Adie's wrist. "You're the one with the fancy watch, suppose you should. I'll tell you if we're going too fast." She gripped a hand around it this time and lowered her voice. "Or slow."

They started with a gentle jog over mud that had dried and cracked in the sun, moving in and out of the shade cast by a line of trees. On the other side a wheat field blew in the gentle breeze. Even so, it was hot, and within minutes Adie could feel sweat dripping down her back and into the waistband of her shorts. She had no idea where she was going so followed the path into the next field, out into open sunshine. Morgan remained always a step behind, and it was disconcerting to find she didn't even appear to be out of breath yet.

"Is this too slow for you?" Adie called back, turning her head momentarily before almost stumbling on a loose rock and having to steady herself. "We can crank it up a notch if you like?"

"I'm easy," came the teasing reply. "I presumed this was a warm-up."

It was, but a little effort would have been nice, and Adie looked down at her watch. They were running under her usual pace, so she kicked off until it came closer. "How about now?"

Morgan panted a little. "Yeah, better."

As they reached the end of the second field they paused to climb over a stile, then ran on again. A wooded area appeared on the right-hand side and Adie followed the arrow, hoping for more shade. What she found was not only that, but a stream trickling along the side. She paused her watch and bent over, her hands sliding off her quads.

"Time for a break, I think." She jumped in, the water seeping into her trainers and stinging her burning toes.

Morgan frowned, shielding her eyes again, but then laughed. "We've only run for twenty minutes. Are you knackered already?"

"No, but I thought this was the benefit of a trail. We're exploring, aren't we? And this is beautiful."

She reached out a hand and Morgan glanced down at her feet before taking a tentative step into the stream. "Well, at least you look more relaxed than when you arrived." She winced as the cold hit, bouncing up and down a few times. "Everything okay?"

"Yeah, just thought a run might help clear my head."

"Sounds ominous."

"Not really. My mum had a bit of a wobble, but she's okay now." Adie realised they were still holding hands and let go, but they ended up with their fingers tangled when Morgan didn't. "When there's a problem I get a call. Keeps me fit, given how many decompression runs I need, so I suppose I shouldn't complain."

"I'm sorry. I don't want to pry, but you can talk about it if you like."

There wasn't much to discuss, she just hated seeing her mum so distressed like in the car park. In the past couple of months, she'd phoned in tears over a leaky tap, an incorrect phone bill, seeing a dead cat on the ring road, and about a million other things. It was still better than when she went quiet, but it wasn't easy.

"I'm alright, just wish she was happier. She's getting there, but it's hard to know how to help. Sometimes she seems perfectly fine. I had dinner with her on Tuesday and she was in a great mood. You get lulled into a false sense of security." Adie sat on the edge of the stream, letting the water lap over her feet. "It'd help if she had some proper friends, but she lost touch with a lot of people when Dad had the affair. Think she was embarrassed."

He'd been rumbled having it off with a woman from the sandwich shop. She was younger, almost inevitably, and it'd made them the town's key source of gossip for a solid six months. All the couples they used to know and spend time with had quietly distanced themselves, and there was an underlying anxiety about what people knew or thought whenever she met anyone new, even years after.

"What about you?"

Adie rest back on her elbows and frowned. "What about me? I've had no affairs with sandwich shop employees, so far as I remember." She squinted, pretending to think. "Nope."

Morgan swiped her shoulder. "You know what I mean. Must have affected you, too."

"Nah, not really." She was already an adult and able to put it in perspective. It's not like they'd had to navigate weekends with the other parent and child support payments. The only time it got tricky was at Christmas, and since Liz was on her own, she usually won the toss. "The way Dad went about it was shitty and I've told him what I think of that, but they're both far better off now they're a minimum of a hundred metres apart."

Neither was happy, the affair was just a catalyst, but something had bothered Morgan because her eyes widened in shock. "There's a restraining order?" When Adie spluttered with laughter at the idea, she shook her head slightly and rolled onto her front, picking a daisy from the grass. "Maybe not, then. You hear things, though."

"You do, but my dad isn't that kind of asshole. In fact, most of the time he isn't one at all, I think he just struggled to know how to end it. Particularly given they worked together, too."

"Hmm."

"What?" Adie flopped over and poked daisies into the top of Morgan's ponytail, the tips of her trainers still dipped into the stream. She was as easy to talk to as her mum but gave away far less.

"Plan forming. You said your mum has struggled to make friends, and my mum is trying to meet new people." She sucked her teeth then smiled. "Reckon we should set them up?"

"You can try, but it won't be easy. Not least because Jenny works for my dad."

"What you mean is *we* can try. I'm not doing this on my own."

The irony that she was trying to set up her mum on a friendship date when Jenny had almost certainly been trying to do the same thing wasn't lost on Adie, and she chuckled to herself for a few moments before relenting. Of all the people who seemed likely to show sympathy and might be an intellectual match to Liz, it was Jenny.

"How are we doing this, then?"

Morgan pushed up on her forearms as if she were doing a press-up and her triceps popped. "Perhaps they could bump into each other at the fair?" She jumped up, and the daisies spilled from her hair. "Is your mum going?"

It was unlikely, given who else would be there. Convincing her would be a struggle. "Doubtful. Dad."

"Ah. Let's think on then, I'm sure we can come up with something."

Adie rolled to her feet in a far less graceful manner and shook her legs again, sending out shards of water which glinted in the sun. "We should move, or you'll stiffen and pull something."

"Good thinking, I wouldn't want to pull anything." Morgan stepped backwards and stumbled on a rock. She twisted as she righted herself and put out a hand, but it slipped down Adie's arm.

"You okay there?"

"Yeah, that was just a test to see if you'd save me." She turned and set off the way they'd arrived, peering over her shoulder. "You failed, by the way."

Adie gave chase, grunting with laughter every time she came within a couple of metres and found her target pulled away again. Before she knew it, they were back at the stile and Morgan vaulted it but caught her shorts on a splinter of wood and ripped them. She carried on running with blood trickling down her leg, and Adie called to stop her. "Hey, slow down. I think you've cut yourself."

"Nice try," Morgan yelled back. She sped up, clattering through the gate, and only stopped when her hands hit the wall of the annex. She panted as she leant forward, blood soaking into her sock and the back of her trainer.

Adie shut the gate and walked up the path, pointing to the cut. "Can I look now?"

Morgan twisted and tugged the fabric of her shorts. "Don't worry, it'll be alright." She stretched against the wall, but a stream of crimson continued to trickle from the wound. "I've had worse. I'll clean it in the shower."

"There was a nail sticking out and I'm worried you've caught it. You might need a tetanus shot or something."

"I won't, don't fuss."

Her tone had hardened, and Adie stepped back, but the worry remained. "It's no bother to drive you to get it looked at, just to be sure."

"But I don't need you to, I said drop it." She wore a forced smile as she turned, wiping the ribbons of sweaty hair from her forehead. "Sorry, I didn't mean to snap. Thanks for caring, but it's honestly fine. Do you want a drink? Mum's bound to have something good stashed."

"Okay." Adie tried to avert her eyes from the mess, following her into the main house.

Jenny stood in front of the fridge, unpacking bags of shopping, and jumped when they walked into the kitchen. "I didn't realise we had company."

Morgan stepped in front of her mum and pulled out a couple of cans. "We don't, Adie just came to run."

"No bother. Would you like to stay for some dinner?"

Adie took the drink and tried to catch Morgan's eye, but she wasn't receptive. "Thanks for the offer. I've got plans with my mum, so it'll have to be another time. This was fun, though." She meant it, despite the rather abrupt ending. They'd been getting along like old friends until a few minutes ago, but she got the impression she'd outstayed her welcome, and shuffled towards the door. "Let me know if you ever fancy doing it again."

"How about next Sunday?" Jenny pressed.

"I'm not sure..." She trailed off, trying to work out how Morgan would feel about that from her body language. Her shoulders had tensed, and she hadn't looked at anything but her drink since she'd opened it. Neither were good signs, but her mum was persistent.

"Don't be silly. You'll come next Sunday, and then I hear there's a football match the week after."

"Yes, are you coming?"

Jenny smiled, holding up two bags of apples. "Wouldn't miss it. I haven't been to a fair in years, this is just the sort of thing I wanted us to get involved in when we moved." She set them on the counter and then leant forward, resting on her elbows. "Everyone's been so kind."

Adie zoned out while she continued to talk about the party and people at work, giving only murmurs of response. She was far more interested in whatever was wrong with Morgan, who now looked about ready to burst into tears. It couldn't have been too serious, given Jenny wasn't at all bothered, but she seemed miles away. Adie prayed for Morgan's return almost as hard as Liz's.

8

There had been no time to breathe all week between work, sorting new locks for Liz, and trying to clean the house ready for Morgan to start. Everything from the kitchen was now in boxes, the task having been completed that morning, and Adie was meeting Josh for a quick drink before dinner with Jenny. It was meant to be a chance for them to catch up, but for some reason she couldn't concentrate on a word he was saying.

"Are you listening to me? Earth to Adie."

Josh waved a hand in front of her face and she blinked rapidly. "Sorry, I was miles away. What was that?"

"Pub quiz. While we're in here, shall I try to set a date?"

She smiled, glancing at the bar. "Good plan."

He got up and wandered over, leaving Adie with her thoughts. She gave up on any notion of relaxing and submitted to worrying about spending the evening at Jenny's, given how things had been left with Morgan. They'd spoken a few times in the week, mainly about the house, but there had been nothing said about that abrupt shift in mood. She was half tempted to cancel, if it weren't for morbid curiosity and a good dose of that old British fail-safe: not wanting to appear rude.

She groaned as her phone flashed up her dad's number, finding it was far easier to do that where he was concerned, and hovered over the accept button before tapping decline. They could catch up properly at the match next week, but despite having agreed to see him, she didn't have the energy to feign interest in his holiday. It'd only be a run-down of all the restaurants they'd eaten in, what the hotel was like, and how it never lasted long enough. As someone who hadn't been abroad in several years, it would be hard to find sympathy.

Josh grinned as he sat down, tucking a scrap of paper into the pocket of his jeans. "Success. They're already running a fundraiser next month, so I've booked us for the first Wednesday in September. I've said you'll be the quiz master, but I'll write the questions. Is that okay?"

"Yeah," Adie replied absently, typing out a message to her dad. She set the phone down and ran a finger around the rim of a pint of shandy, her head propped in a hand. "Wait, what?"

"Which part has confused you?"

"Quiz master. You can forget that." She was happy to shake a tin for donations on the night but wasn't committing to standing up and running things.

"Why not? You've got the gift of the gab."

"No, I haven't."

"Have."

"Haven't." He went to repeat, but she banged her forehead on the table, her palms coming to rest on either side. "This is infuriating. I'm not doing it. You're perfectly capable, or you've got Emma and the other volunteers."

"They won't take a forty-minute train ride out here, though, just for a pub quiz."

Adie tried desperately not to roll her eyes as she pushed herself up on the sticky wood. Most of the time she found boundless patience for him, but today it had worn thin. "You haven't even asked them, have you?" She knew he hadn't because she knew Josh. He'd have decided not to bother anyone, except for her, despite what they'd said last week. "Honestly, I want to help but I've got a lot on right now. If you get really stuck, come back to me, but please will you just speak to Emma? Either that or tell me what's going on with her, I know there has to be more to this and I can't keep playing guessing games."

She was a nice woman who chaired a youth group, but even as Adie said it, she felt like a total bitch. It gave her the same low grumble in the pit of her stomach she'd experienced on Tuesday night when Liz had wanted to stay up way too late playing games, clearly as a stalling tactic not to be on her own again, and it had been necessary to hold firm. It was either that or end up zombified at work the following day.

"Okay, sorry," Josh mumbled. "The thing is, I think Emma likes me."

Adie sat dumbstruck. How was this a problem? "That's great, isn't it?" Then the penny dropped. Emma had a new boyfriend. "Oh, but there's an extra wheel on this party wagon?"

"No, she broke up with him. Turns out man buns and Doc Martens aren't as desirable as we thought. Sorry." He shot her a cheeky smile and she might have fought back if it weren't so nice to see.

"Double great. Go for it, then. What's stopping you?"

"I don't know." He shrugged, then seemed to reconsider.

"It's just, I've known Emma for over a year and in that time, I've only seen her date cis men and cis women. What if she's disappointed?"

Adie softened at the fear and nerves written all over his face. She hadn't even considered he might be worrying about that and berated herself for being so naïve. "Why would she be disappointed? I'm guessing she just thinks you're hot and sweet and... hang on, you're starting to sound like a mug of tea."

There was another little smile forming, but it was quickly quashed. "The dynamic is different. I won't be what she's used to, how can I be?"

"You don't have to measure up against anyone. If she's interested, it's in *you*." Adie dug out a warmer smile for reassurance, pleased to see his gradually growing again. "I need to go but think about it. Okay?"

She squeezed his arm and strode towards the door with renewed enthusiasm. Having finally made some headway with Josh's problem, she was hopefully about to go two for two and find out what the hell had happened with Morgan.

* * *

Fifteen minutes later she pulled up on the farmhouse drive and checked the date on her phone. Yes, it was Sunday. Yes, Jenny had invited her for dinner. So why were there five other cars here? She inched up the gravel and knocked on the front door, scuffing her feet on the step with a bottle of white wine in hand. Jenny appeared, mid laugh and half turned to talk to someone behind her.

"Sorry, did I get the wrong day?" Adie tried to peer past to see who was inside.

"Not at all, everyone else is already here. Come on in."

Jenny stepped aside and ushered her past, then slammed shut the front door before placing a hand on each of Adie's shoulders to guide her forward. The kitchen was full of noise and laughter from the people sat around the big oak table, and no one seemed to have paid much mind to the newcomer. Beyond them in the garden Morgan was running around with a swarm of kids at her feet, kicking a football at a small goal that'd been erected by the line of ferns.

"Are you sure it's okay for me to be here? It looks like this is a family thing."

She said 'looks like' because she didn't often experience it, and the amount of joviality was also perplexing. Family gatherings were usually more angst than enjoyment, but these people seemed genuinely happy to see each other.

"Of course. You're not the only interloper, Rebecca's brother is here."

Rebecca's brother? Who the hell was Rebecca? Adie took a deep breath and tried to smile. This would be fine; she could talk to anyone. "Well, then I'm honoured you invited me."

She set the wine bottle down on the counter and frowned as she stared out of the patio doors. Morgan had just executed a turn with the football that'd left every kid on their bum, and it looked like this was another thing she was about to excel at next weekend. She stopped dead and waved, then beckoned Adie outside, smiling and then turning to hoist a toddler over her shoulder.

"You go ahead. I'll introduce you to everyone else later." Jenny had already started fiddling with something on the hob and Adie wandered out to the patio.

The kids were all bare foot and she couldn't stomp on them in her boots, so she sat on the step and untied her laces, setting them neatly next to a terracotta pot. When she stood again and Morgan passed her the ball, she felt a wave of panic, compelled to do something fancy with it so she didn't think she was the only one with some skills. She managed a few keep-ups before lobbing it over the clump of children.

Morgan applauded. "Very nice, I'm glad we're on the same team next week."

"We'll show those old blokes a thing or two." Adie bowed, as relieved not to have cocked that up as she was to find Morgan in a better mood this week.

"Too right we will. These little monkeys have been helping me practise. Haven't you, guys?" None of the four boys answered. They surged across the lawn and lost the ball under the hedge, then shimmied about on their fronts trying to retrieve it. Morgan left them to it, sticking her hands in her pockets as she kicked daisies. "How have you been?"

"Great. Busy. House is clear for you to start this week."

"Good." She paused, glancing at the boys now prodding their ball with a stick and arguing over who had the longest arms. "Listen, about last Sunday. I'm sorry I was a bit weird."

Adie nodded as Morgan bumped their shoulders together. "I didn't say anything to offend you, did I? I was worried you might not want me here today."

"No, definitely not." She smiled, her eyes fixed on her feet. "It's all me, you were lovely. Promise."

"Okay, that's all I need to know." Adie leant sideways to knock shoulders again. "For the record, I had fun too. It did occur to me though that I've spilled my guts, but I know next to nothing about you." Besides her being annoyingly athletic. Somehow on the flip side Morgan had heard all about Liz and Robert's divorce, his affair, her mental health problems, and God knows what else.

"To be fair, I don't know much about you either, only your parents. You know, those people who apparently don't impact your life whatsoever." Morgan smirked and prodded Adie in the stomach.

"Untrue. You know I run."

"Oh, well. Say no more, I know you perfectly now."

"It's a biography compared to what I've got out of you. Your mum has told me more."

She regretted that the instant it was out of her mouth as Morgan folded her arms and peered down her nose. "Has she indeed? And what is it my mother has told you about me?"

Adie cupped a hand to her ear. "Oh, I think I hear her calling us in." She lowered her voice to a whisper and stepped into the kitchen. "I'm coming, Jenny. We'll have to continue this chat later, don't want to seem rude."

Morgan appeared alongside and put a hand on Adie's shoulder. "Want me to catch you up so we're even? Think fast because I'll only say this all once." She pointed to a tall, slim guy with a flop of brown hair. "That's my twin brother Tim, and next to him is his wife Rebecca. She's eight months pregnant with their first kid."

Adie turned to stop her. "You have a twin?"

"Yes, keep up." She continued to point, moving onto the next guy. "Then Rebecca's brother, my brother-in-law, and finally my older sister. All the kids outside are hers. You could say she's been busy."

Tim stood and held out a hand the size of a steak, smiling warmly. "Welcome to the family, Adie."

"Blimey, you lot don't muck about. Am I going to find a horse's head in my bed?" There was a distinctly Corleone vibe going on. The fact Jenny's husband was still nowhere in sight and hadn't been mentioned raised suspicions further. Perhaps he was busy smoking cigars in Sicily while they all hid out in the English countryside. It'd certainly explain where the money for this house came from because accountancy wasn't that lucrative.

"Maybe. Once Mum's decided she likes you, there's no escape. Believe me, many have tried..." He turned pensive for a moment, then laughed, sitting back on his chair. "I'm only messing. Take it as a compliment, she's pickier than you'd think."

"Yeah, I heard about Morgan's ex."

He threw back his head and laughed again. "Mm, Lou. Poor girl."

"Tim!" Morgan rubbed her hands along her face. "Jesus. Just when I thought Mum was the most embarrassing member of the family."

"What's there to be embarrassed about, sis? You saw sense and dumped her, eventually."

Morgan let out a noise somewhere between a laugh and a sigh, then stepped back onto the patio. "If you've quite finished, I think this was a bad idea." She dragged Adie out by her T-shirt and folded her arms in a challenge, but the smile indicated none of this had bothered her too much. "Come on then, what did my mum tell you about Lou?"

"Not much. Just that she didn't like her. What was she, an axe murderer or something?"

"Don't be ridiculous. She was just... not particularly understanding of a few things." Morgan thumbed towards the annex. "Do you want tea?" She made a move for the gate. "Come and tell me about your week."

Adie followed her in and squinted as she adjusted to the cool, dark corridor. There had been some progress in the living room, and the walls had a fresh coat of magnolia. She leant against the doorframe and took in the view again, still not quite believing somewhere so beautiful existed only a ten-minute drive from the estate full of ex-military houses where she lived.

"I do believe you're deflecting." She wagged her finger as Morgan took a pint of milk from a small tabletop fridge. There had to be a reason she was so desperate to get them away from her family. "My week was shit, why don't you tell me about yours?"

"Not much to say. I went to London three days to do some jobs, then I worked on this place for my parents."

"Great, well that's a start."

"A start?" She rooted around in a drawer, pulling out a teaspoon, then held up the milk and squinted at the label. "Expired. How stringent are you when it comes to run out dates?"

That all depended on how lumpy it was, and Adie took a few paces forward, grabbing the carton from her and tipping it upside down. When the milk didn't move, she threw it at a bin under the counter. "I need it to be liquid."

Morgan poured some water from the tap into one of the mugs she'd left on the side and held it out. "Liquid it is."

"Thanks."

"You're welcome." She filled her own and took a few sips, cradling it like tea. They were silent for several moments, each drinking as they leant against the work surface, but then Morgan mumbled a few times before speaking again. "Lou isn't a bad person, despite what my mum will tell you." She turned, making eye contact but then dropping it again. "Sure you want to hear this if you've already had a bad week?"

"Of course I do."

"Okay, and there's me doing it again." Morgan dumped her mug down on the counter, grinding her palm into her forehead. "This is exactly what I did with Lou, which is how we got into a mess in the first place."

Adie frowned, fiddling with the handle of her cup. She had no clue what was happening here, or how to help. "I'm totally confused," she confessed. "You may need to go back a step." Or ten, if necessary. There was clearly some sort of story with Lou, and apparently everyone knew it but her.

"I have a few issues with anxiety." There was a big gaping pause, as if Morgan might be expecting a reaction, but she wouldn't get one. Who didn't? "Panic attacks, intrusive thoughts... it's why I freaked on you last Sunday. I can't go near hospitals, they're just too stressful. I had a ruptured appendix as a teenager and ever since it's just..." She let out a sigh, her arms falling to her sides. "PTSD apparently, but I was always a bit high strung, even before that."

She was finding it hard to get the story out, fidgeting with her hands and staring at the floor, and Adie shot her a smile for reassurance. "Sounds like a pile of dog crap. How does the ex fit in?"

"Lou really struggled to cope with this stuff. Everything became about her, how much she hated to see me have a panic attack or how difficult it was when I didn't want to do something. I ended up hiding how I was feeling from her most of the time because it was just easier."

"And then you broke up?"

"Yeah." Morgan shrugged. "She wanted us to live together, but I knew it wasn't right. When Mum and Dad put in the offer on this place, I decided it was a chance for a fresh start. Time to do things differently. Except I'm not, because I seem to always default back to this position of assuming no one wants to hear my problems and I need to just keep them to myself."

Adie considered her words carefully, not wanting to over-step given they'd only met a week ago. She felt like a lot of trust was being placed in her. "I know I said it's tough seeing my mum struggle, but I'd never want her to stop sharing it. For what it's worth, you don't need to hide anything from me."

"I appreciate that, but it's been tough. A lot of my friends ended up being her friends and most of them couldn't see the problem, so I feel a bit adrift." Morgan picked up her mug again and raised it to her mouth, but then paused and stared at the water. "I know she wants us to get back together, and I occasionally wonder if I was too hard on her."

"I can't tell you that, but I can tell you your gut is usually right." It's the one thing she'd learned from her gran: follow your instincts. "If you had concerns, and your family didn't think the relationship was healthy, perhaps that's a sign it wasn't. Only you know for definite, though." Adie waited for Morgan to reply but she only nodded, listening intently. "Thank you."

"What are you thanking me for?"

"Trusting me. I could see how tough that was for you to share. I know I'm no substitute for the friends you're missing in London, but I can also offer you Josh. When he's not stressing about youth clubs and girls, he's actually a pretty good laugh."

Morgan's face contorted, but it looked more like embarrassment than any great aversion to the suggestion. "Oh God, are you sure he'll want to hang around with me? I think he was trying to ask me out last week and I had no idea what to say."

"Don't sweat it. Josh was thrilled when you weren't interested."

Morgan's jaw dropped open a little. "Rude."

"On the contrary. You correctly identified that he is a man, and as a lesbian you did not find him attractive." She still looked confused, her lip hooking up slightly, and Adie laughed. "Josh is trans. That validation was worth a hundred dates." Besides which, he was clearly only interested in Emma.

Morgan's shoulders dropped as if they'd just been relieved of a great weight. "I understand now. Okay. I had no idea."

"Why would you?" Adie smiled, her mind connecting the dots. Their situations weren't dissimilar. "I reckon you have quite a lot in common with Josh, actually."

"How's that?"

"He needs to believe he can find someone who loves the whole of him, and I think maybe you do too."

9

It was barely light when Adie left for her run on Wednesday morning. A large yellow skip had arrived while she was at work the day before, and she'd needed to set three alarms to rouse herself early enough to complete her usual routine before Morgan arrived at eight. When she made it back, hungry and shaking after pushing it hard over the final mile to get back in time, the rest of the world had started to move. She waved to a neighbour as they loaded their kids into the car for nursery and then crept through the front door so as not to wake Monica. She was out late on a date and hadn't come in until the early hours.

"Who the fuck are you?" Adie whispered as she stepped into the kitchen, jumping back with fright to find a half-naked man fiddling with the sink.

"Roy. How do you do?"

Adie blinked a few times, wondering if she was still asleep and this was a nightmare. "How drunk was I at the weekend? I don't remember ordering a geriatric strip-o-gram."

"Oh no, I gave all that up years ago." He ran the tap for a

second before pulling two mugs from the cupboard wearing nothing but a pair of jeans and a wry smile. Then he grabbed a third and held it up. "Tea?"

"You're offering me a drink in my own house? You seem to have missed the point here. What is the purpose of your visit?"

He laughed, deciding to go for the third tea regardless, and set the mug with the others. Then he picked up the kettle and filled it. "I'm a guest of your grandmother. She is a remarkable woman. Did you know she used to sing on cruise ships?"

Was he joking? She'd heard every sordid detail. Anyone could, for the price of a gin and tonic.

Adie opened the fridge and pulled out a bottle of milk. She still needed breakfast and a shower before Morgan arrived. "What were you doing with my sink?"

"Fixing a drip."

"She didn't tell you I have a professional coming to rip out the lot today?"

Roy turned to lean against the work surface with his arms folded just below a silver pendant hung on a piece of black leather. It was hard to discern his age; she was terrible at figuring out men. Early sixties perhaps? It was all guess-work. "I'm sure he won't mind me horning in on his profession."

"*Her* profession. My plumber's a woman."

"A female plumber? Lord, you lot will want the vote next."

Adie narrowed her eyes as she grabbed a box of cereal from the cupboard but chose to take his smile as a sign that it was a joke. "This has been fun, Roy. Perhaps we'll meet again, but I need to get ready for work." She handed him the milk, having completed her bowl of cereal, and he made a quick show of finishing her tea. "Can you remind Gran that she won't have access to the bathroom after eight o'clock?"

The implication should have been that she found herself somewhere else to stay for a few days, for her own convenience as well as everyone else's, but she didn't always take the hint. Liz would be glad or at least willing to have her.

"Will do."

He whistled as he slid the other two mugs of tea from the work surface and sprang across the floorboards, hopping up the stairs as Adie trudged behind. She waited until he'd opened the spare room door with his elbow, slopping a little liquid and then kicking it closed again, before taking a mouthful of cornflakes and sitting on the edge of her bed trying to listen to their conversation. It was a waste of time; the house was built like a nuclear bunker.

She took a quick shower after breakfast, cursing her gran for the second time that morning for not tidying away her bottles as requested. They needed the room clear, so she grabbed the cardboard box she'd left out in anticipation and filled it with night creams, shampoos, make up and all the other paraphernalia Monica used to put herself together. If she needed it any time soon, she was out of luck.

As eight o'clock approached, Adie sat on the sofa watching breakfast television, ready besides the small matter of the love-in concluding in her gran's bedroom. Explaining this one to Morgan would be a laugh. She was probably unused to horny old men in the kitchen on a Wednesday morning and might need some warning.

When her van pulled up a few minutes early, Adie tugged open the front door, wandering down the path with her hands dug into her trouser pockets. Morgan wound down the window and leant over, her hair scraped back into a ponytail and the usual pair of aviators perched on top of her head.

"Are you ready for me?" She reached around to grab a thermos and took a swig before slotting it back.

"Yes, ma'am." Adie nodded and saluted her. "A word of caution, though. Gran's got a bloke in her room. If they give you any trouble whatsoever today, give me a call. I can come home at lunchtime."

Morgan laughed, peering up at the first-floor window. "What kind of trouble are we talking?"

"Oh, I don't know. Anything's possible. Drugs, loud sex games, satanic rituals."

"I love your gran already. Can I keep her?"

Adie shrugged, considering for a second. "Sure." She stood back as the door popped open and Morgan jumped down, straightening her cargo shorts and grabbing her thermos again. They both crept into the hallway, sniggering as they stopped to listen for signs of life overhead. "Whatever you do, though, don't invite her to stay in that annex with you. It'll start as one night and she'll still be there a year later."

* * *

Monica's dulcet tones filled the house when Adie returned at six. She had Janis Joplin's 'Piece Of My Heart' on full blast as steam and a heavy spice scent erupted from the kitchen. It'd be one of her famous curries, its origin changing every time she told the story, no doubt as a peace-offering for the morning.

"You're in a good mood." Adie chucked her bag on a chair and pulled a can of orangeade from the fridge. A bang overhead startled her as she tugged the ring, and it fizzed down her hand. "Is Morgan still here?"

"Yes, I invited her to stay for dinner."

"No Roy?"

"I'm meeting up with him after we've eaten."

Monica turned down the volume, and they both laughed as the sound of Morgan singing along floated down the stairs. It came to an abrupt stop and when she appeared in the doorway ten seconds later, her face was a deep crimson colour.

"Looks like I got the water back on just in time." She held up her hands to show the grout. "Mind if I use the sink? You won't have one upstairs until tomorrow."

"Go ahead," Monica offered, turning it on for her and then resuming her task. She drained the rice into a sieve once Morgan had finished washing her hands and distributed it across three plates. Then she spooned generous helpings of chicken and vegetable curry on the side and set them on the table.

Adie pulled a couple of naan breads from under the grill before they burst into flames. "You've got a great voice by the way, you two should team up." She dropped them on the work surface and shook her burning fingers.

"Oh, we've been duetting all day. Perhaps we'll become a trio."

"Forget it." She'd been trotted out as entertainment for her gran's friends enough times and wasn't being dragged in again. Especially in front of Morgan, who really would think they were all barking mad.

"You sing?" Morgan sat and dipped her little finger into the curry, licking it off. "Let me guess, soaring rock ballads."

"Very funny. No, I do not sing."

Monica scoffed. "Rubbish, you've a lovely voice. Get it from your grandmother."

The look of delight on Morgan's face was clear, and she leant forward on the table. "What else can you tell me about her?" It was payback for Sunday, and the prospect had brought a glimmer to her eye. "Spare no detail."

Adie shovelled rice and submitted to being thoroughly embarrassed as they ate, hoping the quicker she made her way through the meal the faster her gran might leave for her date with Roy. They were one step away from pulling out the baby photos when she wiped around the rest of her sauce with the last chunk of naan and quickly bussed her plate to the sink. "Well, that was fun, but you should go and meet your boyfriend, and I'm sure Morgan needs to get home."

They both laughed, and Morgan reached into a carrier bag hung off the back of her chair. "Afraid not. I've got a whole tube of filler here, so we can start patching up your living room walls ready for painting. Another idea you can thank your gran for."

"Ah, see, I would but I haven't shown you around the fair yet." Adie shrugged and ran the tap, filling the bowl with warm water to wash their dishes. "I haven't earned any help. It'll have to wait until next week."

"I think we can make an exception just this once."

Could they? Because filling holes in a wall sounded about as much fun as sticking her wet fingers in the plug socket. She grappled for another excuse, but before she got there Monica slipped her plate into the bowl and kissed her cheek.

"So long. I may see you later."

"May? Does that mean you might stay out with Roy?"

She shrugged. "Who knows? The night is young, and we are—"

"Old?"

Morgan spluttered with laughter, but Monica only scowled. "No." She placed a hand on Morgan's shoulder and kissed her cheek. "It was a pleasure to meet you, my dear. If you could ensure my granddaughter gets all the very hardest and most laborious tasks, I'd be eternally grateful. Ta-rah."

Once she was sure her gran was gone, Adie left the washing up and sat back at the table. "Sorry about her, I did warn you she's a nightmare."

"Don't apologise. Monica is a very interesting woman; we've had some fun chats today."

"That's one word for it. Can you do me a favour and not let slip to Jenny or my dad that she's had blokes back here? I hate to ask, but he's a bit sensitive. I think a childhood of random uncles has fucked him up a bit."

Monica was great as a gran, but Adie couldn't imagine what it had been like having her for a parent. Robert had spent a good portion of his childhood living with his grandparents because she was off on cruise ships or tours and was always back with someone new in tow. It made for exciting anecdotes, but probably not a stable childhood.

"Noted. I did get the impression there was some friction there. How do you get on with your dad?"

Adie shuffled on her chair. "We largely leave each other to our own devices. I don't particularly like his choices, and he doesn't condone mine. It's not ideal but we sort of agree to disagree."

At times it was more disagreeing than agreeing, but the less time they spent together the easier it was to manage. The double-whammy of his affair and her coming out four years ago had created a shit storm of bad feeling and they were past it, but their relationship had never fully recovered.

"What on earth have you done to offend him?"

"Well, for a start I figured out I was gay. That was the real sucker-punch." Robert was a pretty traditional guy, which she'd reconciled was probably a result of Monica being the complete opposite. "He wasn't exactly jumping for joy when I told him I was in love with a woman." She inclined her head and smiled. "But then I'd just found out he was in love with another woman, so we were kind of even."

"What happened?"

"He tried to tell me I was too young to make such a big decision, and that it wouldn't make me happy in the long run. That's why I said I'd have to be sure before getting into another relationship. If I'm bringing it all up again, it'd have to be for someone really special."

Margot Robbie dipped in chocolate, perhaps, or some tattooed goddess. Adie's mind drifted, and her eyes wandered up Morgan's arm, but then she averted her gaze and tried to return to safer thoughts. Morgan needed a friend, and she'd get one.

"So, you don't have a girlfriend now?"

"Nope, free as a bird. I'm not saying I don't see anyone, but I always make sure they know where they stand, and I keep my private life out of this town."

Morgan covered her mouth as she laughed, pushing back her plate. "Oh, I see what you're trying to tell me." She munched through the last of her dinner, bobbing her head. "You're one of *those* lesbians."

"Excuse me?"

"You know the type. Brooding, want you to think they're desperately sad and deep, so you'll sleep with them and understand when they never call."

Adie spluttered with laughter. "Brooding? No. Not calling? No. I have perfectly healthy, honest relationships, which we *both* agree will remain casual."

"Mhm. If you say so."

"I do. One day I'll meet someone special, but for now it's easier this way. When you meet my dad on Saturday, you'll understand why."

10

True to her word, Adie stood on the edge of the football pitch at one o'clock on Saturday, nervously waiting to see who turned up first. She'd spent the preceding half an hour helping Josh set up his stand and then left him to it, swearing blind he'd invited Emma and reinforcements were on the way. She'd be back to check that out later.

For now, though, she was trying to push down a wave of pre-emptive nausea. It was a long time since she'd let Robert meet any of her friends but given the connection to Jenny it was an inevitability. Hopefully, his desire to get in her good books would make sure he kept a lid on any of his less savoury opinions.

"You are alive then?" He stood with his hands on his hips behind the turnstile in a pair of tight black shorts and a fluorescent pink football shirt, the faintest hint of a gut protruding and his hair slicked back like he belonged in an old Brylcream advert. "I've been trying to get hold of you for weeks; we need a chat."

"For someone who thought I might be dead you don't seem very bothered."

His brow furrowed slightly, and he shook his head. "Where have you been?"

"New York, Paris, Tokyo. You know my life is non-stop glamour." Before he had a chance to reply, she cut him off. "I did come in, but you were away. Met Jenny, though." Adie caught sight of her out of the corner of an eye, with all the grandchildren, Tim, and Morgan in tow. "Speaking of which, we got chatting. I invited one of her kids to join us today, is that okay?"

The turnstile clunked as she pushed through into the old Town FC ground where the match was being hosted. The club had long since folded but the facilities were still in use by anyone who wanted to hire them, including the local rugby team and various companies who used the bar and function rooms.

"Of course, we could do with some young blood. It's Tim, isn't it?"

"No, actually. Morgan's playing. Jenny's daughter." Before he had a chance to make further comment, she switched it back to him. "How was your holiday?"

Robert frowned momentarily but then it turned to a smile. "Lovely. We were in Tuscany with a couple I met through the golf club. Far too much wine consumed, I'm not sure how this will go today." Two weeks drinking wine had nothing to do with it, but the twenty a day smoking habit he'd kept up for the best part of forty years might slow him down. "If you've time for dinner this week, I'll fill you in properly. There is something I wanted to tell you."

This time she had a genuine excuse. Morgan had finished the bathroom and, whilst she fitted the new kitchen next week, they were going to spend their evenings making a start on the painting. "Sorry, got plans. It might be a couple of weeks, but then we can have dinner or something."

"You can't even spare your old man a quick drink?"

She shrugged. The only day she'd told Morgan they couldn't do was Tuesday, because of Liz. Given the decorating help was a freebie, she didn't want to muck her about. "Sorry, but I'm finally doing up the house. You should be happy about that, I'm sure the only thing you and Mum agree on is how much of a state it is."

"Did you have the sense to at least book in Tim for that? I presume Jenny mentioned he's a plumber. You'd do well to keep in with that family."

"Morgan's doing that too." She held his gaze, challenging him to say anything, but he soon dropped it and his eyes were on his boots.

"Good, good. Listen, if we can't meet, I should probably tell you this now. It's not the way I wanted to ask, but you haven't left me with a lot of choice." Morgan and Jenny smiled and said hello as they walked past, trying to wrangle all the kids who were surging across the pitch and trying to join in with the opposition team's warm up. It seemed any football was fair game. Once they were back out of earshot, Robert shuffled and continued. "The thing is, I asked Sarah to marry me when we were in Italy."

Adie's eyes widened and her stomach lurched. This was supposed to be a fling. Granted, a fling that'd lasted nearly five years, but marriage? That made it permanent. Or, at least, it should. "Wow."

"I was hoping you might agree to be my sort of best man. Best lady, I suppose."

"I don't know, can I think about it?" She adjusted the bag on her shoulder. "Sorry, but I'm not sure how I feel about this. I want you to be happy, and of course I'll come to the wedding, but I'm not sure about the rest."

He nodded, a smile softening his worried features. "Of course. I wouldn't want you to feel uncomfortable."

Perhaps he should've thought about that before proposing marriage to the woman he'd had an affair with, then, but saying so wouldn't help. They didn't need to rehash the past, especially on the side of a football pitch.

"Does Gran know?"

"No, I wanted to tell you first."

That was something, at least, but then Adie felt another swift blow hit her stomach and the colour drained from her face. "And Mum?"

Robert shrugged. "I don't think it's wise for me to contact her, we haven't spoken in a long while. How do you think she'll react?"

Who knew? Last Tuesday Adie would've said she'd take it okay, but the way she'd been on Sunday after having her purse stolen it could easily swing in the other direction. "I'm not sure, but I'll tell her. It'll be best coming from me."

"Thank you, sweetheart. I'm sorry if it makes things difficult for her, or you, but we've held out a long time. We could all do to move on."

She didn't disagree with that and began to amble along the side of the pitch with him alongside, the metal studs of his boots clacking on the concrete. When they reached the pavilion, she tried to put it out of her mind. Jenny had found a spare ball for the boys to play with and they were chasing each other around the grass while Morgan sat on the step changing her shoes.

She looked up and waved as they approached. "Hello, Mr Green. Nice to meet you." Leaving a boot lace untied she stood and shook his hand. "Adie told me you sponsor this event; it must be where she gets her charitable side from."

Robert smiled. "My daughter has a charitable side?"

Before Morgan could say any more her mum jumped in. "Youth group. She came by to talk with you, but I presumed it wouldn't be a problem, so I've already arranged a donation. I was left in charge, and I was certain you'd want to support your own daughter."

Adie tried to hold back a grin. They hadn't discussed a donation at all, and a conversation must have taken place between Morgan and Jenny. After the bombshell Robert had just dropped it was the boost she needed, and she could hug either one of them.

"No, no. Of course," he muttered. "Anyway, I should leave you to get ready. There are shirts in the changing room. Don't be too long, we kick off in twenty minutes and I want us warmed up."

They left him to chat with Jenny and pushed through the double doors, Adie bursting into laughter. She nudged Morgan with a shoulder, then stopped in the corridor. "What was that all about?"

Morgan shrugged. "What?"

"Oh, please. The ambush."

She bent to tie the flapping boot lace. "We talk. I'll say no more."

Adie laughed again and went to open the changing room door, but a deep booming voice resonated from beyond. Shit. It was going to be full of hairy old blokes. "They won't have laid on separate female changing rooms." She let go and slumped against the wall.

"That's okay, we only need shirts." Morgan adjusted her shorts and reached to pull up her socks. "Grab them and we'll change here."

"Must I go in there?"

"Yes, don't be such a wuss."

Adie sighed and covered her eyes with both hands, turning and pushing the door open with her back. "Okay, lads," she called. "Someone chuck me two shirts."

There was a loud cheer, and she was hit by two pieces of fabric which were presumably the shirts, although she couldn't see. When one dropped off her shoulder, she had to remove a hand to pick it up and caught a glimpse of a hairy back. She made a hasty retreat, shuddering and causing Morgan to laugh.

"I think that's just reconfirmed my sexuality." When Morgan tugged off her T-shirt and stood in only a sports bra, the tattoo creeping up her broad shoulder and under the strap, Adie stole a look to replace the image. "It's just happened again," she mumbled. When a slap landed on her arm she winced and laughed, pretending to shield her eyes again. "Sorry. Yuck, put it all away."

She let her hands drop, relieved to see Morgan was still smiling and her cheeks had turned a dusky pink. The shirt in her hand hung limp, and she tugged at the bottom of Adie's loose running vest. "Take this off. I can't stand inequality."

Adie complied, taking care not to mess her hair as she pulled it off and dumped it on top of her kit bag. She leant forward and flexed her bicep, but when Morgan did the same thing she had to stop. There was no competition. "How the fuck did you get so strong?"

"Weights. I told you that."

"Yeah, but... wow." There were muscles popping in places she didn't know they could.

"You're strong, too, just leaner from all the running. Our

bodies are suited to different things. Don't you ever think how cool it is that they're so adaptable?"

She didn't, really. It wasn't even what she was thinking about Morgan's; the wow wasn't envy, it was desire. She knew friendship was safer ground for them both, but she had enough self-awareness to realise there was a physical attraction. Jenny hadn't been wrong about that.

"No, I just think it's hot." Adie shrugged and picked up her football shirt. She wouldn't deny anything to Morgan; pretence wasn't healthy. "I love women with muscles. In fact, strength in any form is a massive turn on. What about you?"

Morgan seemed a little taken aback at the candour, but then she also shrugged. "Yeah, I have to agree. Show me a strong, compassionate woman, and I'm putty. After Lou I think the second part is probably more important, but they go hand in hand."

This was turning deep for a conversation in a sports pavilion corridor, but Adie didn't mind. It was a great distraction from what had transpired before, and what would happen next when she had to deliver the news to Liz. For now, she was happy to continue it. "Compassion is good. Patience is another thing any future girlfriend of mine will need in spades." She laughed as she adjusted her shirt. It was way too big, and with the sleeves rolled up it had formed ruffles. "Damn it. I'm going to trip over this thing, it's a dress."

Morgan took a step forward and unrolled the sleeves, then began neatly folding up the left arm. "Maybe you're the one who needs to learn some patience." She tapped the right arm to indicate she wanted access, and Adie turned sideways. "Although come to think of it, the girlfriend might need that too. You'll be worth the effort, though."

It was Adie's turn to blush a little. "Will I?"

"Of course you will. I know life has made you guarded, but you're a massive softy. You were right last week when you said it'd be different one day, but I don't think this is easier for you, I think it's very hard indeed." Morgan smiled and reached for her own shirt. "When was the last time you had one of these mutually casual relationships with a woman?"

Adie squinted as she tried to recall. "I dunno. Last year some time. Autumn, I think, so what's that? Maybe ten months ago." It was someone she'd met in a bar in Manchester. They'd ended up chatting, then spent a night together a few weeks later. They both knew nothing could come of it, though, when they lived so far apart.

"I rest my case." Morgan pulled on the shirt and then tied her hair back with the band around her wrist. "You know that you deserve it, right? Not just me and Josh."

Adie had been lost in thought, trying to remember if there was anyone since, but besides a few random fumbles in nightclubs there was no one else springing to mind. Perhaps it was time to remedy the situation, but it'd have to wait until life calmed down and the house was finished. "What's that?"

Morgan smiled warmly. "Never mind. Come on, let's go and teach these guys how to play football."

11

Josh held out a tub of lollipops as they approached the stand. "How did it go?"

Adie took a red one. It'd been hard going trying to carry an entire team, so a little sugar boost was needed. "Won. No idea what the final score was, there were too many goals in both ends, but we definitely came out on top." She twisted off the wrapping and licked, surprised to find it was cherry rather than strawberry. "How's it going here?"

Emma wasn't there, big shock, and Josh sat on his own. There were a few people slotting coins into the collection box, though. That had to be a good sign.

"Great, Emma's just gone to grab us an ice cream." He wore a satisfied smile, as if he knew she'd doubted him.

"Good, I'll say hi later. You remember Morgan?"

She gave a shy wave and delved into the tub for a green lolly. Then she pulled a fiver from her bag and stuffed it in with the other donations. "Most expensive sweet I've ever eaten, so it'd better be good."

"Can I ask you about something?" Josh gestured sideways with his head while Morgan thumbed through the leaflets, and Adie scooted over a few steps.

"What's up?"

"Do you mind if we don't meet for a drink later? Emma's asked me for one and—"

"Say no more. How are you feeling about it?"

Josh ran both palms down his face, stretching the skin and rolling back his eyes. "Still terrified, and totally out of my depth. I'm not ready for anything physical yet, and I can't stop worrying that when we do get there..." His lips vibrated as he expelled a deep breath. "Every time I think about it my brain slowly explodes."

Morgan sidled over; the lolly hung from her mouth leaving a bright green stain. She pulled it out and pointed it at Josh. "Not my place, but can I say something?" She waited until he'd nodded. "She clearly likes you, and you like her, so what's the issue? I understand maybe it's more complicated down the track, but why don't you just see where it goes? Try to enjoy this."

Adie shrugged. "Exactly what I said. I totally understand why you held off dating while you had surgery last year, but perhaps it's time to get back out there. You don't have to rush in, just dip your toe in the water."

Josh smiled and slumped back into his deckchair. "Okay, but what shall I say?"

"The truth? It's often a good place to start. Just tell her it's your first time dating in a while and you're a little nervous. Women eat that shit up."

Morgan nudged Adie's shoulder. "Do they indeed. That's interesting to know."

"Don't twist my words, you know what I mean." Showing some vulnerability never hurt, he'd just look sensitive. The irony of who was dishing out this advice was not lost on her, though, given her complete lack of emotional intimacy with any woman. Ever. "Do as I say, not as I do, and you'll be fine."

When Emma came towards them carrying two dripping cones of whippy ice cream, Adie put an arm around Morgan's waist to draw her away so Josh could have some privacy. She seemed to get the message and surreptitiously pointed, smiling at the nod of confirmation, and they ducked into the next stand.

"She's pretty," Morgan whispered, peering around the tarpaulin. "I'm having definite hair envy; I can only get mine that colour with a lot of dye."

Adie hooked a finger into Morgan's waistband and dragged her back. She was terrible at undercover work. "Yeah, Emma's great. Super clever, too. She's a PhD student at Goldsmiths. We chatted at their Christmas party last year, I like her a lot and I think she's good for Josh. He needs someone who's on his level intellectually, but the trouble is they're both shy and—" She was still rambling on about how great Emma was when she clocked Morgan's smirk and came to an abrupt stop. "What?"

"Perhaps Josh isn't the only one who goes for redheads."

"Behave. She hasn't got nearly enough muscles or tattoos, weren't you listening earlier?"

Morgan went to reply but then her bag started ringing. She fumbled to pull out her phone, sticking a finger in her ear and squinting. She'd said "I can't hear you" a lot before she finally gave up and wedged it back in a pocket. "That was Mum, she's in the fair with the boys so I said I'd meet her later. Are you coming? You owe me a tour first and I've been looking forward to this."

She swirled the lolly around her tongue with a devilish glint and pinged the remainder into a bin bag tied to the side of the table, then they waved goodbye to Josh and Emma. He gave them a double thumbs up but was still engrossed in conversation and it'd be cruel to interrupt if he'd made progress. This was not a relationship that needed any help derailing itself.

They sauntered down the line of stalls. There was a tombola, raffle, information stands, guide dogs, and all sorts, with people bustling around in the mid-afternoon sun. Morgan pulled her aviators from the bag and perched them on her nose, then threaded her arm through Adie's, stopping them being parted by the crowd.

When they reached the next field, separated by a line of trees, the stalls turned to rides. There was a kiddie area with roundabouts and mini rollercoasters, then beyond that the thrill stuff meant for older children and adults. It was packed out already, even though some of the rides didn't open until later in the evening, and they could barely hear over the screams and blaring music.

"What do you want to go on first?" Adie yelled.

Morgan looked down at her bag. "We might be a bit limited with all this kit. Didn't think of that." Then something caught her eye, and she pointed off into the distance. "Isn't that your gran with Roy? Do you reckon they'd hold our stuff for a few minutes?"

It seemed the least they could do, and Adie nodded, pulling Morgan towards them. They dodged in and out of kids with candy floss and cones of chips, waving until Monica spotted them and held up a pink cuddly toy. Sometimes it really was difficult to tell who the seventy-two and who the twenty-nine-year-old was.

"Congratulations, we watched your victory earlier. I don't pretend to understand much but you seemed to make quite a good team, when you weren't tackling each other."

Morgan laughed. "Someone got a bit competitive."

"Me?" Adie protested. "You had blinkers on."

She shrugged. "Scored three goals, though, compared to how many?"

"None. In fairness I did end up playing in defence for most of the game."

"I spoke with your father afterwards, too." Monica had been smiling but her lips tightened. He'd clearly delivered his news, and by the looks of things it hadn't gone down well. Not that it was a surprise, because Monica had never liked Sarah, and after the affair debacle she'd been steadfastly in Liz's camp. Her line was always that you didn't divorce family, and the stance annoyed Robert no end.

"There's nothing we can do about it, but will you come with me to tell Mum on Tuesday?"

"What's this?" Morgan interjected.

"Oh, my dad's getting married. It's fine, it's—"

"No big deal? Yeah, I know."

"Well, it's not. He wants me to be his best woman or something, though, and I'm not sure about that."

Monica's eyes widened in full force fury, and she clutched the cuddly toy so tight she almost popped off his head. Apparently, that had been the wrong thing to say right now. "He's what? Where is he, did he stay for the fair?"

"Calm down, I'll sort this out with him later." Blowing a fuse wouldn't help anyone. In a way it was sweet that he'd asked.

"I will not. It's wholly inappropriate."

Adie rubbed a hand over her eyes. She could see this needed resolving sooner rather than later before a full family feud erupted. "Do you mind finding your mum and we'll finish in a bit once we've dumped our bags?" She shrugged at Morgan, hoping for mercy. "You'll get your tour, but right now..."

"It's fine." Morgan squeezed the top of Adie's arm. "We'll find each other later. It was good to see you again, Monica."

She waved as she set off the way they'd come, and Adie watched her disappear into the crowd. It was tempting to follow and forget any of this had happened. How, four years on, were they still having the same arguments and holding identical grudges?

When she turned back to face Monica, her features had at least softened a bit. "Dad said if I was uncomfortable it was fine, and I didn't have to do it. He was actually pretty nice about the whole thing, so whatever gripes you have with him and Sarah, can you leave me out of it?"

"Is he letting you bring a guest?"

Adie shook her head with confusion. "What's that got to do with it?" Then the realisation dawned that he'd probably said she couldn't. If Roy had been at the football match, it wouldn't have gone down well. "Has he objected about you two, or something?"

"No. Well, I doubt he was thrilled, but it's not my point. I'm sure he was very nice about it, but is he letting you bring a date?"

She shuffled and patted the sweat running down her back so that it soaked into her T-shirt. "We haven't discussed it."

"Then you should, because I don't know how you can say you'll accept this and go to the wedding if you don't know whether he's now prepared to do the same for you."

Adie blanched, her discomfort rising. She'd never seen it as tit for tat and didn't understand why any of this meant they had to drag all of that up again. "It doesn't make any difference. He's my dad, of course I'm going to his wedding."

"Why do you have to go?"

She scuffed a trainer into a patch of dried dirt, covering the white leather in dust. It would cause all manner of trouble if she didn't go, and Monica knew that. Perhaps that's what she wanted, though. A bit of drama. "Because it'd crush him if we weren't there. Do you always have to be so hard on him?"

"Perhaps that's what he needs. I'm sorry, I don't ever mean to upset you, but sometimes I don't think you're hard enough."

They'd reached a stalemate. All Adie wanted now was to get out of this heat, and away from her gran, who was the only person she found objectionable. Despite everything she'd been having a good time, but now Morgan was gone, and she was being quickly sunk into a foul mood. "I'm heading home for a shower. I'll catch you later."

With a low groan, Adie pulled herself onto a barstool and flagged down a barman, ordering a burger and a pint before slumping forward with her head on her arms. After heading home to shower she'd fallen asleep for an hour but only woken more tired. If it weren't for Morgan, bed is where she'd have stayed, but they'd texted and agreed to meet at eight. She'd lured herself out at seven with the promise of food, but less than fifteen minutes later two hands dug into her shoulders.

"Struggling already? I thought you were a massive party animal," Morgan whispered next to her ear.

Adie grunted out a laugh, her eyes still closed. "I am, watch out later." The hands pulled away, and she grumbled. "Oh no, don't stop. That was nice."

"Dream on."

She rallied when her food was dropped on the bar with a knife and fork wrapped in a napkin. Before she had a chance to ask for ketchup, the server was gone again so she hauled herself up onto her knees and leant over, grabbing a bottle from under the counter. She repositioned herself on the seat, pulled off the lid, and banged hard on the bottom of the glass to release some sauce.

Morgan grinned as she took a chip, smothering it in ketchup, but her face fell when Adie slid the plate out of reach. "Are you always this tight with food?" She went to take another chip and her hand was batted out of the way. "Rude."

"Take the hint, I don't share."

"Not at all?" She narrowed her eyes in a challenge. "How would someone change your mind?"

Adie laughed a little, wiping her hands on the napkin. "It's hard to say, it's never happened before."

"Then this is a good way to really get to know you, bear with me for a minute. Theoretically, what would I have to do for half of your burger?"

"For the burger?" She thought for a second, trying to work out how best to keep her food safe. "Marry me. Even then, it'd be touch and go. For the chips maybe a little less."

"What, like a long engagement or just cohabiting?"

Adie laughed again as Morgan took off one of her rings and held it up expectantly. She put out her left hand and let Morgan slip the band of silver up her ring finger, flinching as it caught on her knuckle where it was too small. "That's a lot of commitment just for a chip."

"Oh no, I'm all in. I want your burger, too."

Adie picked up a chip, dipped it in ketchup, and held it out. "I'm prepared to give you one bite of the burger, but that's my first and final offer. You can take it or leave it." She cut off a piece and pushed it across the plate with her knife. Morgan's eyes narrowed again, but she took it. "Two engagements in one day. Who would've thought?"

"How did it go with your gran?"

"We argued some more, but she eventually calmed

down and texted to apologise. She's coming to help me sort my mum out on Tuesday, which I think is some sort of peace offering. Now, though, I plan to get wrecked." Adie's eyes widened as she drained half her drink.

"That's one option. Alternatively, we could start a little early. I know it's not so much fun before dark, but I'm feeling pretty confident my company is better than that beer glass."

Adie smiled. "I'd have to agree." They finished the food together and headed back out onto the street where the noise of screams and crap music were just about audible. There were several entrances to the field and the closest was on a lane off the top end of the Market Square. "How did you know I'd be in the pub?"

Morgan shrugged as they wandered past Robert's office. "It seemed the safest bet."

"Am I really that predictable?"

"Maybe. I was worried. Drinking seems to be your way of coping with things and I wondered if perhaps what you really needed was to talk."

Adie laughed, nodding her head in agreement. She wouldn't argue with that, although the longer it went on, the less it worked. At first, going down to London and drinking all night had been Josh's suggestion to take her mind off everything, but four years later it was more of a habit neither of them seemed able to shake.

"Don't forget, I run as well. Been every day this week, sometimes twice." She'd expected Morgan to regard that as a positive but was only met with a frown. "What?"

"You don't think that's a little excessive?"

"No." The drinking was a poor way to cope, and she already knew it was time to do something about it, but running was a healthy response.

"Okay. Out of interest, if I told you that for one week you could neither drink nor run, what do you think would happen?"

Adie stopped at the entrance to the field and leant against the gate. It was louder now, and she had to strain to hear or talk over the noise. "Nothing, I'd watch Netflix or something instead."

"If you say so."

"Would you stop saying stuff like that?" She knew what it meant. It was code for "I don't believe you".

"Sorry, but I just don't buy it." When a couple came up behind them wanting access, Morgan pushed Adie backwards with a hand on her stomach. There were a few moments pause while she held the gate open, then carefully bolted it. She wasn't letting this go, though, firmly rooted to the spot until she'd finished. "You're supporting your mum, and despite everything your dad's done he can't accept something that's fundamental to who you are. I don't think there's any world in which that hasn't affected you."

That's what Monica had been getting at earlier and hearing it from two people in one day stung. "You're very annoying."

"I know, it's a shit when someone calls you out."

She smiled, and it was irritatingly disarming. Adie noticed the dimples in her cheeks for the first time and felt an overwhelming urge to poke fingers in them but resisted. Instead she turned and looked out over the fair. The light was fading, enhancing the garish effect of hundreds of fluorescent bulbs, all flashing and strobing. She'd promised Morgan a proper tour, and it was time to deliver. Not least because it would end this conversation.

"Where do you want to start?"

Morgan pointed to the stalls along the side of the field. "I like games. Let's shoot something."

"Do I need to worry?"

"Maybe, I have a tendency to get a little competitive."

A little? That had to be the understatement of the century, and Adie scoffed. "Now who's kidding themselves?" She pulled Morgan towards a plinth with rifles attached and grabbed a fiver from her pocket, paying the man. There was a target on the wall that'd been near enough ripped to shreds by bullets, and Morgan cocked her head as she fired, not even bothering to use the eye piece. "Remind me not to get on your wrong side."

"You didn't already know that?" She pulled the trigger again and hit the bullseye. "I used to shoot on my grandad's ranch."

"Used to? It looks like you're still pretty well practised."

"Those days are long gone. He had a stroke a few weeks ago, my dad's out in California moving him into a care home."

Adie had lifted her own rifle but let it drop. It explained the mystery of Jenny's husband, but she almost wished the mafia thing were true now. "I'm sorry."

Morgan shrugged. "It is what it is." She stuck out her tongue a little this time as she peered down the barrel and fired, then set it back on the stand. "He's okay, just not able to live on his own anymore."

"Will you head out to visit him?"

"Nope."

Adie expected her to follow that up, but when she only stood with her hands on her hips selecting a prize, she decided to probe. "Did you fall out or...?"

Morgan pointed to a grey stuffed dog and tucked it under her arm. "No, but I hate flying. Don't say anything, I know it's selfish." Her eyes were on the floor as she continued, all the earlier confidence lost. "I've Skyped with him, but a twelve-hour flight would just push me over the edge right now. I feel guilty enough, so whatever you're thinking just keep it to yourself."

"I was only going to ask if you're alright, I wasn't judging you at all."

"I'm judging myself."

Adie knew when a raw nerve had been hit and went back to her target. She pulled the trigger but missed altogether; this might have to be one thing she conceded Morgan was better at. "I gathered, but lots of people are afraid of flying." The man handed over a consolation prize of a crappy plastic keyring, and she stuffed it in her pocket. "Josh, for one. When we went to Portugal two years ago, I practically had to sedate him. He was freaking out all the other passengers going on about every noise and what would happen if the engine caught on fire." It was ridiculous, air travel was one of the safest forms of transport, but sometimes fears were just irrational. No amount of talking would win him around on the idea, he just needed a little support to get through. "Don't beat yourself up."

"I'm not afraid the plane will drop out of the sky, it's more about being trapped. I don't like that I can't get off."

"Is this something to do with your appendix stuff?"

Morgan nodded, looping her arm back through Adie's and pulling her over to the coconut shy next door. She paid for a load of balls and lined them up on the plinth. "When I got ill, I was on the ranch. My grandad didn't realise how serious it was, and we were in the middle of nowhere." She handed over the dog and hurled a ball, smashing a coconut off the stand. "By the time I got to a hospital I was so unwell that I could've died." There was a pause as she missed and cursed. "And now the thought of being in a contained space with no help freaks me the hell out."

"Makes perfect sense to me."

"Glad it does to someone. I've had a *lot* of therapy, but this is the one thing I've never come close to getting a handle on. It's time to change that." She smiled and prodded Adie's stomach. "See, I call you out, but I also do it to myself. Fair's fair."

"And we're at a fair. Yes, very funny." Adie rolled her eyes but couldn't help returning Morgan's smile. She hadn't been annoyed earlier, only uncomfortable, and she was glad Morgan had explained this time rather than going moody and weird.

They took in the rest of the fair, mainly sampling all the games until Morgan had an army of teddies tucked into every available space, but it turned out she wasn't one for big rides. It seemed her fear of flying extended to roller-coasters, but she enjoyed the atmosphere and watched everyone else. When they'd completed a slow lap, Adie was yawning again and struggling to do any more without dropping a stuffed animal.

"Do you want to head for a drink?" She stopped at the gate and waved to a little boy who was staring at all their teddies. "Do you mind?" She held one up and Morgan nodded. The boy grinned and grabbed the little brown bear as it was offered, hugging it tight to his chest and mumbling a quick "thank you" before running off.

"Remember how I called you a big softy...?" Morgan held open the gate, and they began to wander back towards the Market Square. "You're also tired, though, so I'll get a taxi. Mum was my ride."

"No need, I was lazy and drove. Would've dumped the

car in town overnight if we were drinking, but now it means I can take you home."

"Sure you don't mind?"

The question was whether Morgan would mind when she saw the state of the car. Adie turned left at the bottom of the lane, rather than right, and along a side street to where she'd parked. The roof was still down, and she bundled the toys over the top, letting them fall behind the seats.

"Hop in if you dare." She popped the driver door and the wing mirror rattled again. "Don't worry about that, it's been broken for ages. Someone hit it."

"Is it even legal?"

"Who knows?"

Morgan hopped in and clicked her seatbelt, then leant forward and fiddled with the stereo. "Is this a tape deck?" She smiled, opening the glove box to pull out a cassette. "Amazing, but The Spice Girls? Are you serious?"

"Deadly. Whack it in."

Adie cranked up the volume and pulled out of the bay with a jerk. They zipped through the town centre and out onto the ring road, the sun setting to a pink haze as they veered over the hump bridge and onto country roads. All the while they'd been singing along, Morgan raising her arms to feel the rush of air over her hands.

When they crept onto the lane, Jenny's farmhouse in sight, she turned it down and poked Adie's leg. "Your gran was right, by the way. You can sing."

She shrugged as she pulled up on the drive and cut the engine. "I'm okay at karaoke."

"Then one day we're definitely doing karaoke. Thanks for today, I had fun." Morgan unclipped her seatbelt and leant over to kiss Adie's cheek. "See you on Monday to start the kitchen?"

Adie's face warmed at the unexpected show of affection but was already so sunburnt she hoped Morgan wouldn't notice. She reached over and began pulling out teddies, lining them up on the dashboard for Morgan to take. "Looking forward to it."

13

Two weeks later, she had both a new kitchen and functional bathroom. Most of the rooms were painted, too, but since Morgan had been caught up on other jobs after the paid work was complete and needed to make headway on her mum's annex, the two bedrooms were prepped but bare. It worked out well, since Monica had also chosen this week to head south and inspect her own house while catching up with a few friends, so they wouldn't need to worry about splattering her stuff in paint.

Adie had been promptly banned from decorating on her own, after layering so much emulsion on the wall that Morgan had needed to fix it, but that didn't mean she wouldn't show some willing. Straight after work on Monday she changed into her painting clothes, laying out the sheets and supplies before Morgan arrived to help.

"Adie!" Morgan's footsteps banged on the bare stairs at half six. Carpets would be the final flourish, but they couldn't book them until the risk of spills had passed. "I'm hungry, had to come straight from a job. Can we order pizza while we start on this?"

Adie looked up from the tin lid she was struggling to lift off with a screwdriver. "No need, I'm cooking you one from scratch." There was no point wasting money on takeaway when they could do it themselves. She hadn't paid a fortune for a new kitchen not to use it. "Dough is already prepared." Morgan appeared in the doorway, grinning manically, and leant against the frame. "You're in a good mood today."

"That's because I have a present for you. It's in the living room."

There was a gift? She seemed to be confused, because after all the help she'd given, Adie was trying to find ways to pay her back. "Are you kidding?" She grunted as she hauled herself off the floor and followed Morgan downstairs. On the side table was a brown cardboard box and she ripped off the tape, pulling out a new wing mirror. Well, it was probably second hand, but it wasn't broken. "This is the strangest present I've ever received. Thank you."

"Not sure if I can fit it, but if not you're at least halfway there."

Adie held the mirror in her palm. "You know, you're the first person who hasn't told me to scrap that car."

"Scrap it? No way, she just needs a little TLC." Morgan squeezed Adie's arm as she wandered through to the kitchen. It still smelt of fresh paint, all the surfaces gleaming. Apart, that was, for the one covered in flour. "Did you have a good weekend?"

Adie set the mirror on the kitchen table and grabbed the bowl of dough from the fridge. She'd made it in the morning after her run, so it had time to rest. "Average. Spent yesterday in the pub with Josh catching up on his unfolding romance." It'd been officially upgraded to a romance since their drinks date had gone well, and they were spending the day together on Saturday. He'd been angling to use the house, since he didn't have anywhere of his own, but it wasn't really in the right state yet. "Also helped write these quiz questions. Seems a bit unfair since I'm taking part, so mine is the team to join. Yours?"

Morgan nodded and peered into the bowl, looking vaguely impressed by the contents. "Went to the gym, then met up with some friends in London on Saturday night. Was good to see them."

"Go okay?" By which she meant, was the ex there?

"Surprisingly. Lou wasn't mentioned once."

Adie tried to hide a smile. "Great." She paused, her head back in the fridge as she pulled out sauce and mozzarella. "Have you heard from her recently?"

"Not a peep. I'm hoping she's finally given up and moved on."

She wasn't the only one. Adie's advice had been genuine and unbiased when she'd given it a few weeks ago, but she had to admit that the idea of them getting back together now generated pangs of jealousy. It wasn't an emotion she enjoyed, and she still didn't believe it was wise for them to get into anything, but nevertheless the feeling persisted. Not least because they were getting on so well and she couldn't imagine it lasting with Lou back on the scene. Everything she'd heard implied she wouldn't want this friendship to continue.

Morgan washed her hands and rubbed them together, her eyes full of glee. "Tell me what I need to do, I've never made my own pizza before."

"Never?" Adie was incredulous, tipping the dough onto the floured surface and slicing it in half with a palette knife. "It's really easy and much better than store bought." She pushed one ball of dough aside and handed Morgan the rolling pin. "Technically we shouldn't use this if we're being authentic, but it's easier and I don't want to ruin my new kitchen by throwing dough all over it."

"Whatever gets me pizza quickest." Morgan went to work, shaping a perfect circle, and then stood back. Adie handed her a circular tray with holes and she carefully picked up her base, moving and reshaping it to fit. "Now what?"

"Toppings. I have sauce, cheese and meat."

"No vegetables?"

"Wash out your mouth right now."

Morgan laughed and took a scoop of sauce, splatting it onto her base and spreading it around. Then she ripped mozzarella and dumped on a liberal helping of Parma ham and salami. "Happy?"

They repeated with the second ball of dough and slid them both into the oven, setting a ten-minute timer and scraping the sticky remnants from their hands into the sink.

"Are you eating that?" Adie frowned as Morgan ran her finger over her front teeth to dislodge the dough.

"Yeah, it's tasty. Try some."

She held out a finger and Adie took a nibble, then grimaced. "No, it's not."

Morgan laughed, then nudged in and ran her hands under the tap. "I need to ask you about something." She peered to the side, a hint of apprehension in her voice as she spoke. "Tim and I have got a friend out in Spain who runs a property maintenance company. Luke."

She paused while she dried her hands, and Adie's stomach lurched. For some reason, the first thing that flashed through her mind was Morgan being offered a job out there and moving, however ridiculous the idea was when she struggled to get on a plane. It was even worse than the thought of her going back to Lou.

"Yeah?"

"After our chat at the fair I got in touch. Tim sometimes goes out there to do bits of plumbing work for him, although it's more of an excuse for a few days away, so I asked if he had anything for me. I figured if I had a job to do it might be an added incentive, so he's sorted a bathroom for me to replace. It's like for like so won't take long, only a weekend."

Adie was flooded with relief for the second time in half an hour and smiled. "But what, you're worried if you can manage the flight?"

"Yeah, which is where you figure. Luke says I can take a friend and he'll pay for us both to fly, given I'm not being paid much for the actual work. Would you come?"

"Me? Don't you want to ask one of your friends from London?"

Morgan shook her head. "No, not really. I want to take you. What do you reckon? We get to stay in the villa, so it won't cost anything. Well, besides a bit of spending money. Could you get Friday and Monday off work?"

Probably, given she hadn't used any of her annual leave yet, and the idea of a weekend break did appeal. She hadn't been away since the trip to Portugal with Josh two years ago. After everything that had gone on recently, a few days on the beach would be a good break, and she'd get to help Morgan into the bargain.

"Expect so. It does seem a bit wrong that the way I finally get to repay you involves a free holiday, though. It's not much of a sacrifice."

"Oh, you wait. You haven't seen me at an airport yet."

As the timer pinged Adie opened the oven and let out a gush of hot hair which almost burned off her eyebrows. The pizzas bubbled and she grabbed a glove to pull them out, setting them on the hob. "When are we going then?"

"Weekend after next, just before this quiz of Josh's. Mum is more excited about that than I can adequately describe, she's a major quiz buff." Morgan wore a sheepish smile as she carried her pizza to the table. "Does that mean you'll come?"

Adie considered for all of two seconds. "If the boss says yes, I'm in."

They ate and loaded their plates into the new integrated slimline dishwasher, but as they were about to head upstairs there was a loud banging noise and Adie jumped. "No idea who that is, sorry." She jogged out to the hallway and yanked open the door. It was still sticking but minor details like that hadn't been tackled yet. The number of favours required to get the house perfect, she'd owe Morgan forever. "Mum, what are you doing here?"

"Hello, love. That's a nice greeting." She held out a rectangular package wrapped in brown paper. "House-warming gift."

"Housewarming? I thought that was the plant?"

"And you killed it." Liz stepped in and hooked her bag on a coat peg, then walked straight through to the living room. "This is for your nice new walls. I told you, they need pictures."

Be that as it may, they were about to paint upstairs and Morgan was now standing in the kitchen doorway, leant against the frame with flour down her polo shirt. Liz didn't notice her at first, tearing off the wrapping and holding up her offering against the far wall.

Adie shuffled with discomfort. "Looks good, where did you get that?" She glanced at the still life of a vase of sunflowers. It wasn't something she'd choose for herself, but then she'd lived with nothing for over a year and it was clearly important to her mum. "It's pretty."

"I painted it." Liz glanced over her shoulder. "Oh, hello Morgan. Didn't realise you'd be here."

"Hello Mrs Green." She bit her thumbnail, that same sheepish grin back on her face.

"Have I missed something?" Adie frowned. She must have because last time she checked her mum and Morgan were not acquainted.

Morgan shrugged. "I went into the garden centre with Mum a couple of weeks back to buy a few bits and your mum served us. We both recognised the name and you look pretty similar, so we got chatting."

"Yes, and Jenny invited me to a painting class she'd seen advertised on the bulletin board," Liz added. She carefully leant the frame against a wall and sat in the armchair, crossing her legs.

"In my defence, I didn't know that part, otherwise I would've mentioned it. You know what Mum's like..."

"Why are you defending yourself? It's been a Godsend, with everything that's happened lately. I would've said something myself, but then the painting wouldn't be a surprise."

Adie perched on the sofa. "I thought you said you were okay with Dad and Sarah?" They'd talked it through, and she'd been surprisingly blasé about the entire thing, wishing him luck if he wanted to go down that route again. "Or has something else happened?"

"Being okay with it and finding it confronting that your life hasn't moved on a jot are not the same things."

That was ridiculous, of course her life had moved on in four years. She was far better off now than she had been then, she couldn't be suggesting otherwise. "You're doing really well now, aren't you?"

"I'm surviving, not thriving. This has been a kick in the bum, and the painting classes are only the start of it. I've got a new man in my life."

Adie choked on thin air, her lungs constricting. What was this, invasion of the body snatchers? A couple of weeks in Jenny's company and her mum was an entirely different person. "What?"

"Is it really so incredible? His name's Charlie."

Soft grunts of laughter emanated from Morgan's direction, but they stopped when Adie shot her a worried look. She covered her mouth, but the twinkle in her eye implied she was struggling to hold back.

"I want to hear all about this, but first I think we need a drink. I'm making tea." Adie stood and scuffed into the kitchen, still not quite believing what she was hearing. Morgan stepped aside to let her pass, then sidled up to her as she filled the kettle. "Is this for real?" Adie whispered. "My mum has a boyfriend? I don't think I can cope."

"Why not? If she's happy, surely that's the main thing?"

"What if this guy's a creep?"

Morgan smiled and rubbed a hand in Adie's lower back, stroking soothing circles. "I think it's sweet that you're so protective, but she's in her fifties. You may have to let this go."

Adie grunted but nodded, setting down the kettle and pulling out some mugs. It was one thing knowing that, and another acting on it. She finished the tea and gestured for Morgan to grab one, but then froze to the spot. "Um, this is awkward, but I need another favour. My mum doesn't really know I'm gay, and I'm sure it won't come up, but—" She watched Morgan's eyes widen in shock and then shrink just as fast. "I'll explain later, but for now. Please."

"It's not like I was going to straddle you in the living room, relax."

Adie took a deep breath and tried to do just that, but she now had two things to worry about. Three if she counted the image of Morgan straddling her, which seemed to have stuck. Trying to muster a smile, she wandered through and set a mug on the side table for Liz, then sat next to Morgan on the sofa. "Come on, then. What's he like?"

Liz pursed her lips as she considered, staring at a point on the ceiling. "He's warm and loving. Enjoys snuggling up on the sofa of an evening after dinner." She laughed as Adie shuffled. "And he's a cat. Your father would never let me get a pet, so I thought sod it. If he gets a younger woman, I'm finally getting what I want. I can tell you one thing for certain, he's got far better manners, and I never have to worry about what he's up to in the sandwich shop."

Morgan was in fits of laughter this time, bent over double on the sofa with a hand firmly grasping Adie's knee to keep from falling off altogether. Liz was chuckling too, and it seemed Adie was the only one who hadn't found it utterly hilarious.

"Well, I'm glad you've both had a good giggle at my expense," she muttered. "To think I could've been painting for the last five minutes."

"Oh, is that what you were doing? Sorry." Now she seemed to care, when it meant the house wasn't being finished, but not when she was giving her daughter a heart attack. "I'll leave you girls to it, don't want to interrupt progress. Say hi to your mum for me, Morgan. I'll see her Thursday."

Who was this woman who'd just breezed in and out of the house? When they'd last seen each other six days ago, she was dealing with it but not exactly jumping for joy. Now she was attending painting classes and adopting cats. She hadn't even bothered with her tea.

Adie sat dumbstruck. Not, however, as dumbstruck as Morgan. "How on earth does she not know you're gay? Have you met?"

"What's that supposed to mean?"

"Nothing, it's just..." She gestured up and down Adie's body. "I don't know if it's because I'm also gay, but the first time we met it was like a little antenna started pinging in my brain."

"Just your brain?"

Morgan's eyes rolled a little as she smiled. "She must suspect, at least?"

"Probably. She may even know, people talk, but we never have. When I came out to Dad, he seemed to think she wouldn't take it well on top of the affair, so I decided to wait. Four years on and it never happened."

It wasn't even intentional. Time just passed and it never came up. With there not being a girlfriend to introduce her to, there didn't seem much need. Now, though, she had to confess a little anxiety had developed. Not so much that Liz would object to her daughter's sexuality, because she was fine with Josh and always quite liberal, but that it hadn't been disclosed for so long.

"Very convenient for him," Morgan muttered.

"Yeah, well. You're probably right, but here we are. I'll tell her eventually, but right now I have bigger things on my mind, like painting the bedroom before we lose all the light. Shall we crack on?"

Getting into another discussion about Robert, the

divorce, and her coming out held no appeal. Notwithstanding the weird cat interlude, they were having a good night, and she had a holiday to look forward to. Nothing in the world was going to derail that.

14

She was still holding on to that thought as she arrived for lunch with her dad on Wednesday. After promising to meet up properly when the house was finished, and with the only remaining big task now getting the carpets fitted, the excuses had run out. At least this way, it was time limited and didn't involve Sarah.

After managing her appointments to give a bit of wiggle room, she made her way over the Market Square and pushed through the doors into Robert's office. This time the receptionist recognised her immediately and smiled. Jenny was also loitering, though, so she didn't get a chance to speak.

"Been on a shopping spree?" Adie pointed to the bags in Jenny's hand.

She opened one and pulled out a baby grow patterned with elephants. "First granddaughter; couldn't resist. After four boys on the trot she'll be spoilt rotten. Lunch has become a dangerous time of day for my credit card."

"Lucky girl, when's she due?"

Jenny folded it over her hand and placed it back in the

bag, her expression turning quizzical. "The weekend you two are in Spain, conveniently. Out of interest, has Morgan said much about the baby?"

"A little, why?"

There was a pause, then she let out a soft grunt. "When she first found out Tim was going to be a dad, she was extremely excited. Now she barely even mentions it." She wandered through to her office and set the bags on the desk while Adie leant against the door frame. "I know you two have become close, I wondered if she'd said anything."

They'd talked about a lot while they'd worked on the house together, particularly how much she'd enjoyed splitting her time between the UK and the States growing up and how much she missed her dad while he was over there. Whenever family was mentioned she spoke of them with love and appreciation, and she adored her nephews, but she hadn't really enthused over adding a niece.

"Maybe when you've already become an aunt four times, it loses its shine a bit."

"Mm, perhaps."

"You don't seem convinced."

Jenny rolled out her chair but only stood behind it and drummed her nails on the plastic backing. "No, I'm not. I know my daughter very well, and when she's quiet there's usually a reason. Tim and Rebecca had a lot of problems conceiving and it's been a tough pregnancy, I think perhaps it's caused her some anxiety. I shouldn't ask, but would you keep an eye out for her?"

Adie turned her head to find Robert coming out of his office with a client and flashed him a quick smile. "Of course." She managed a warmer one for Jenny. "I'd better go but try not to worry." Although Morgan hadn't said a great deal, what she had commented had all been positive. "She seems happy enough, from what I can tell."

"I can't disagree with that; this move has done her the world of good. If I don't see you before, have a good holiday and we'll catch up at the quiz."

A hand landed on Adie's shoulder and she took a deep breath, preparing herself for whatever was about to unfold. She needed to tell him she wouldn't be his best man, or best woman, or whatever the hell it was, and hold a boundary.

"Are you ready to go?" Robert pulled the wallet from his pocket as if he needed to make the point that he was buying his daughter lunch, then said a quick hello to Jenny and ushered Adie out of the door. "Where would you like to go?"

She didn't really care, so long as it was quiet and didn't take forever. Her appointments wouldn't wait for a three-course meal. Sarah's sandwich shop was also off the menu. "Burger on a bench?"

There was a greasy spoon on the edge of the square which served them over lunch, and they were an occasional indulgence if she couldn't get by on her sandwiches. Robert didn't look convinced, though.

"I don't know. Supposed to be watching my weight." He patted his stomach and sucked it in.

"One won't kill you." And if it did, that was a sacrifice they'd both have to make.

She tugged his shirt sleeve and paused on the kerb until the traffic cleared, then they crossed and walked past The Anchor, which had posters up in the window advertising Josh's quiz in a couple of weeks. You could smell the café before you saw it, and Adie's stomach grumbled in anticipation. It'd been another early run day, and she was starving.

Robert stopped to chat with the owner as he served them, handing over a couple of polystyrene boxes beading with condensation where the steam had begun to escape. Then they pulled out a chair each and sat around a circular chrome table by the window.

"Thanks for finally making the time to see me, I know it's been a real struggle." He leant forward and narrowed his eyes, then winked and smiled.

"Don't get sarky. The house looks great, so it's been worthwhile."

"Perhaps Sarah and I could pop over one evening and take a look. Or do we need to book two months in advance now?"

Adie let out a soft grunt of laughter, but it didn't last long. It never even seemed to cross his mind that they could spend time on their own anymore. "Sure." She grabbed her burger in both hands and took a big bite, ketchup sliding out of the back. When she'd finished chewing, she set it back down. "I did want to talk to you about the wedding, while we're on our own. The best woman thing..."

"You don't want to do it?" His voice was tinged with disappointment, but then he rallied. "Sure I can't change your mind?"

"I don't think so, no. It'd feel like I was betraying Mum. I'll be there, but only as a regular guest."

Robert nodded. "Okay, sweetheart. It's only a small thing, anyway. We'll do the registry office and then I managed to swing a favour and book the golf club for a reception. Start of November, it's all sorted."

That soon? Adie tried to hide her shock. She didn't think they'd do it until at least the new year. "You don't hang about."

"No, well. It's taken on a new importance."

She'd gone to take another bite of her burger but left it

hung suspended in front of her mouth. Dear god what else could there be? "Has it?"

"Yes." He shuffled in his seat and wiped his fingers on a napkin. "Sarah's turning forty in January and she's always wanted children. It might not happen for us, we'll have to wait and see, but we've decided to try."

He looked about as sick with nerves as she did. A baby? He was well into his fifties and talking about retirement. If they had a kid now, he'd be seventy before it turned eighteen. They'd always been about nice holidays and fancy meals out, not nappies and puke.

"Is that really what you want?"

Robert nodded. "We've talked about it a lot. It's funny, I always thought I'd be a grandparent at this age, but I want to try. It's not like that'll ever happen, what with—"

"Before you finish that sentence, it won't happen because I don't want children, not for any other reason." She'd always been entirely clear on that fact. Kids weren't on the agenda whether she was gay, straight, or anything in between.

"Everyone says that when they're in their twenties."

"Do they? Well I mean it. Nothing against them, but babies really aren't my thing."

He had the sense not to push it and instead worked through half of his burger in silence, then wiped his fingers on a napkin and stared out the window. "You know I only want you to be happy, don't you?"

She managed a brief smile. "Yeah. Same." Monica's words echoed around her head, and she shuffled on the chair. Perhaps if that was the case, she should check what the situation was with taking a date to the wedding. "So, how big will the reception be? Are guests allowed to bring a plus one?"

Even as she asked, she could feel the bile rising, and with the addition of burger grease it was not a pleasant sensation. Why had she started this? It's not like she even had anyone to take.

"If your gran asks, the answer to that question is a very definite no." He shook his head slightly, lobbing his burger into its box. "I hope she hasn't had that bloke back to your place. It's ridiculous, she's in her seventies. You'd think she'd grow up and act like a responsible adult." He folded his arms and glared out the window again. "Although I've been waiting fifty-four years for that to happen."

The regrets just kept on coming. She really hated getting in the middle of her dad and gran, given he always ended up looking like a hurt child. Perhaps that's all he was, though, deep down.

"Have you told her how you feel about this?" Adie pushed away the remains of her burger and gave him her full attention, but his gaze remained fixed on something outside.

"What's the point? You can't change the past."

"No, but it might help if you understood each other a little better. I've had quite a few conversations with gran about her early life and why she made some of the decisions she did. She's quite open."

"Oh, I know she's open," Robert mumbled. He tapped his foot on the tiled floor and then pushed back the chair. "Sorry, but I didn't come here to talk about this. Can we pick something a bit cheerier?"

Adie nodded, but was struggling to come up with anything. They didn't really have much to converse about these days and finding topics for discussion was a challenge. When she was younger, they spent quite a lot of time together, but now everything involved Sarah or the golf club. That only gave them so much mileage.

"How are you getting on with Jenny?" It should be safe ground. She was the only person, discounting Monica and Liz, who they had in common and both probably liked. Even so, it felt like clutching at straws.

"Oh, fine. She's quite taken with you, keeps asking how you are. Seems like she'd know better than me, though. Yesterday I found out you're going on holiday with her daughter."

So much for that theory. Adie considered her options and decided to shrug it off. "I like Morgan." She left it at that, hoping he wouldn't probe any further. "I also like Jenny and the rest of the family, they're good people." Gathering up their rubbish, she stood and lobbed it in a bin. This seemed like an ideal point to call it quits. "Should probably get back to work, I've got a busy afternoon."

"Yes, it's funny how you're always busy whenever you see me," Robert muttered.

He got up and tried for the most awkward hug on record, and Adie patted his back before taking a giant step towards the door. He could sulk all he wanted, but what exactly did he expect?

15

A week later the house was finished, and Adie was bouncing around the living room on plush new carpets in a much better mood. It'd been a last-minute booking, which meant a bit of begging and eventually agreeing to use what they had in stock, but she didn't want to wait. Experience told her that another year would pass, and she'd still have a paint stained mess.

Josh arrived straight from work and pressed his cheek to the floor. "I can't believe this is your house. These are so soft."

"I know. That's still weird, though. Stop it."

He laughed and put a hand on the sofa to push himself up, brushing away some loose carpet fibres that'd stuck to his T-shirt. It was moulting where they'd only laid it a few hours ago. "Morgan's done a great job."

"She's been an absolute legend. It's cost a few takeaways, but she was here almost every night last week helping finish the decorating. I'd have been fucked without her; I haven't got a clue what I'm doing."

"Uhuh."

She'd started leading him up the stairs, insisting on the full tour experience so she could get her money's worth, but paused with a hand gripping the now securely affixed handrail. "What's that uhuh for?"

He prodded her back to make her move again. "You and Morgan. Whenever we've spoken lately you've mentioned her name about a million times, and now you're telling me you spent every night together last week." When they reached the landing, he went straight through to the bathroom and shut the door. "Sure it's not more than a bit of help on the house?"

"Of course it's more, we've become friends. I told you, she's invited me away for the weekend."

"What? No, you didn't. You haven't mentioned that at all."

Even muffled, she could tell she hadn't gotten away with it. "Oh, didn't I? Well, we're going to Spain for a couple of days. It's no big deal, she hates flying and asked me to go with her." Adie shrugged to no one, trying to convince herself more than Josh. "I'm just there for support."

The sound of rushing water gave her a moment's reprieve, then he reopened the door with a glint in his eye. "You really want me to believe there's nothing going on between you?"

"Yes. She's just come out of what sounds like a really shit relationship. I can't imagine she's looking for anything new right now and I'm..." Adie gestured up and down her own body. "Well, I'm me. Who wants to go from that to being with someone who can't even come out to their mum?"

He jabbed his finger. Perhaps some of the advice she'd been dishing out was coming back to bite her in the butt. "No. Let's not play that no one wants me because it's too difficult card."

"Alright," she conceded, stepping back to avoid being poked in the eye. "Maybe someone will want me. It won't be Morgan, though, she's on a self-improvement kick and trying to straighten out her life. I'm not saying there isn't a little attraction there, but it'll fade."

"What's a little attraction?"

Was he really asking after his performance at Jenny's party? Josh knew Morgan was hot. Smoking hot. "I don't need to tell you that. She's gorgeous, and clever, and kind."

Josh clasped his hands together and his voice shot up at least an octave. "And perfect, and wonderful, and I love her."

"Grow up." Adie slapped his arm, but perhaps she'd need to accept he wasn't completely off the mark. "Fine, so I have a teensy crush on her." She tried to halt it there by leading him into a bedroom. It had the same plain magnolia walls and mottled beige carpets as the rest of the house, though, and wouldn't distract him for long.

Sure enough, he wandered straight back out and down the stairs. "Enough of this, come and spill."

"I've spilt it all." She trudged behind him and flopped into the armchair. "Your turn. Tell me how it went with Emma. You know, the woman you actually had a date with. Two, in fact."

"It was good. Did as *Morgan* suggested and just tried to relax. In fact…" Josh picked at a loose thread in the cushion he was now hugging and then tucked it down the side of the chair when it went too far and almost unravelled. "If you're going away with Morgan, could I use your house?" When he saw she was about to reply he quickly cut in again. "You did only say no last time because it wasn't finished."

She'd set herself up for that. "Fine. Gran will probably be here, though, so you'll need to negotiate with her."

"No problem, I'll send a quick text." He'd wriggled to

pull out his phone before there was a chance for Adie to change her mind and was busy tapping out messages.

"Have you ever considered you could just get your own place? It's great, you can even have girls over without asking your mum." Although the irony, given Monica's presence, wasn't lost on her. Not that it was Adie who was having the torrid trysts. "Does Emma have her own place?"

"Of course."

She found it baffling he could say that so casually given his own living situation, but it was easy to see why he stayed. His mum and dad had supported him through everything since he moved home from university six years ago, although even they probably didn't expect he'd still be there when he was knocking on thirty.

"So..."

"I'll get to it, one thing at a time."

"You don't think one would sort of help the other? It's not just about Emma. You might like having a bit of space to yourself, so you can wander around in your undies and drink beer at ten o'clock in the morning without anyone judging." Again, not things she ever did, but her point was sound.

"Money, though."

He couldn't play that card. He was only ever skint because he wasted it. She'd placed him in his job and knew how much he earned. It wouldn't take much management, if he were willing to cut back on the nights out a bit, and his liver would probably also thank him.

"I can help with that, and you always said you wanted to do this when you felt more settled."

Josh dropped his phone on top of the discarded cushion. "I know, but—"

There was a loud thump on the door, and they both

jumped. As Adie leant over, she spotted Morgan outside, her eyes bleary. She bolted off the sofa, pulled the window wide open, and climbed through. "Are you okay? What's happened?"

Morgan gripped tight around Adie's waist; her voice muffled by a shoulder. "Did you just climb through the window?"

"Yeah."

"You're weird." She pulled back but didn't let go, sniffing as a tear rolled down her cheek. "Sorry, but I didn't know where else to go."

"Always come here. Tell me what's upset you."

"Rebecca and Tim's baby was born this morning and no one told me. Everyone presumed they were doing me a favour not giving me a chance to go to the hospital, and I didn't find out until Mum called half an hour ago. There's still time to visit, but I was so upset I just ended up driving around in circles."

She'd blurted it out seemingly in one breath, then gasped and her lip trembled. As she cried in a burst, Adie drew her back into the hug. If this was Jenny's answer to worrying Morgan was anxious, it wasn't a good one. "Want me to come with you?"

Morgan shook her head as much as she could with it still pressed tight against a shoulder. "No, I just needed to vent."

"Okay, then do you want to come in and talk some more before you go?"

There was a long pause before she spoke again, her voice thick with emotion and almost a whisper. "No, I want you to come."

Adie laughed as Morgan groaned, banging her forehead. "Why is it a problem if I come with you?"

"Because it's another thing I should be able to do on my own."

"And you can do it on your own, I have no doubt whatsoever. Let me just get rid of Josh."

Morgan rapidly wiped under her eyes. "Shit, sorry. I didn't realise you had company. Don't tell him to go, I'll be fine. Honestly, I didn't mean to interrupt your evening."

"You haven't, I was only showing off your handiwork. The carpets were fitted today, do you want to see?"

Adie climbed back through the window while Morgan took the door, removing her work boots and leaving them on the front step. She leant against the door frame, a nervous smile directed at Josh, and gestured to the floor. "Looks good."

Josh rolled to his feet, needing no excuse to permanently end their previous conversation. "I'm just heading to the gym. I'll leave you to it."

"Please don't on my account." Morgan's tone was pleading, and she rubbed a hand over her face.

"I'm not, don't worry."

With Josh's warm smile, Morgan gave a slight nod and began to turn into the hallway. "Okay then. I'm just going to tidy myself up in the bathroom."

He waited until she was out of earshot, the door closing above them, and lowered his voice. "Teensy crush my ass. Adie, you just climbed through a window. I've never seen you climb through a window before."

"Nothing I can't handle. You can see she's not in a head space for anything, I'm just being a good friend." Adie grabbed hold of his T-shirt sleeve and pulled him forwards. She didn't particularly want to revisit any earlier discussions either. "Relax and bugger off. Oh, and feel free to use either the door or window."

* * *

Listening to tapes and making plans for their holiday seemed to have the desired effect of calming Morgan's nerves. That was, until they got to the hospital forty-five minutes later and she was peering up at a stark white building.

"Sure you don't want me to come in?" Adie leant an arm on the car door, still seated, and rest her chin on top. "I could wait in a corridor or something."

Morgan was silent for what seemed like an eternity, raising a hand to shield her eyes as she stared across the car park. Her lip was trembling again, and she seemed more upset still than anxious about anything. "I'm so pissed off. I get they want to protect me but if they hadn't made such a big song and dance this would all have been fine. Why is it everyone always thinks they know what's best for you?" She didn't seem to want an answer to that, pulling out her phone and jabbing at the screen before holding it to her ear. There was a brief exchange, presumably with Tim, and then she shoved it back into her pocket. "He says you can come in, and it won't be weird so long as you get him a Coke from the machine on the way past."

Adie laughed. She liked Tim, from what little she knew of him, and his sense of humour. They'd chatted at dinner a few weeks ago and he was like a less intense version of Morgan, always making jokes and digs at his sister's expense, but never with any hint of cruelty.

She locked the car and wrapped an arm across Morgan's shoulders, the other dug into the pocket of her jeans. Instinct told her that without a firm steer, they wouldn't get very far. After a quick stop by the vending machine for a selection of cans and some chocolate, they called a lift and rode up to the seventh floor, then asked for directions from the nurse's station.

"Are you okay?" Adie whispered, noticing Morgan had hold of a chocolate bar with such intensity that it was losing shape.

She nodded and nudged Adie's shoulder. "Yeah, don't panic." There was a little glint in her eyes as she smiled. "Just excited. I'm so happy for them. I'm making sure I've corrected my mood so I don't ruin their day."

"I think a few hours with a screaming infant is more likely to do that."

Morgan whacked her in the stomach, and she winced. "Careful, you'll lose that big softy title."

"I'm a big softy with you, but I'm never going to be someone who gushes over babies." Not that she'd had much opportunity. As an only child whose sole experience of them was when someone brought one into the office, she had no idea what she was doing. It might be time to start making headway with that, given her dad's latest news.

"You are not just a big softy with me, that's absolute rubbish. You'd do anything to help Josh, and your mum, and your gran, and even your dad."

Adie laughed rather than arguing and put a hand on Morgan's lower back to gently encourage her forward. She'd stalled again and there was only half an hour before kicking out time. They hadn't driven all this way to miss out before last orders.

Rebecca was in a private room at the end of the corridor, and Morgan peered through a window in the door, holding up their treats. She didn't seem to want to go in, though, and began pulling funny faces.

"Am I coming inside, or waiting here?" Adie pushed the door handle, trying to encourage her to move.

Morgan bundled the chocolate into the crook of her arm, then with her free hand wrapped her fingers around Adie's and gave them a squeeze. It'd been a long time since any woman had properly held hands with her and Adie chewed the inside of her cheek to keep from smiling. It felt strangely intimate, more so than the hug they'd shared earlier.

"Hello auntie Morgan," Tim whispered from a chair in the corner. He had a bundle of blankets in his arms, which presumably contained a baby. "Are you coming for a cuddle so I can stuff my face with chocolate?"

She dropped the bars and cans onto the end of the bed and gave Rebecca a quick kiss. All the while Adie leant against the wall, still feeling like an intruder. This was an intimate family moment, and she barely knew these people.

Morgan cradled the baby and did a weird, half-danced walk. "Do you want a hold?"

Adie inched sideways. Did all babies look like this? A strange hybrid of raisin and alien. "Um, no. Wouldn't want to spoil this moment for you by dropping her."

That was the last of her concerns, though. She watched the smile creep across Morgan's face, her insides melting to create an uncomfortable sick feeling somewhere between excitement and panic. The line was so thin that she couldn't tell where the two sides converged, and that was a problem given they were about to spend a whole weekend together. Alone.

16

It was some ungodly hour on Friday morning and Adie took a deep breath as she looked up at the departures board. They didn't take off for another two hours and she needed to find a way to occupy the time. Morgan had insisted on arriving ahead of schedule and now sat scrolling through her phone on a seat, tapping a foot and looking like she needed to vomit. Despite her own rising anxiety about where their relationship was heading, right now Adie needed to offer some support, and it would at least give her something to do.

"Are you okay?" She sat on the adjacent seat and hitched up her knee. "What can we do that would help you relax?"

Morgan continued to stare and scroll. "Nothing, I'll be fine. I just need to focus on anything but the flight."

"A drink? I can go and pay a million pounds for a can if you like?"

"That'd be nice. Something orangey. Do you want some money?"

Adie laughed as she grabbed her rucksack from the floor

and pulled out her wallet. "No. I'm sure I can stretch to a can of drink, even here."

She wandered into a newsagent and grabbed a couple, then some chewing gum for descent and a giant bar of Toblerone for fun. After forking over a whole month's mortgage payment for the privilege, she re-joined Morgan, offering her a triangle and then slowly munching through a piece.

"Do you have to make so much noise with that?" Morgan snapped, inching sideways. She dropped the phone into her lap and massaged her temples. "Sorry, I'm just a little stressed."

"Are you? Hadn't noticed."

Adie took another chunk and stuffed the whole thing into her mouth, wiping away a trail of chocolate infused saliva as it dribbled down her chin. It was an odd time of the day for sweets, but when you'd been up since three o'clock time lost all meaning. They were already five hours into the day, and her body thought it was lunchtime. When they arrived at one o'clock Spanish time, it'd cause all manner of internal confusion.

She shoved the other half of the bar into her rucksack and sat back, watching people scuttle past. It was easy to see why Morgan found the experience stressful. It felt a bit like being in a hospital waiting room, all clinical and bright white lights. The shops even looked like the ones you got near waiting areas, so you could grab a newspaper or a drink to calm your nerves.

Adie shuffled sideways and wrapped an arm across Morgan's shoulders almost without thinking, trying to give the experience some warmth. A bit of human connection, so she didn't feel like another number in the cavernous system of transport.

Morgan leant into the embrace, resting her head on Adie's chest. "Thanks for coming."

"Are you kidding? Free holiday with my best new buddy. This is no hardship, trust me."

"Best new buddy, huh?"

Adie poked a finger into each dimple, deciding she no longer needed to resist the urge. "Yeah, you're growing on me. Sort of like a fungus." She winced as a slap landed on her leg. Trying to push the friendship card had backfired. "Or a pretty flower. Is that better?"

"I think it's a bit too late."

Morgan tucked the headphone buds back into her ears and closed her eyes, shuffling to get comfortable. They remained like that until their gate was called, and Adie tapped a shoulder to rouse her. She jumped, rubbing her face and yawning, her features falling and the colour draining as she realised that they needed to board.

Adie intervened before she had a chance to descend into full-blown panic. "Come on, let's get this over with. Two hours on a plane, and then we can reward you with a trip to the beach."

"Are you kidding? I'm going to work. Today and tomorrow are designated to bathroom fitting."

"But we can go to the beach after, right?"

Morgan laughed, squeezing their fingers together. "Yeah, we can go to the beach after." Her grip tightened again as they passed plane after plane in the floor to ceiling windows. "I've actually planned us something for Sunday. I think it'll be worth the wait."

It was hard to tell who she needed to convince, and when they reached a set of toilets, she insisted on going in. Adie stood outside with their bags, watching couples walk past in loud shirts rolling cases behind them. When a good five minutes had passed, she took a deep breath and carried their luggage through.

"Are you alright?" She called to no one in particular. A woman turned from the sink and smiled, but there was no reply. "Morgan?" she enquired again, dipping her head to look at the shoes in the stalls. She found a pair of glittery silver trainers in the end cubicle and knocked on the door. "I'm sorry if you're just taking a shit, but is everything okay?"

Morgan's eyes were raised in enquiry as she appeared, clutching her phone to her chest. "Yes, sorry. Just got caught up reading an article." She slid it into the pocket of her shorts and shrugged, stepping past to wash her hands. "You never do that?"

"Oh yeah, I do it all the time when I'm avoiding something. Is there anything I can do to help, besides sedating you? I'm afraid I'm not licensed to dispense medication, but I do good hand holding, hugs, and crap talk if any of that is useful."

Adie passed over Morgan's rucksack as she wiped her hands on her T-shirt, biting her lip and betraying her unease. Her skin was pale and clammy, and the pendant around her neck was going up and down at a rapid, uneven pace.

She shook out her hands and glanced towards the door. "No, I just need to put on my big girl pants."

"I've got a pair of those. They're Wonder Woman print." Adie reached under the waistband of her shorts and hooked her thumb into the briefs beneath. They snapped back and she took Morgan's hand again, leading her out of the toilets.

"Don't take this the wrong way, but I didn't have you down as a novelty underwear kind of girl."

"No? I don't wear them all the time, but they're comfy for

travelling and sports. What did you picture when you were fantasising?"

Morgan threw an elbow into her stomach. "I wasn't." She grunted out a laugh, the conversation seeming to take her mind off the flight. "But if I had to guess, I would've said plain black cotton."

"Really? I suppose I do wear that day to day, but I have some nicer stuff. You know, for the weekend."

"Oh yeah? What sort of nicer stuff?"

"By nicer I mean sexier. Sometimes even if I'm heading out in jeans and a T-shirt, I'll put on a lace bra. It makes me feel confident knowing I've got that on underneath."

Morgan stopped and looked Adie up and down, biting her lip again with a far sultrier expression. "You are full of surprises. Now I'm fantasising. Thanks, it's given me something to think about on the flight."

"Glad to be of service. We'll talk about your underwear later."

* * *

A warm blast of air engulfed them as they peered down the staircase at the shimmering runway. Heat rose from the tarmac and Adie pulled down her sunglasses, letting out a loud whooshing noise as she recoiled. It'd been warm at home for weeks, but nothing like this. How Morgan planned to fit a new bathroom in this weather was a mystery.

They took care as they descended, then filed onto a bus that would take them to the terminal. After getting through passport control, and not needing to collect hold luggage, they headed straight to the foyer where drivers in white shirts fanned themselves with rectangles of paper attached to clipboards. There was no one waiting for them, though, they just had to chance it.

Morgan sidled up to a car, catching the attention of the driver who had his arm hung out of the window as he listened to the radio on full blast. He shouted over the rapid intonation of the DJ rather than turning it down, and when she responded in Spanish Adie frowned with concentration, trying to work out their conversation and when she'd learned a whole other language.

"Um, excuse me," she ventured, as they slid across the back seat. "You didn't tell me you spoke the lingo."

"I studied it at school."

"Yeah, but when I learned languages in school, we never got to the point of being fluent. It was considered a success if you could say hello and ask for a beer."

Morgan tugged the door and it slammed shut. The early start and the stress of the flight had taken it out of her, and she yawned before responding. "I had friends in California whose first language was Spanish, so I got a lot of practise. I'm not actually fluent, more intermediate, but I can hail a cab."

"Wow." Adie sat back as the car pulled away, watching the airport disappear into the distance as they whizzed along a highway flanked by enormous shopping centres and billboards. "I have never felt less accomplished than I do right now. All I learnt at school was how to roll a joint."

Morgan laughed through another yawn, then closed her eyes and wriggled back against the seat, resting her head on the safety belt. She stayed like that for all the twenty-minute journey, her face scrunching on occasion when they hit a pothole.

Adie was wide awake, wired from the early start and not ready to crash. She spent the time watching their surroundings change as the Mediterranean came into view on their right and they passed a mixture of bars and novelty shops selling inflatable unicorns. They were amongst the British and German tourists here, licking ice cream cones while strutting along the esplanade in next to no clothes until their skin scorched bright red with sunburn.

When they stopped, she nudged Morgan, unsure if they were at the right place. "Is this the house?" She turned to peer from the window at a high white-washed wall with a brown gate. There was a ceramic sign reading 'Villa Bella', which sounded familiar, and the driver had turned to demand money. When Morgan opened her eyes and blinked a few times, Adie probed further. "Before I pay the man, has he brought us to the right house?"

The nodded response and fumble for the handle signalled he had, and she reached to pull a wedge of Euros from her pocket before hopping out and grabbing their bags from the boot. There was a key box on the wall, and they used it to let themselves in, stepping onto a patio with a rectangular pool sunk into the middle. Three sun loungers were turned on their end and rested against the side of the villa, and there was a table covered with a green tarpaulin.

Morgan hauled open the sliding doors, leading them inside, and Adie squinted in the dim light. All the shutters were closed and there was a beautiful chill, but it had the undesired effect of sending a wave of tiredness crashing over her body and reducing her limbs to a quivering wreck desperate for sleep. She threw their bags at the sofa and crumpled down, closing her eyes and groaning.

"Have you reached my stage of tiredness?" Morgan rallied, prodding Adie's stomach until she was slapped away. "Let's get some lunch and then we can start work."

Adie peered out of one eye. "We?"

"Yes, we. You didn't think this was a completely free holi-day, did you?"

"Ugh." She pushed off the seat and wandered into the kitchen. There was a loaf of crusty bread on the side with a note, which Morgan picked up to read.

"That's sweet. Luke has left us milk and stuff in the fridge." She opened it and laughed. "By stuff, it seems he meant cheese and beer."

"The basic food groups. Sandwich and a drink?"

"Tempting, but I meant it when I said I had to work this afternoon. If I don't start now, we won't be able to do what I planned on Sunday."

Adie rummaged for plates and began preparing lunch. "How can I help, so that we get to the fun part sooner?"

"I've seen you attempting DIY, you'd be most help keeping out of the way and bringing me drinks."

"I won't argue with that. I'll feed you, keep you hydrated, and then show you the time of your life."

Morgan laughed again, taking the sandwich that was being handed to her and ripping off a chunk. "Now there's a promise. I'll get changed and started while you chill and use the pool." She pointed the bread in Adie's direction. "Take whichever room you want."

Adie gripped her sandwich between her teeth and carried her bag down the hallway off the lounge, her trainers squeaking on the marble floor. There were four doors, which she presumed meant three bedrooms and a bathroom. She opened the first and didn't go any further. It had a second set of sliding doors onto the patio, a double bed, and a chest of drawers. There wasn't much else the other rooms could offer, and she just wanted a nap.

The mattress creaked as she sat and tugged off her shoes and socks, but then the banging of renovation works foiled any plan to sleep. She slipped them back on and decided to head out instead. If she was going to stick to her promise, she'd start by fetching more supplies and preparing dinner.

When Morgan finally re-surfaced at eight, Adie had been waiting for so long that she'd fallen asleep on a lounger. Even the sound of banging had no longer been enough to keep her awake. Sprawled face down, she felt something tickle the back of her leg and slapped it away, then slowly lifted her head to find a pair of knees in her line of vision.

"Must be all that hard work," she mumbled.

"Yeah, it's funny how the sound of someone else doing that can really tire you out."

When she sat up, she had to do a double take. There was a giant inflatable lobster in the pool, which she'd forgotten all about. "Oh, I got us a friend while I was out this afternoon. Fancy a dip before we eat?"

"Absolutely. Let me just go and get changed."

Morgan wandered off, and Adie wafted some fresh air under her T-shirt. Even now it was scorching hot and her front was covered in sweat where it'd been pressed into the lounger. She tugged open the patio doors and delved into her bag to pull out a black bikini, then peeled away her clothes.

After dressing she headed back out and dipped her toe in the water, flicking it over the lobster. "I think I'll call you Sebastian." She launched into a medley of songs from the Little Mermaid and Morgan joined in, stopping at the lounger to check her phone. "How on earth are you wearing a T-shirt? Aren't you hot?"

Morgan didn't answer at first, she was still busy scrolling. Then she muttered a few times and let out a quiet "shit".

"What's up?"

"Baby's back in hospital." She still didn't have a name, despite the multiple excellent suggestions they'd each made a few days ago.

"How come?" Adie took care not to slip as she jogged over the terrace.

"Something to do with jaundice. I don't know, Mum says it isn't serious, but she has to go under some sort of special light."

"Oh. Sounds like she'll be okay then."

Morgan didn't look reassured. She was fiddling with the bottom of her T-shirt, and then perched on the edge of the lounger tapping her foot. "Yeah." She squeezed her fingers into her eyes. "Sorry, it's just been a big day."

"You don't need to apologise." Adie sat next to her and rubbed reassuring circles on her back.

"I can feel myself overreacting. I'm trying to push it down, but it doesn't always work, especially when I'm tired."

"That's okay. If it needs to come out, it can come out. You did a big thing today, I'm proud of you."

Morgan sunk sideways, and Adie kissed her temple. They sat like that until her breathing had calmed. Then she stood and tugged the T-shirt over her head, hiding the scar on her abdomen with a palm. "It's like a constant reminder of how this all started. Sometimes I think I'll cover it with a tattoo."

Adie reached out her first two fingers. She nudged away Morgan's hand, tracing along the faded pink line. "Just a battle scar, like any other." She smiled and pulled herself off the lounger. "I know what'll cheer you up. Get in the pool and I'll let you beat me in a race." They each narrowed their eyes, then turned and dived under the water. When Adie came up, she had Morgan backed against the wall and placed a hand either side. With a cheeky grin, she lowered her voice. "Don't expect special dispensation forever, though."

Morgan stepped forward, raised on her tiptoes with a defiant look in her eye. "Dream on. I don't need it now."

Uncomfortable sitting on her butt relaxing while Morgan worked, Adie insisted she was helping with the bathroom on Saturday. She showed up for work, sweetening the proposition with some fresh pastries from a shop on the corner, and promised not to break anything. Despite a few moments of regret when she was covered in sweat and being bossed around in a confined space, there was a certain amount of satisfaction in manual work where you could see the product of your efforts.

She'd found it with the house, too, even if it was frustrating when you were dreadful at every task you tackled. In the bathroom, where there were no paintbrushes with which to wreak havoc, she'd fared a lot better. Instead it involved a lot of heavy lifting and they were both exhausted by the end of the day, rolling into bed early in preparation for their Sunday fun.

When Adie woke, she was feeling surprisingly fresh. She dressed in shorts and T-shirt as directed, then grabbed a banana for breakfast before cleaning her teeth. With two minutes to spare, she was sat on a lounger, patiently waiting.

For some reason, this surprise had turned her into a kid on Christmas morning. She tapped her foot on the floor, her heart racing and a daft grin plastered on her face.

When Morgan emerged, Adie sprang up. "Will you tell me what we're doing now?"

"All will be revealed." Morgan had her aviators on and peered over the top. Then she beckoned with a finger and disappeared around the side of the building, dragging out a long boat.

"What the hell is that?"

"It's a kayak." The delivery was dripping with condescension, but she wore a warm smile. "I got Luke to bring it when he came to inspect the bathroom last night. Said we'd have some fun, and here it is."

"Cool, I've never kayaked before. Where are we going?"

"Traditionally they're used on water, and there's a big body of it somewhere in that direction."

Morgan pointed over the wall, her continued teasing not enough to bring down Adie's high spirits. She was already grabbing the paddles, which were propped against the villa, and had taken hold of a carry handle.

"Hurry, then. We only have one day." Her heart did a little dance and happiness almost erupted in a squeal. She didn't even recognise herself, but Holiday Adie was fun and could stay for as long as she wanted. "Can you tell I'm excited?"

"There have been a few giveaways, yeah."

The kayak was lightweight and easy to transport, even if they did get some strange looks wandering along the street with it before most people had eaten breakfast. The temperature was bearable at this time of the day, though, and they were able to beat the crowds.

Luke had given Morgan directions to a good place for

them to get in the water. They found it and pushed off the beach, wading up to their knees. When they were sure they wouldn't end up grounded on the sand again they each climbed into the boat, then Adie tried to work out her paddle. "Which way up does this thing go?"

"They should act a bit like scoops." Morgan held up hers, showing the position of her hands, and peered behind to make sure the message was received.

Adie got into a rhythm once she stopped panicking every time they bobbed over a wave, but then they steered around a mass of jutting rocks and she felt a jolt of adrenaline as she realised how far they were from the shore. It was amazing Morgan wasn't completely freaked by this, given what usually caused her anxiety.

"Is this not bothering you?" Adie shouted.

Morgan shrugged. "No, because I'm not trapped. I may feel a little differently when we're in this cove Luke told me about, given the only way out is by sea, but I'm doing okay right now." She carried on for a few strokes, then turned her head. "You are a confident swimmer, aren't you? I've only seen you in a swimming pool."

"You didn't think to check before we were hundreds of metres out?"

"Would you believe I didn't?"

Adie laughed, enjoying the sea spray in her face and the sun on her back. She was a little sore still and unused to working her upper body, but Morgan was having no such problems and powered them along. Once they'd rounded the rocks, steering a wide berth so as not to end up pummelled, the water became shallower and they slowed. Adie dipped in her hand and watched the little fish glitter and dart away.

The kayak slid up the bank, but as they jumped out it

was almost drawn back and she grabbed onto a handle, hauling it up the beach. The last thing they needed was to lose their vessel because then Morgan really was screwed. They both were.

She flopped back, starfishing in the warm sand. Unzipping her pocket and grabbing her phone, she opened the camera to send Josh a photo. When she'd shot a few funny faces, and one of the clear blue sky, Morgan shuffled in beside her and they got a couple together. She fired them off and added them all to Instagram for good measure.

"What now?" Adie tucked away the phone and rolled onto her front, glancing up the beach. They were hemmed in on all sides by scrub covered cliffs, and completely alone.

"We stay here for a bit, then paddle back. I've booked us a table for tonight, but until then we're free to go wherever we want."

"You have to let me pay for dinner. I still owe you for all the help, and I'm not taking no for an answer on that, either."

Morgan stroked her little finger up and down Adie's forearm so that the hairs stood on end. Then she bumped their shoulders together. "Have I ever said no to you before?"

"Yes, frequently, but don't do it now. Holiday Adie is also Generous Adie."

"Holiday Adie?" Adie quickly jumped to her feet, standing with both hands on her hips like a superhero who was only missing a cape, and Morgan rolled onto her back, propping herself on her elbows. She wore the same amused look she had when they'd first met. "Oh, you mean Happy Adie. Okay. Will I see her again when we get home?"

"Tough call. Maybe."

"How can we ensure she returns to the UK with us?"

That was the million-dollar question. Was it possible to pick up the beach, the sea, the sun, and the beautiful scenery, or was that going to push them over the weight limit in economy class? Before Adie had a chance to answer, Morgan was off again. "I wonder whether—and this is just a thought—UK Adie needs to spend more time having fun."

"What a novel idea. Why don't I just quit my job, tell everyone else to naff off, and spend every day at the zoo?"

"Don't be ridiculous, but there's plenty you could do. You could join a running club. You're also a great footballer so you could join a team. You could sing in a band, or—"

"You're coming dangerously close to telling me to get a life."

Morgan nudged Adie's foot with her own. "I'm not telling you to do anything, only you know what'll make you happy."

"I did play for a team when I was younger but I sort of just stopped." She squinted, trying to work out when and why, but couldn't quite remember. It must have been at least seven years, because she wasn't playing when she'd started her current job.

"Well maybe you should start again."

Adie had still been lost in thought but was quickly snapped out of it when Morgan stood, brushing the sand from her shorts. Then she began to pull off her T-shirt and Adie swallowed hard, following the line of Morgan's tattoo as it curled over her shoulder. Her gaze continued into the barely constrained cleavage, but the sight had set off an uncomfortable chain reaction in her stomach, something like the sensation she'd experienced in the hospital. "What are you doing?"

Morgan lowered her shorts and kicked them aside. "I

want to swim. Are you standing there checking me out all day or coming in?"

"What?" Adie shook her head slightly, her face blanching. "I wasn't—" She was. Her eyes still hadn't left Morgan's torso as she stretched to tie back her hair. It begged to be touched, stroked, kissed, and her mind was already there doing it. One step forward and she could run her hands over every inch. Morgan closed the gap but Adie couldn't quite make herself move, as if her feet had slipped into quicksand. Instead, she tugged off her T-shirt and pointed at the sea. "Ready then?"

Morgan nodded, her eyes travelling over Adie's chest. "Yeah, I'm ready." She wore a shy smile and bit her lip, then ran off down the beach.

Adie watched her dive into the water and tried to return her enthusiasm. At least one of them was.

After a morning of exploring and an afternoon sampling ice cream, Adie wandered through to her bedroom to change for dinner. The rucksack she'd brought didn't have room for many clothes, but she had packed something a little smarter. The navy cotton shorts and matching short-sleeve shirt had creased in transit but would look better than her tank top and old ripped denim.

She changed and ran a brush through her hair, pulling it into a loose bun, then sprayed some perfume and resumed her place on the lounger. It was almost eight, and the evening sun shimmered over the pool. The noise had died down too, as the surrounding families all left their villas in search of food, and it was so tranquil that she almost fell asleep again.

She jumped and rubbed her eyes when something nudged her, then they popped out of her head. Morgan was in a flowing skirt and strapless top which showed off her shoulders and arms, laughing as she peered over the top of her aviators.

"Are you ready for dinner, or ready for bed?"

Adie tried to divert her gaze and form a coherent sentence. "Yep."

Morgan raised her eyebrows. "What are you saying yes to?"

"Dinner." Definitely dinner. Until she'd worked out where this hesitation was coming from, things needed to stay strictly platonic. She stood, stuffing her hands into the pockets of her shorts. She'd felt like a fidgeting, gibbering mess for most of the day and it was like the more relaxed and flirtier Morgan became, the more Adie tensed and faltered. Suddenly her totally in control crush on a friend was spiralling into a not so in control crush on a friend who might want her back, and she didn't know how she felt about it. "How far is this place?"

"About a ten-minute walk away."

Morgan unlatched the gate and they wandered down the hill, a light breeze now taking some venom out of an otherwise scorching day. As the path reached the main strip, Adie nodded to a couple eating alfresco at a tapas bar and followed Morgan down an alley onto a more secluded street lined with whitewashed buildings.

The smell of grilled fish made her stomach lurch with hunger and she inhaled deeply, taking in the aroma mixed with coconut sunscreen and perfume. They stopped at the penultimate restaurant and Morgan lifted her sunglasses, perching them on top of her head. As she spoke to the waiter in Spanish, Adie resumed fidgeting, unable to understand a word. All she could do was follow through the heaving room to a terrace on the back and then stand in awe at the view.

"Bloody hell," she muttered, squinting over the edge of a cliff down a sheer drop into the sea. "This is gorgeous."

Morgan laughed as the waiter pulled out two chairs. "You didn't think I'd bring you to anywhere less than absolute perfection, did you?"

"No, I didn't. So far, every moment I've spent with you has been just that." She meant every word, however unwise she was to voice them. Water sprayed and misted as a wave crashed into the cliff, showering her with a delicate coating of salt as she sat and scraped the chair forward, her eyes still focussed on the scenery.

"Let's enjoy it then." Morgan reached out her palm. "Give me your phone."

"Why?"

"Because I'm putting them aside so we don't get distracted. It's just you, me, and the sea."

Adie handed it over and they were stacked on one another at the side of the table. She could hear hers vibrating with notifications, no doubt from Josh commenting on every single photo from their kayaking trip, but after a few minutes of interruptions she asked for permission to turn it off. The only trouble was that Morgan's was the angry phone.

"Sorry." She picked it up and glanced at the screen, her face falling. "Shit."

Adie felt a jolt of panic. "It's not the baby, is it?"

"No, it's Lou. Did you tag me on Instagram earlier? I've got about a dozen WhatsApp messages wanting to know who you are."

"Oh. Bugger. I didn't know I shouldn't do that." The

mention of Lou's name had caused an eruption of something only discernible as jealousy and protective instinct, which made Adie's fist clench.

Morgan put a hand flat on the table. "You know what? It's not your fault and it doesn't matter." She had the same defiant look, just like in the pool, tapping out a message and then turning off the device. "I've told her it's none of her business who I see, and I've blocked her."

"Really? Are you okay with that?"

"Absolutely. You were right at Mum's party. That relationship was never good for me, and I don't need her in my life."

"I'm not sure that's quite what I..." Adie trailed off, unsure why she was about to defend Lou. Frankly, she'd be happy never to hear the woman's name again, regardless of what had happened between them.

The waiter delivered a bottle of wine and they ordered, enjoying their meal without further interruption. Adie was relieved when they fell into their usual easy conversation and as their bill arrived, they were both staring out into the abyss. Vibrant pink and orange swirled across the sky and she rested forward with her arms propped on the wall, immersing herself in the scenery again until Morgan pushed back her chair and she jumped.

"Do you fancy one last walk along the beach?"

Adie grabbed her wallet and dumped down some notes. Then she stood, wobbling a little under the influence of all that Priorat. She followed Morgan out of the restaurant and back onto the strip, finding there were still people sat around on loungers even at this hour. Further along it was quieter, almost deserted, and quiet besides the roar of the sea. She squelched her toes into the wet sand, her good mood tinged with a sense of foreboding that tomorrow they'd head home. Even with the intrusion of Lou, and the uneasy state of her stomach, it'd been one of the best weekends she'd spent in ages.

She stopped in the sea, waves lapping over her feet, and squinted out across the horizon. "Do you think we could just stay here?"

"Sure." Morgan gathered her skirt in her hands as she splashed Adie's knees. "We can pitch a tent on the beach and fish from the sea. It'd save having to get on a plane again tomorrow."

"You worried about that?"

She shrugged. "A little."

"Do you feel better, though? Now you've managed to do it."

They continued to follow the line cut by foam and Morgan stroked the back of her hand down Adie's forearm, then entwined their pinkie fingers. "Yeah. I've always wanted to travel more. It's one of the reasons this was so important to me, besides wanting to see my grandad at some point."

Adie closed her eyes and slid her palm into Morgan's, her chest contracting when it was squeezed tight. It still felt good to hold her hand. "Me too. Never really got around to it, probably because I'm such a scrooge." She let out a brief laugh, partly with nerves. "Amazing, given what my gran's like."

"You never go away with her?"

"No, I'm usually working. Her sister is in Canada and she goes quite a lot, but I've never made the trip."

"I'd love to visit Canada." Morgan tipped back her head and let out a longing sigh. "My dad travels a lot too, with work, and it's one of his favourite places." She came to an abrupt stop. "Shit."

"What?"

"Can I have my phone?" She held out her palm and wriggled her fingers. "Mum was supposed to text me an update on the baby but it's off."

Adie dug it out of her pocket and pressed the power button as she handed it over. The device flashed into life and Morgan tapped it against Adie's stomach while she waited for everything to load. "Okay? You seem a little stressed."

"Yeah. I'd just forgotten, and now I need to know everything's alright." She nudged closer and rested her head on Adie's shoulder, a little giggle escaping with the kiss of reassurance on her temple.

"What?"

"Nothing, you're just soft," she whispered.

The brush of air against Adie's ear sent a shiver down her spine and she dropped Morgan's hand, wrapping it around her waist to hold her exactly where she was. It was a good job, because she stumbled slightly in the half light, still feeling a little squiffy, and had to grip tighter. She pressed her lips to the soft skin on Morgan's shoulder. "What's the verdict?"

"My niece is coming out tomorrow so all is well." Morgan let out another little laugh and then sighed. "Okay, I can relax now. Shall we keep walking before it's pitch black? Don't want you falling down a hole some kid's dug, you're struggling enough to stay upright."

Adie stalled for a second, torn between wanting to get off the beach and her desire to pull Morgan into a kiss. The cover of darkness and the wine in her system had combined to do a pretty good job on her inhibitions, but what exactly was she asking for by submitting to this? A relationship? Some sort of friends with benefits situation? Even as she considered it, she knew that wasn't an option, because they already cared too much about one another and Morgan didn't seem the type. Hell, even *she* wasn't the type these days.

"Yeah."

"Yeah? You don't sound convinced. I'm not sure we can actually sleep out here all night because we don't have the tent." Morgan tugged on Adie's hand, pulling her up the beach. She still had her phone and it flashed up with another message, causing Adie to squint.

"I—" What was she? Fumbling for the right words, her mouth hung open. She was in the quicksand again and, although the sick inducing mixture of what was presumably guilt and anxiety wasn't there, couldn't find the answer. Lou was out of the picture, Morgan had given her more than enough hints that this was okay, but something still stopped her. "Yes, let's go back. Early start in the morning."

Before they moved any further, Morgan was inspecting her phone again. Her face was illuminated with a garish glow as she stepped back. "Oh."

"Oh?"

There was a long pause while Morgan studied the screen again. "Yeah. I had a chat with Luke when he came to inspect the work and told him more about what's been going on." Another moment of hesitation, and she tapped the phone against her hand. "He's just offered me a job for two months while one of his guys goes traveling."

Adie's heart lurched as she dropped onto a patch of compacted sand, the thud echoing her sudden turn in mood. "Right," was all she got out, trying to still the tremor in her voice. "That's great, congratulations."

"That doesn't sound convincing either."

It wasn't. Images of Morgan stood in the airport departures lounge panicking on her own or sat in that villa in the dark were the first to enter her brain once the initial shock had subsided. She shook her head and tried to deliver a more enthusiastic response. "Sorry, I guess I'm just worried about you. It seems like a big step when you struggled to make it out here for a weekend." Besides which, two months? The thought of not seeing her for that long was unbearable. She wasn't quite sure what she'd expected to happen next, but all scenarios involved them spending more time together, not less. "Do you think you'll take it?"

"I have no idea. I told him I wanted to get outside my comfort zone and try some general maintenance stuff. I guess this is his solution."

Adie stared at the blank horizon, unable to make eye contact. She focussed on a dot of light, trying to hold back a wave of sickness. So much for that having disappeared. "If moving to Spain is what you want, go for it. You don't have anything keeping you at home, right?"

"I wouldn't say nothing, that's—"

"No, of course. You've got your friends and family, but they'll still be there in two months." She resisted the urge to specifically include herself, given she hadn't even been able to work up the nerve for a simple kiss. It was hardly compelling.

"That's your opinion, then? You think I should take the job?"

Adie nodded. What else could she do? She'd be a terrible friend if she tried to talk Morgan out of this, especially when she had selfish motivations. Some dumb crush was not a good enough reason to turn down a great opportunity, if it was what she needed to do for herself. "If this is what you want, yeah. You know I'll support you either way, so long as it makes you happy." She rolled back up, a sharp pain stabbing her gut. "Do you mind if we go? I'm not feeling great."

"Are you okay?"

Adie rubbed a hand on her stomach, trying to work out whether this really was the same feeling she'd experienced in the hospital or if she was ill. Nausea flooded her entire body and she felt a rush of warmth in her throat. That definitely hadn't been there last time.

"I'm not sure..." She trailed off as Morgan stood, squeezing her shoulder.

"Okay. It's alright, let's get you back."

"Thanks. I think Holiday Adie pushed it a little too hard and needs to go home."

18

When Wednesday and Josh's pub quiz rolled around, she was still struggling to correct her mood. She'd been up half of Sunday night either vomiting or trying to halt another wave of sickness and hadn't felt entirely right ever since. Whether it was emotional or simply the fish, wine, and sun, she couldn't tell, and at this point it didn't really matter. All she needed to do was get through the evening.

Despite everything, she was back at work and rushed home to change. Unable to bear anything but plain food she set a pan onto the worktop and chucked in a handful of pasta. It needed boiling but she couldn't muster the inclination and swiped it back towards the tiles, deciding to go hungry. It'd only make her feel ill again, anyway.

"What's all that noise?" Monica shouted from the living room, which was ironic given how loud she had the television. She turned it down and called again. "Are you alright?"

"Yeah, fine," Adie yelled back, slumping onto a chair and pulling out her phone. She scrolled through the messages, but there weren't any. Then she turned to social media, but there was no solace there, either.

Monica appeared in the doorway. "You can't fool your old gran. Come on, out with it. Otherwise I'll get the pliers and use torture tactics."

"There's nothing to tell, I'm just feeling a little unwell still. Are you almost ready to leave? Josh will kill you if you're late, now you've offered to be his quiz master."

"Whenever you are." She shrugged and pulled out a seat, but only rested a hand on the back of it. "I thought this holiday would improve your mood, but you're more miserable than ever. What on earth happened?"

"Nothing happened besides getting sick. Let's just go to the pub, Mum will be waiting."

Adie grabbed her jacket and pushed her gran out of the door, striding off in the direction of town as if the faster she got there, the quicker she could leave. She wouldn't go at all if this weren't so important to Josh, and she couldn't let him down.

"Roy's not coming." Monica adjusted her sunglasses and delivered the statement with minimum emotion.

"Isn't he? That's a shame."

"I ended it; things had become stale."

Adie scoffed. "You say all of this as if it should be news to me, but I never thought for a second the relationship would last. It's not what you do."

"No." She paused, glancing in Adie's direction every few seconds as if she wasn't sure whether to speak. It made a change, given she never usually held back. Perhaps their argument at the fair had taught her a lesson. "I presume this has something to do with Morgan." Or, apparently, it hadn't.

"Drop it, Gran. Honestly, we will fall out over this."

They walked the rest of the way in silence, and Adie tried to put on a smile as she pushed through the doors of The Anchor. Josh was with Emma by the bar fiddling over a microphone, and Liz had already bagged them a table. There were drinks lined up ready and waiting, and Adie took a liberal swig before she'd even finished her greeting.

Monica slipped into the booth and unwrapped her scarf. "She won't tell me what's wrong."

"I did tell you. I've been ill."

Liz wore a sympathetic smile. "Probably also a touch of the post-holiday blues." She shrugged and took a sip of her wine. "I was chatting to Jenny before you arrived and heard Morgan's news. You must have had a good time before the unfortunate vomiting incident if she wants to live there."

"The penny drops," Monica whispered.

"Don't," Adie warned, shooting her gran a stern glance. With any luck, it had enough daggers attached. "Are they joining us?"

"No." Liz lined up her various sheets of paper and made sure the pen sat straight beside them. "I think Jenny gets a bit competitive." And she wasn't the only one.

A text flashed up from Morgan asking if she was here and why she hadn't said hello. Tapping out a quick reply that they'd catch up during the break, Adie tried to get into it and take her mind off the impending awkwardness of feigning happiness. It didn't seem to be working because Liz kept frowning in her direction.

Forty-five minutes later Adie hadn't touched the rest of her pint, and her mum was pushing it across the table. "Don't you want your drink?"

"Can't stomach it. Thanks for the thought, I might grab some water in a second." She managed a weak smile and continued to stare at the picture round, trying to work out which member of One Direction she was looking at. It was no good because she didn't have the faintest clue what any of them looked like and didn't particularly care.

As the interval approached, she became more jittery, knowing it was an overreaction but struggling to calm her tapping foot and sweating palms. She couldn't let Morgan see her like this, it was ridiculous, so she squeezed out and went to the garden for a breath of fresh air.

"There you are." She'd been outside for a few minutes when Liz dropped down onto the wall next to her and shuffled over. "Morgan was looking for you. Is there a reason you're avoiding her? Did you have some sort of falling out on this trip?"

"Mum, I'm not twelve."

"Could have fooled me the way you're acting tonight." She smiled warmly and stared down the garden. "Come on, spit it out because I don't buy this is just a tummy bug." When Adie still didn't respond, she changed tack. "Emma seems nice. I'm glad Josh has met someone."

"Yeah." They'd also decided to form their own team so they could sit and drool over each other. That sort of thing wouldn't usually be a problem, but right now Adie wasn't in the mood to play third wheel to a happy couple.

"I like Morgan a great deal, as well."

She sniffed into the sleeve of her T-shirt and wiped under her eyes, hoping it'd go unnoticed. "Me too."

There was an uncomfortable silence, and Adie had to quell the desire to flee. This was the last conversation she wanted to have with her mum, especially now she was onto the fact it was about Morgan. For three days she'd been swinging between telling herself the move was a good thing, to feeling like someone had just declared the beginning of the apocalypse. It didn't matter where she landed, nothing brought her any respite.

"I know we don't talk about these things, but we can." Liz was more hesitant now, as if she could sense how close

Adie was to breaking. She shuffled closer, then let out a brief sigh. "Is this because you're falling in love with Morgan and she's moving away?"

Adie's stomach heaved but there was nothing to come up this time. "I'm not." Even as she heard herself, she knew it wasn't convincing.

Liz wrapped her arm across Adie's shoulder. "Do you want my advice?" With the nod of approval, she continued. "Tell her how you feel."

Adie took a deep breath, trying to work out whether to push through the discomfort and tell the truth or lie like crazy and hope her mum bought it. In the end, she knew she was doomed. It was written all over her tear-streaked face. "How can I do that now? All the reasons she has for going are sound. I won't try to convince her to stay."

"Who says you need to ask her to stay? You could still be together if it's what you both want."

"How, if she's in Spain and I'm here?"

"Trust, communication, visits. It's only a couple of months, and it'll prove to her that you truly care. You're considering her needs and being supportive. I'm sure she'll see that; she seems a level-headed woman."

Maybe, if she was even interested. If that was the case, though, why had she agreed to move away? "If she wanted me, she would have told me on Sunday. When I said there was nothing keeping her here, she didn't even begin to argue, and—"

"Oh, Adrienne Green, you didn't say that." Liz's arm fell away, and her head dropped into her hands. "How did you expect her to reply? If someone made a statement like that do you really think you'd argue? I expect she was extremely hurt."

Adie blanched, then her stomach grumbled again. She hadn't even looked at it that way, she'd been too upset in the heat of the moment. Not to mention a little drunk, and so damn preoccupied with figuring out her own feelings that she hadn't properly considered Morgan's. "I'm such an idiot."

"Perhaps that's a little harsh, it sounds like a miscommunication on both parts. From what Jenny's said, Morgan's about as love-sick as you are."

"Really?" The upturn in Adie's mood was short-lived. Of course Morgan was upset, she'd spent two months getting close to someone and then been told she wasn't important to them. "Buggering fuckery, I've really ballsed this up. How could I be so stupid?"

"I'll resist the urge to say you must get that from your father."

Regardless of where it'd come from, she had to fix it, and quickly. The break would be over soon, and she needed to speak with Morgan. No wonder she'd decided to split onto a separate team with Jenny, who probably knew exactly what had gone on and would be considering the best way to mount Adie's head on a stick.

"I need to talk to her."

Liz smiled for the first time. "Yes, you do. We'll chat about this some more in a few days once you've cleared things up with Morgan." She peered over her shoulder as the door creaked. "And here's your chance."

Adie stood and brushed the back of her jeans, then offered her mum a hand and hoisted her up. She wiped under her eyes and took a deep breath, trying to compose herself. This would take far more courage than Sunday night, and she really couldn't muck it up a second time or she'd need hospitalisation. No words had formed yet, but she hoped a few might occur to her once they were face-to-face.

"How are you doing on the quiz?" was the best she came up with in the end, and at least Morgan managed a tight smile.

"Yeah, good. Mum was a bit confused by the musical theatre round when it included no Andrew Lloyd Webber or musicals produced more than ten years ago, but we're getting by. Are you okay?" Morgan frowned, inching forward with her hands stuck in the back pockets of her jeans.

Adie shuffled and cleared her throat. "Not really. I think there's something we need to talk about."

"Yeah, I think you might be right."

There was another uncomfortable silence and she fiddled with her fingers, then stuffed them in her pockets and tried to make eye contact. She didn't have a clue where to start, but an apology seemed as good a place as any. "I'm so sorry for what I said on Sunday night, about you not having anything to stay for. It's no excuse, but I was hurt when you told me about the job. Beyond hurt. It felt like someone had just whacked me in the gut with a baseball bat. In any case, it was the wrong thing to say."

The wait for a reply was interminable and when it came, Morgan could barely even look up from the floor. "I understand why you said it, but you still crushed me when you said I had nothing to stay for."

Tears pushed hard on the back of Adie's eyes. "I'd been plucking up the courage to tell you how I feel, but I couldn't quite work out what to say, and then you dropped that bombshell and I panicked."

The earlier flash of anger seemed to dissipate, and Morgan moved a little closer. "Thank you for apologising, but you weren't entirely to blame. It took us both by surprise." She bit her lip, her eyes still fixed on the paving slabs. "Can I tell you why I also panicked?" Adie nodded. She wasn't entirely sure she'd enjoy hearing this but had to submit to the discomfort. "Because I realised on Sunday that things between us have gone way past friendship. When Lou texted I didn't even care. The only person I've thought about for weeks is you."

"Yeah me too—"

"Wait." Morgan glanced up and held out a hand. "Just let me finish, that isn't why I panicked." She perched on the wall, rubbing her palms down the front of her jeans. "I didn't panic about having feelings for someone else, or that it was you. It's a good thing, and I wanted to tell you that in the cove, but you seemed to back off and I chickened out. Then I was going to try again before Luke texted, but you were drunk. I had a moment of terror that if something happened, I'd end up a holiday fling." There was something in her eyes as she looked up. Remorse perhaps. Sadness, more likely. "I couldn't trust your reaction, and I couldn't be a convenient one-night stand you wanted to hide when we're back here. Can you understand that?"

Adie felt the tears welling again. "Yeah."

"I have real feelings for you, and I would love it if we can see where that goes, but I see your hesitation. It makes you sick, for god's sake. You let your guard down for a bit and then I think you realise you've done something wrong and you pull away again. I don't want you to pull away from me, though, because you haven't done anything wrong. Most of the time you do everything right."

Adie nodded and took Morgan's hand in a moment of bravery, hoping it wouldn't be immediately withdrawn. "I'm not drunk now, so can I be honest about how I feel? I promise it'll be the truth." She smiled briefly, and when it was returned with the faintest hint of dimples her stomach gave a little flutter. "I love these." She poked them gently. "I'm falling in love with all of you, actually, and I'm so sorry I hurt you with my careless words. You're the last person I ever want to cause any pain." A little shot of nervous laughter and the dimples deepened in reply.

"Where does that leave us, though? Tell me what you want."

Trying to straighten a smile that was wide with exhilaration and relief, Adie took a deep breath. She finally knew exactly what she wanted, even if there was a little voice still nagging that it wouldn't be easy. "I want you, and I'm very patient." She squeezed Morgan's hand, grateful when it tightened in return. Anticipating another wave of sickness, she paused, grinning when it didn't come. "I'm not asking you not to go. All I need to know is whether you want to be with me. If you do, I've got loads of holiday owed still and it's not a long flight. I've also started talking to my mum, she knows how I feel, and—"

She was stopped again when Morgan stood and raised a finger to her lips. "No. I didn't ask how you were prepared to compromise because I already know you're really good at that. I asked what you want."

Adie kissed the pad of Morgan's finger then pulled it away, entwining their free hands. "Okay." She took another deep breath, wondering how explicitly honest was appropriate. "I don't want you to go. I want you to stay right here, with me." She thought she'd finished but then added a last bit, sensing the mood had lightened enough. "Oh, and I want us to have lots of sex. In case that part wasn't a given."

Morgan bit back a smile, a deep red extending down the V of her T-shirt. "See, was that so difficult?"

"Yes, it was excruciating."

Morgan leant forward, pushing their hands so they ended up in the small of Adie's back like a prisoner under restraint. "Here, this should be a little easier." She glanced up to meet Adie's gaze and then pressed their lips together. It was the lightest of touches, but it still sent a thousand volts through her chest. "Think you can manage this part?"

When their lips met again the kiss was harder, more insistent. Morgan let go of Adie's hands and they spread up her back to hold her close. Then she cupped Adie's cheeks to guide their mouths together, her soft palms and fingertips stroking across Adie's face with such tender affection that warmth shot to every part of her body. When their lips broke apart, her hands continued clasping Adie's neck, both thumbs rubbing gentle circles.

"What now?" Adie whispered, hugging Morgan close and dabbing kisses on her shoulder. For some reason, she just couldn't let go.

"Now, we have a pub quiz to go and win," Morgan whispered back, tousling the loose hair that'd escaped Adie's bun. Her lips grazed Adie's neck now and the warmth of her breath sent out a shiver of excitement.

"Then shall we talk about what'll happen when you're in Spain? We could go for a drive, or..."

"Oh, I'm not going." Her mouth was pressed tight against an ear, but then Adie abruptly pulled back her head. "I did consider it, but then I called Luke this morning to tell him no."

"What?" Shock and confusion were written all over Adie's face.

"I've already got plans for what I want to do, and they don't involve becoming another person's skivvy on less pay than before. I want to do something for *myself*, I told you that weeks ago."

Adie stuttered out a few words, but none of it was intelligible, mainly because she was smiling too much. "Why didn't you say?"

"You didn't ask. You assumed. As for what we're doing next, I have to pick my dad up from the airport tomorrow, but do you want to come over on Friday and spend the weekend?"

Still too dumbstruck to answer properly, Adie nodded. She wasn't even going to worry about the prospect of an entire weekend in the annex, or what Morgan's other plans might be. For now, all she knew was that she felt well, and happy, for the first time in days. Maybe a glimmer of Holiday Adie had come back with them after all.

19

There was an array of vehicles on the drive again when she pulled up on Friday evening, but at least she was prepared for the onslaught of Morgan's entire family this time. She hopped out of the car, her wing mirror now securely attached, and wandered around the side of the house with a now familiar but uncomfortable mix of nerves and excitement disrupting her stomach lining. The hot weather wasn't helping, and she dabbed the T-shirt into her back to mop up a drip of sweat. Given it was early September, it was unseasonably warm.

When they'd left each other on Wednesday evening it had been with the promise that they'd figure out everything else this weekend, but she didn't really know what that meant. She could only presume the overnight invite was a good sign, but hadn't wanted to probe further, given she was exhausted enough from getting that far.

As she wandered down the side of the house, she was confronted by a dripping wet boy in swimming shorts with a large water pistol cocked towards her. She held up her hands and stepped back, then Morgan appeared behind with a bigger gun, something more akin to a missile launcher, and pumped the handle.

"Get her," she whispered, and they both let rip, spraying Adie with a jet of cold water that made her gasp and cover her face. "Show no mercy."

When the deluge stopped the boy ran off and Adie peered through her fingers. The discomfort she'd felt only a few minutes before had gone, but in its place was a flutter of excitement which tingled up her chest and left a big fat grin on her face. Morgan stood there in a pair of cut off denim shorts and a black bikini top, the aviators perched in her hair.

"Hi," Adie mumbled, hoping to regain control of her senses. It might be okay to let her guard down now, but probably not so obviously with relatives in range. She pulled the wet fabric away from her torso and shook it out, trying to subdue her grin. "The ambush was a little unfair, given I'm unarmed."

"It could've been a lot worse but we've already used most of the water bombs. Mum's had to go upstairs and change, they really did a number on her." Morgan's smile was warm and inviting now, far more so than the initial greeting. "If you want to get your own back, I can find you a weapon." She raised her eyebrows just a touch, her dimples deepening.

"Depends, am I with you or against you?"

The question was loaded with subtext, and the colour raised in Morgan's cheeks as her smile turned bashful. She shrugged, then fiddled with the trigger on her gun. "With me, I thought." A step forward and it was pressed into Adie's stomach. "Unless you've changed your mind?"

There was a big gaping pause, the only thing separating their bodies a giant lump of white plastic, and Morgan didn't seem to want to back away again. Her eyes flicked up to meet Adie's for only a fraction of a second. She was being awkward and weird as if she didn't know quite where to put herself.

Adie put a hand on the gun and took it from Morgan, setting it on the floor. "You alright, there?" A little nod, and she smiled. "You're being all cute and odd."

The comment only seemed to bring more colour to Morgan's cheeks, and she fixed her gaze on the splatters of water on Adie's T-shirt, tugging it away from her skin again. "Did you just call me cute?"

"Yeah. That a problem?"

Morgan shook her head. "Nope."

"Then shall we go so I can take revenge on your nephew?" Adie went to move but Morgan still had hold of her T-shirt and she had to stop. She put her arms around Morgan's waist, drawing her closer still. "You're going to have to tell me what's wrong."

Morgan shrugged, her voice now a whisper. "I wanted to kiss you, but for some reason I got nervous."

Adie smiled again, trying not to laugh. She closed her eyes and felt Morgan's palms cup her cheeks. Her breath tickled as she lingered and circled until their lips met, then Morgan's arms wrapped around her neck and they pulled each other closer into a hard, passionate kiss. Adie felt as though she hadn't drawn breath in minutes, her heart pounding and her cheeks flushing as her hands roamed over the exposed skin on Morgan's back. All her awkwardness seemed to have dissolved as she let herself go, submitting entirely and sinking into the embrace.

Morgan pulled back, tugging on Adie's bottom lip and almost taking her along too, and she touched a thumb to it, tasting iron. "You got over your nerves pretty fast." As a slap landed on her shoulder she jumped back and knocked over the gun, which clattered and scraped down the wall. They both looked at it, but Adie reached first, hugging it tight to her body and fumbling for the trigger. "You'd better run."

Morgan's eyes widened and she turned almost in slow motion, bolting around the corner as Adie gave chase, pumping the handle and preparing to fire. As they ran through the garden the high-pitched squeal rendered the four boys statues. When they got over it, they all ran after Morgan, spraying their guns and hurling a remaining water balloon so that it popped at her feet. She did a loop at the end of the lawn and ran towards the gate, the annex door open beyond. If she got there they were screwed, so Adie let rip on the bazooka, launching a jet of water at her back.

"What on earth is going on here?" Jenny boomed, stopping the boys in their tracks again.

It had the same effect on Adie momentarily and she ceased fire. "Just a little revenge."

"Say no more. I won't stop you, but these boys need to get dressed. Come on."

They all skulked off, leaving their pistols by the door, and Morgan continued to the patio. She grabbed a towel from the back of her deck chair and wrapped it over her shoulders. "I could change my mind about you."

"Really? There was me thinking you'd quite enjoyed this wet T-shirt contest."

"I'm not wearing a T-shirt."

Adie grabbed the towel as it was hurled in her direction and rubbed it over her face. "No, I know."

When they'd dried off and Morgan had found a dry top, it was time to face the family inside. Tim was at the table cradling the baby but besides that it was relatively quiet for a Cartwright family event. It came as a relief, because much as Adie looked forward to meeting Morgan's dad at some point, she wasn't sure she could stomach the stress this week on top of everything else. There was a good chance he was also handy with a gun, and she had visions of being chased off the property by Yosemite Sam.

"Where's everyone else?" Adie pulled out a chair and peered at the wriggling bundle in Tim's lap. She'd yet to see her eyes, which seemed to be permanently closed, and ten days on from their first meeting she apparently still didn't have a name.

"Gone to the pub to catch up with Dad. The three of us have been on kid duty while they're off enjoying themselves." Tim looked up expectantly. "Would you like a cuddle?"

"Is that possible while you're holding the baby?"

He laughed, shuffling in the chair as if he intended to make a handover. "Just support her head, she won't bite."

Adie relented, awkwardly placing her arms in what looked like the right position to hold a baby, her shoulders tense and her back oddly twisted. "Are you sure she doesn't bite?"

"No teeth, you're grand." Tim pushed back the chair and stood, stretching then taking a sip from his glass of lemonade. "Right, that's me away."

"Don't you dare."

The look of abject fear made him laugh, and he squeezed Adie's shoulder. "I only want to use the bathroom. Auntie Morgan will help if she attacks and tries to gum you to death."

"Auntie Morgan," Adie called. She repeated, her voice now pleading. "Come and see your niece."

Morgan had been getting them each a beer from the

fridge and laughed but ignored the request. The caps pinged across the work surface and she whistled to herself.

Adie examined the sleeping baby and tried to relax her shoulders, clearly stuck with her. Perhaps if they spent a bit of time together, they'd develop an understanding. Who knew? This kid might like running. She definitely enjoyed drinking.

When Morgan did come over and set a bottle on the table, she also had her phone in hand and held it up. "Say cheese." Adie obliged and Morgan snapped, smiling as she tapped on the screen and pulled out a chair. "Now, what shall I caption this?"

"How about irresponsible woman leaves niece with incompetent girlfr—" She twisted her mouth and let out a series of strangled sounds. That word should not have issued, and the amount of cringing caused pain in her jaw.

"As you wish." Morgan spoke as she typed, accentuating every word. "Irresponsible woman leaves niece with incompetent person who wants to be her girlfriend. Great."

Adie's mouth hung open. "You didn't post that?"

"Oh, how you underestimate me." She sat on the chair and hitched up her knee, laughing at the screen and typing again.

"What's so funny?" Adie grabbed at the phone with her free hand, but Morgan lifted it away, raising herself in the seat. Surely she hadn't actually posted that? Not publicly. Adie snatched again but had to stop because the baby stirred. "Tell me."

Morgan squeezed Adie's knee. "Nope."

Her hand lingered, trailing gentle circles while she continued to grin and scroll the screen. When Tim returned, phone also in hand, Adie felt left out. Was there anyone besides her and the baby not glued to a device? "You lot are very antisocial today. Maybe I should just go home."

Tim laughed and then shot Morgan a knowing look. "Are you torturing the poor girl, Morgs?"

She shrugged. "A little. She just wants to see what I posted on Instagram."

There was a pause while Tim checked his phone, emitting soft grunts of laughter. He looked Adie up and down, then did a creepy wink. "Alright, big softy? I'd say that nickname fits."

"Me too." Morgan's hand wrapped around Adie's thigh and she leant forward to kiss the top of her arm. "I think you might need to hand her back now, if you can tear yourselves apart."

Adie scoffed, but then smiled. She wasn't quite that scary after all, and perhaps they could become friends in time. Even so, the thought of this being a brother or sister was still terrifying, and she couldn't quite get her head around the idea. It felt awful to hope it never happened, but a part of her couldn't help thinking it'd be easier for everyone. "Did I tell you my dad wants to try for a baby?"

"What? No."

"Yeah, I'm not sure how I feel about the prospect."

Tim scooped up his daughter and settled her into a car seat on the floor. "Imagine if you have kids first. Your child could have an aunt or uncle that's younger than they are."

It took a moment to process all of that, but then Adie shook it off. "Good job I don't want kids then." She leant forward to tuck in a blanket and caught the look of horror on Tim's face. "What?"

His eyes widened and he glanced up at Morgan before meeting Adie's gaze. Beckoning with his head to draw Adie closer, he lowered his voice to a whisper. "You may have a problem. Haven't you noticed my sister is kid crazy?"

Adie's heart dropped into her stomach. Were they really at that point? They'd only decided to upgrade their friendship two days ago, and Tim wanted to talk about having children. He was right, though. If they wanted different things, it could be a real issue down the line, on top of everything else they already had to contend with. Her heart thudded and her mouth hung open slightly as she descended into a state of panic, but then Morgan burst out laughing and Tim's serious expression turned to a delighted smile.

"Sorry, but he got you there." Morgan rubbed a hand into Adie's shoulder, then stroked a finger up her neck.

Adie slumped back in the chair, trying to calm her racing pulse. "Are you two trying to give me a heart attack? Honestly, you need to leave that to my dad. He's cornered the market in making my life miserable and shocking me at every turn."

"You should take it as a compliment. Tim's teasing is a sign of acceptance. For the record, I am the best auntie on the planet, but I like being able to give them back. You're safe."

"Thank god for that." Although she thought she already had Tim's acceptance when he let her into the hospital room hours after his daughter's birth. With anyone else that would've been the symbolic event, but apparently not in this family.

Tim waved them both goodbye and called up the stairs to say he was leaving, then the door slammed shut. Morgan wasn't finished with this conversation, though. "I think you would make a great sister, for what it's worth."

Adie laughed, but she wasn't quite sure what for.

Perhaps the staggering lack of evidence to support Morgan's assertion. "Why?" Morgan grabbed her phone from the table again and held it up, finally revealing what she'd posted to Instagram. She'd captioned the photo with just a heart and the hashtag 'bigsofty'. It was Josh's comment that made Adie guffaw, though. "You guys are adorable. When's the wedding? Hashtag always right." She took the phone and scrolled through the other messages, and it seemed everyone had the same idea. "I'll wring his neck when I catch him."

Morgan nudged closer, her thumb stroking higher up Adie's leg. "By the way, you're missing something."

"Am I?" Adie had still been distractedly reading everyone's comments but stopped now and handed back the device.

"Mhm. A bag. I thought you might bring one since I invited you to spend the weekend. Does that mean you don't want to?"

It was Adie's turn to do a little teasing, although she feared it'd be less convincing. "Yeah, sorry. I decided we probably shouldn't rush into anything. Perhaps in a few months when we've really gotten to know each other." She leant forward and kissed Morgan's nose. "Is that okay?"

"Oh, I'd love to see you try and hold out that long."

Adie was about to reply when a tongue flicked against her ear and she almost moaned, giving the game away entirely. Morgan lingered there, nipping gently until Adie couldn't resist clasping her neck and kissing her more deeply on the mouth. She took handfuls of hair and then ran her hands firmly down Morgan's back.

They pulled each other tighter and everything became more urgent, Adie's heart thudding again and her hands gliding around Morgan's body. Palms slid down her chest and then up to cup her face, half of the time pushing her away and half pulling her closer.

"We need to stop," Morgan mumbled through another kiss.

"Okay." Adie pressed the soft spot at the start of Morgan's jaw, feeling the pulse throbbing under her lips.

She hit Adie's shoulder, letting out a little laugh. "I mean it, we shouldn't be doing this in my mum's kitchen. Get yourself under control."

"I'm completely in control."

Morgan wriggled out of the embrace, her face flushed and beaming. "I'm glad you are. If you go and get the bag which I know you've left in your car, we've got the whole weekend to continue this." She laughed as Adie sprung out of her seat and jogged towards the door, then shooed her along and called across the patio. "Hurry, before my family come back and we get trapped with them all night!"

20

Morgan was nowhere in sight when Adie got back but the annex door was ajar. She walked straight through and dumped her rucksack in the hallway, then leant against the doorway to the living room. She still loved the view, perhaps more so than the ones in Spain, and stared over the rolling fields, shimmering in the evening light like they'd been touched with a sliver of gold paint. Now the place had been redecorated, it was perfect. You didn't need paintings on these walls because the windows gave you a work of art.

There was a little round table next to them with two places set and a couple of foldout chairs. Morgan had added a tumbler of wildflowers to the middle and lit a candle, which flooded the room with jasmine scent. She'd gone to some effort, working away in the kitchen with focus.

Adie wandered over and wrapped her arms around Morgan's waist, kissing her temple and then peering over her shoulder. "What are we eating?"

"Guess."

"Lobster? Steak? Caviar?"

Morgan laughed. "No. Pizza of course. I'm trying fresh

dough, like we had at your house." She tilted a bowl on the work surface to show off the contents. "See. Looks pretty good, right?"

It looked great, so long as they weren't eating it raw again. Adie let her go and stood to one side, her arm outstretched to lean against the counter. "Are you going to tell me what these big plans are now? You promised to fill me in properly." Despite being glad they'd loosened up with each other, she knew they still had stuff to discuss.

"I've put in an offer on a house." Morgan tipped out some flour and then plopped the dough on top.

Adie's grip tightened on the edge of the work surface. "What? Where did that come from?"

"Property development. It makes perfect sense." She grabbed a rolling pin and began to shape their bases. "I've got all the skills, the only thing I didn't quite have was the money, so I put together a proposal, found an investor, and problem solved." There was a little shrug as if it were no big deal. "We're buying the house outright. I'll live in it while I do it up, then they get a share of the profit."

"You've done all that this week? Since we got back from Spain?"

"Uhuh."

Another shrug, but Adie was still unconvinced by this nonchalant attitude. Going from working with Tim to taking on the responsibility of an investor's money and an entire renovation project sounded huge. "That's a massive step."

"I know, but it's not as sudden as it seems, and full disclosure, the investor is my dad. He says the figures stack up and if this one goes well, he'll reinvest. Everyone wins."

Adie went to comment but then stopped herself. Just because she knew Robert would be a living nightmare in the same situation didn't mean Morgan would have any trouble working with her dad. Instead, she focussed on the practicalities. "So, where is this house?"

"North West London. I'll have to take them where I can find them if I carry it on, but Rebecca's brother—the one you met at dinner—is an estate agent down there and tipped me off about a place that's been trashed by the previous tenants. The guy just wants rid of it now."

North West London was pricey even if the place was a wreck, and Adie frowned briefly before straightening her face. Partly because she was now wondering quite how much money Morgan's dad had to throw around, not that it was any of her business, but also at the idea of Morgan moving back to London. "You're going to live in this house while you do it up?"

"Yeah, but it's only just over an hour away, it's not like—"

"Spain."

Morgan laughed as she reached into the fridge for toppings. "Right. What do you reckon?"

Adie was about to say she was happy if Morgan was happy, but experience told her that wasn't going to fly. "I'd rather you were here, obviously, but you'll always have my full support. When you need somewhere to stay that isn't a building site, I have a nice little house you prepared earlier."

"Complete with soft carpets, working shower, and adorable girlfriend?"

Adie smiled and stared at her shuffling feet as heat scorched through her cheeks. So much for worrying it was too soon to use that word. "Yeah, with one of those."

Morgan finished topping the pizzas and slid them into the oven, setting a timer and then washing her hands under the tap. When she'd dried them, she wrapped the towel around Adie's middle to draw her forward, clearly no longer reserved about getting what she wanted. "We have ten minutes. What do you want to do with that time? Think very carefully."

It didn't take much thinking at all. Adie dipped her mouth, kissing Morgan until she was guided back against the sofa, her calves hitting the cushion and causing her to topple. Morgan straddled her lap and cupped her cheeks again, every time tracing her jaw or the features of her face with a delicate touch. The heat rose through Adie's chest again but this time it was arousal rather than embarrassment. She became so engrossed that she barely noticed when the timer pinged, until her lap cooled because Morgan was gone.

She glanced up at the bedroom while the food was served, her hands tingling with another surge of nerves. It was a long time since she'd spent the whole night in bed with someone, not least an entire weekend, and the intimacy was daunting. That word 'girlfriend' had also set her on edge, even though she was the first to say it, and would take some getting used to.

"Are you coming to eat?" Morgan set their plates on the table and sat down.

Adie shook her head slightly, diverting her gaze from the first floor and any thoughts of what might happen later, then wandered over to pull out a chair. "This looks great. Not to the same level as my pizza, naturally, but with a bit of practise." She ducked as a fork was thrust towards her head. "Steady, I was only joking. I was hoping to have all my faculties intact for..." With a little shrug, she smiled as Morgan's lip twitched. "You know. The rest of the weekend. What are we doing tomorrow?"

"Whatever you want, but I did say we'd have lunch with

Liz. It was very sweet, she cornered me on Wednesday and said she wanted to get to know me better."

Adie grunted out a laugh as she cut a slice of pizza. She had promised they'd chat in a couple of days so probably couldn't argue. She had mixed feelings over how it would go, though, despite how supportive her mum had been mid-crisis. "Yeah, I think the cat's well and truly out of the bag with her. All that time I spent worrying—"

"And she'd known for years."

Had she? There hadn't been much time to think about it, but Adie had sort of presumed it was a recent discovery. Despite having asked Morgan not to tell her, she'd had no such discussions with Jenny, which was probably a massive error of judgement if she didn't want her mum to know. Not that it really mattered now. "What else did you talk about on Wednesday?"

There was a pause as Morgan chewed through a mouthful of pizza. "Not much. She just said we make a lovely couple and how nice it is that our families get on, too." She seemed to clock the worried expression on Adie's face as she struggled to swallow a piece of crust, the dough turning to ash in her mouth where it was suddenly so dry. "What's up? You and your mum are really close, I thought this would be good news?"

Adie got up and poured a glass of water from the kitchen tap. "It is." She grabbed another for Morgan and carried them to the table, then shuffled to get comfy in her seat. "It's just—"

"What? Too soon? Sorry, I know my family operates a bit differently than everyone else. Mum's always been really open and was the parent inviting in half the neighbourhood kids when we were younger. I've jumped the gun by assuming you want me to get to know your mum, we can just cancel, and—"

"No." Adie shot her a warm smile. The babbling was cute, but she was off the mark. "I'd love for you to get to know each other properly." She took Morgan's hand on the table, tracing her index finger in circles around the palm. "And we've known each other for months, so it doesn't feel too soon."

"But...?"

"You're right. You're used to Jenny, who when I first met her fed me lunch and decided I was her new best friend. It's great. I love how close knit and involved you all are, but my family is a little more complex. My feelings about that are also..." Adie inclined her head, trying to find a word to describe the dynamic between her parents, gran and self. "Complex. I've spent four years out of a relationship for a reason, and it does worry me. You being hurt worries me. Me being hurt worries me."

Morgan smiled and squeezed Adie's fingers. "You're getting better at this honesty thing."

"I'm trying." Although they'd already talked about needing any relationship to be secure and feel worthwhile, so was this really a revelation? Adie hoped the implication was clear, on both sides. She faltered, wondering if she should be more explicit. "You do know, don't you? That this is a big deal for me, and I meant every word I said to you on Wednesday." Tears suddenly pressed on the back of her eyes and she had to divert her gaze out of the window for a second, her feet shuffling under the table.

"Yes, I know." Morgan's tone was soft and even. She nudged forward in her chair and wrapped her hand around Adie's knee. "I know you let fear and shame get the best of you sometimes, and I won't tell you it doesn't worry me, but something tells me I should trust you." She stood and rounded the table, draping her arms across Adie's chest and kissing her cheek. "I want to be with you because you're soft, and kind, and loving. You're also sexy as hell." She whispered the last bit and then laughed. "We can work through the other stuff. Together. Okay?"

"Okay."

Morgan kissed Adie's cheek again and then returned to her seat, the mood a little lighter now they'd got it out of the way. It wasn't the sort of first date conversation Adie would usually employ, but she knew that if this stood any chance of working she needed to be honest, and vulnerable, and brave. It was new and terrifying ground but oddly liberating, as if a weight was being gradually lifted from her shoulders and she could finally begin to stand tall. Fingers crossed she'd feel the same way after lunch tomorrow, and not like she was lugging one of her mum's railway sleepers.

They finished a leisurely dinner and Morgan chatted through more of her plans for the house, showing Adie pictures of an old Victorian terrace. Then she cleared away the plates and leant back against the work surface, bending her leg to inspect the sole of her foot. "I might grab a quick shower. I've been running around the garden with the boys all evening." She pulled off her T-shirt and flung it at the sofa, back to wearing nothing but shorts and a bikini top. It was cooler now, the temperature rapidly dropping as the sun set, and goose bumps rose on her arms. "Then shall we go to bed? It's somehow almost ten already."

Adie nodded, another flutter running through her chest. It wasn't nearly ten at all, it was quarter-past nine, and Morgan's rush to get her in the sack was causing sweaty palms. Not because she didn't want to be there—far from it —but due to the length of time between sexual partners and a genuine worry that she wouldn't remember what bits went where. "Let me just clean my teeth." She got up and grabbed her bag from the hallway, fishing out the wash bag and hurrying into the bathroom. The light buzzed overhead, and she leant forward on the sink. "Get a grip," she muttered to herself. "Anyone would think you've never shared a bed before."

"Don't worry," Morgan whispered as she squeezed past, clearly having listened to every word. "I don't snore."

"Oh good, that was my worry."

Adie cleaned her teeth and her mouth hung open when Morgan dropped her shorts, causing foam to drip down her chin. She wiped it away and rinsed her mouth as the shower was switched on, hot water bursting free and filling the room with steam.

"Do you want to jump in, too? It was warm today, I bet you're all sweaty, and it is double width." Morgan tugged at the bottom of Adie's T-shirt, apparently far more casual about them getting undressed in front of each other.

Adie swallowed hard, mint burning down her throat. "Is my invitation rescinded if I'm sweaty? Because if this is an entry requirement, I'm not left with much choice…"

"No." Morgan laughed. "And you don't have to come in with me if it's inducing a full-blown panic, I can just leave it running." She went to untie her bikini top but then stopped with her hands on the straps. "Do you need to look away before I do this?"

Adie reflexively turned to face the doorway, but she could still see behind herself with a sideways glance at the mirror. Morgan pulled away the flimsy fabric, revealing full, round breasts, and Adie had to grip the sink again. She was mid rotation when the bottoms came down, her eyes traveling around Morgan's body.

"Fucking hell." The voice that delivered this statement was rasping and not quite her own, thick with arousal and appreciation.

"I did warn you." Morgan shrugged and stepped into the shower, water beading off her skin as she tipped back her head. "I'll only be a minute, and then you can have it if you want." Adie ripped off her shirt, spraying loose hair from her bun, and slipped down her shorts. As Morgan opened her eyes, she smiled. "You're not wearing your Wonder Woman underwear."

"No, sorry. Are you disappointed?"

As it was stripped away, followed in short order by a black lace bra, Morgan shook her head. "Not in the slightest. Funnily enough, it wasn't the focus of my attention. Please tell me you're getting in."

Adie slid the shower door closed behind herself and stood under the jet of water, pulling the band from her hair to send it tumbling down her back. There were some situations where you just had to jump in and be guided by what your body was telling you. In this case, despite a few nerves, it wanted to be freed from clothes and in a hot shower with a beautiful woman.

Morgan smoothed her hands through Adie's hair, their breasts slipping together as she pressed close. "I've never seen you with your hair down before. Is it symbolic?"

"Possibly, although you've also never seen me naked."

"True." She laughed again, reaching around to pull a bottle of orange scented gel from a wire basket in the corner of the cubicle. Lathering a generous helping onto a shower puff, she gently stroked it over Adie's chest, working down in a circular motion and paying particular attention to her breasts.

"I think they're clean." Adie leant in for a kiss to distract her. If she spent any more time there, she'd wear away the nipples, which were already hard and swollen.

Morgan relented and carried on over Adie's hips, but she raised her free hand to stroke over their curve again. "Don't worry, you can get your own back in a minute."

Covered in soap, her fingers glided over Adie's skin with ease. She pulled them closer when she hooked her arm around Adie's waist to wash her back, then down her legs. Stepping forward to guide them under the jet again, she hung up the puff and stroked away the bubbles, leaving a trail of goose bumps in her wake.

When she dipped her mouth to flick her tongue against first the left and then the right nipple, Adie groaned with pleasure, desperate to have them consumed. It had been a year, and right now she was feeling it. "At what point exactly do I get my own back?" Her hands roamed over Morgan's sides and across her stomach, clawing up her quads until she backed Adie against the cool tiled wall and kissed her, inhaling sharply and pressing their bodies flush together. But when she tilted to slide her hand into the hair between Adie's legs, her wrist was seized. "Not so fast."

She'd meant it playfully, but Morgan's face fell momentarily. "Sorry, I didn't—"

"It's okay." Adie shot her a reassuring smile and the hand that still grasped her forearm slid down to entwine their fingers. "You haven't done anything wrong, I just wanted to get this." She reached for the shower puff again and held it up.

A smile crept across Morgan's face and her chest heaved as she let out a breath. Then she turned, wrapping Adie's arm tight around herself. "I got a little carried away," she whispered, as soap rubbed over her stomach and up the channel between her breasts. "I keep thinking about the pool in Spain and how much I wanted you to press me against that wall."

"Did you?" No longer a flutter, arousal thundered through Adie's chest like an earthquake. She'd thought about it, too, but would never have gone there when Morgan was so vulnerable.

"Uhuh." She groaned with the lusty suck on her neck, pressing her hips forward into the hand that, having dropped the shower puff, now raked between her legs. The other arm still wound around her waist and bent to flick a thumb over her nipple, then rubbed slow circles with increasing intensity.

"What is it you want me to do now?" With the evidence of Morgan's arousal, Adie's confidence grew, and when Morgan placed a hand over her own to lower it, she didn't need the encouragement at all. It was hot, though, feeling where Morgan wanted to guide her fingers, pressing them into her clit, showing her what pressure she liked and how fast.

Morgan gave up control then, reaching back with both hands to massage Adie's bum and grind them together. Then she twisted to bring their mouths together as water beat down on Adie's shoulders. "Do you want more suggestions?"

Adie nipped Morgan's ear. "Mhm." She did it again. "It's very sexy. Feel free to boss me around a bit."

With that, Morgan parted her legs slightly and pressed her palms flat against the tiles. Before she had a chance to say any more, Adie grasped her waist with her left hand, knowing exactly where this was going. Running the pads of her first two fingers around Morgan's opening to coat them, she gradually slipped further inside, her chest contracting when she'd entered fully and was rewarded with a low, throaty moan.

With the hand from Morgan's hip, she stroked down to hold three fingers against her vulva. "Oh fuck, Adie." As her hips bucked forward, Morgan's fingers curled and slid on the wet tile. "You need to hold me. My legs are shaking."

"I won't let you fall." Morgan leant her forearms against the wall and Adie pressed her body against her back. She could smell the orange from the shower gel on Morgan's skin as she dipped her head to kiss the tattoo, then raised her eyes to watch the pleasure play out on Morgan's face as she rubbed against her G-spot with a third finger.

Morgan's low moans increased Adie's excitement and she gained momentum, every thrust causing her clit to throb. Warmth radiated through her chest at the confirmations of pleasure and when Morgan pulsed around her fingers, she groaned with her.

"Don't stop." Morgan's voice was raspy but the thrill it sent through Adie's body was electric. Sliding her arm around Morgan's waist, she thrust as deeply as she could, and when Morgan released an anguished "fuck", her fingers were tightly squeezed. She dabbed the smooth wet skin on Morgan's back as she relaxed, and then slowly slid them out.

"Are you okay?" Adie whispered.

Morgan turned, her chest heaving and flushed with colour. Pressing her lips to Adie's collarbone, she wrapped both arms around her waist. "Tell me why we weren't doing that last weekend?"

They'd already been over that and it would only ruin the mood, so Adie just shrugged and pulled her close. "Doesn't matter anymore. We won't make the same mistake again."

21

It turned out spending the night in Morgan's bed wasn't so daunting after all. The suggestion that they'd be sleeping had also been some way off, and when Adie was woken by a bright beam of light through the porthole window above them, she'd lost track of the time and how often she'd drifted in and out of consciousness. Her naked legs slipped together as she wriggled, then one of Morgan's nudged between them. She had her arm wrapped under Adie's breasts and began to lay kisses on her back, sweeping the mass of hair up out of the way.

"Is it really morning this time?" Morgan murmured. Even without seeing her, it was clear she was smiling.

"I have no fucking clue even what day it is."

"Good, then my work here is almost done." And with that she ran her hand down Adie's stomach, then trailed her fingernails in light waves over the tops of each thigh. "Roll over."

Adie obliged. She closed her eyes and felt the now familiar pulse between her legs as Morgan sucked and licked her nipples, her teeth raking over them gently. Then she worked down and Adie stretched her hands over her head, falling onto her back and shuffling down the bed to get comfy. The covers were thrown aside, and Morgan kissed over her hips.

"Are you going to wake me up like this every day?" Adie laughed a little, her head pressing into the mattress as she mumbled with pleasure.

Morgan rested her chin on the inside of a knee, and when she spoke it sent out a hum of vibrations. "Haven't I already woken you up in a similar way once today? I guess maybe I am setting a precedence." She continued, kissing everywhere but the place Adie needed her to and causing moans of desperation. "Are you feeling a little frustrated, by any chance?"

"Try painfully aroused." How that was possible when she'd had at least three orgasms already she wasn't sure, but right now she didn't much care. She was just about to be put out of her misery when there was a loud thump on the door and her eyes shot open. "Are you kidding me?"

Morgan laughed and dabbed a kiss on her stomach. "Bets on who it is. I bagsy Mum because she's just spotted your car's still on the driveway." She was crawling off the bed and reached to ping a T-shirt from a hanger, slipping it over her head and then grabbing some cotton shorts which hung off the end of the rail. "I wonder if she'll have a bacon sandwich, I'm starving."

"That's great for you, but all my clothes are downstairs. You can't let her in while I'm naked." Adie reached to draw the covers back over herself, feeling suddenly exposed. When Morgan jumped back on the bed and climbed to kneel on all fours over her body, she peered out and pouted.

"Maybe I like keeping you prisoner up here." There was

another thump on the door, and she had to roll off again, running down the stairs.

Adie listened to her feet pad across the living room and out into the hall, then there came the chatter of voices. There weren't just two of them, though, and she let out a loud groan. If Morgan's dad was coming in as well, she'd have no choice but to die.

"You could have tidied." It was Jenny, for definite, and she was now in the same space. "For goodness sake."

"And you could've told me you were coming." Morgan again, and the sound of snapping towels. They'd discarded them on the sofa last night, and she'd be having to collect them.

"Did Adie get a taxi home last night? I hope it didn't look like this when she was here."

A snigger, and then the sink began to whoosh as it was run and presumably filled the kettle. "No."

The laugh which followed was deeper. It was a guy and all Adie's worst fears about meeting Morgan's dad for the first time ensconced in shame and a blue duvet looked to be coming true. But then he spoke, and she let out a sigh of relief. It was only Josh.

"Don't worry, I take it she's upstairs," he yelled. "I'd recognise those Doc Martens anywhere."

Adie laughed as Jenny let out an almighty huff. "Well why didn't you stop us from coming if you had company?"

"Stop you?" Morgan banged down the kettle. "I didn't know you were coming, or I would've told you to bugger off." Her voice became quieter as she presumably left the room, then she ran up the stairs and dumped Adie's bag next to the bed. Jogging back down, she continued the argument with her mum, although her tone was playful. "What on earth are you doing here, anyway?"

"I texted you at least half a dozen times this morning. Josh has come to look at the annex."

Adie reached a hand from under the duvet and opened the bag's zip, delving for some clothes. She pulled out the first pair of underwear she could find and then clean shorts and T-shirt, wriggling to the edge of the bed and quickly putting them on. She stood and inched towards the top of the stairs, peering down to find the three of them in a stand-off. "In her defence, I have no idea what time it is or where our phones are."

"It's almost midday."

"Never mind, right?" Josh stuck his hands in his pockets, and his eyes darted around the room. He had a delighted smile on his face and stepped over to the window. "We won't take much of your time, but Jenny and I got chatting on Wednesday and she said this place would be available in a few weeks." He looked up to Adie and shrugged. "Kismet."

She descended a few steps, still feeling self-conscious. "We can show Josh around if you want?"

"Sounds good to me."

"There you go." A few more steps, but Jenny was giving her an odd look which she couldn't quite discern. She knew what had happened on Wednesday night because they'd talked about it afterwards and joined forces on the quiz, but she didn't look as relaxed and happy about it as she was then.

"Okay." Jenny wore a tight smile and gestured towards the door. "Adie, would you just help me grab something from the house?"

That wasn't a good sign. No one ever needed something fetching, it was an excuse to be alone. Adie nodded and took a deep breath, leaving Morgan to give Josh the tour and following through the living room and out across the patio.

When they reached the kitchen, Jenny leant against the table and folded her arms.

"Everything okay?" Even as she asked, Adie knew it wasn't. Jenny's eyes were still kind, but there was something there she hadn't seen before. A wariness, perhaps.

"I'm sorry to have to ask you about this, but Morgan told me a little about your dad and it's on my mind. I knew he was slightly..." Her eyes flicked up as if she couldn't quite find the right word and was plumping for anything that vaguely fit. "Backwards. But did he really cause such a fuss over you being gay?"

Adie swallowed hard, trying to push down the bile collecting in her throat. She'd worried how Morgan would cope with this but never Jenny. Perhaps that was naïve, given the work relationship and how protective she was, but all the same. "Yeah, he went ballistic, but don't worry because I would never ever let him say any of that stuff to Morgan. Honestly, he'd have to beat me to death before he got near her."

Jenny frowned momentarily, then pulled out a chair and perched on the edge. "I think you've misunderstood me. I only wanted to make sure you were okay and find out how you'd like me to handle this at work." Her smile was warmer, and Adie read the wariness as hesitation now rather than anything else. "I wouldn't usually be comfortable lying but if you need for me not to say anything in the short term, I will."

Adie's lip trembled with relief, and she rested back against the cool wall of the kitchen. "Um, thanks Jenny." She sniffed, unsure why she was reacting so strongly, but it had been an emotional week. "I would appreciate that, actually. I intend to tell him, but maybe in a little while when things have settled. We're heading to my mum's shortly because

I've never come out to her or had a conversation about what happened." She stopped, noticing Jenny's widened eyes. It was the same look Morgan had given her a few weeks ago.

"Okay, well if you run into any problems, our door is always open."

Jenny stood and held out her arms, and Adie shuffled forward. What did she want, a hug? No one ever gave her hugs, apart from the odd occasion her dad tried it. She could do this, though, it should be the simplest thing in the world. Why then did it feel awkward and, oddly, undeserved?

"Thanks again, Jenny." Adie gave her back a gentle pat as they embraced, then pulled away and stepped towards the door. "I do appreciate it. Everything, really. I appreciate everything."

Cursing her own awkwardness, she strode across the patio and back into the annex, where Josh was relaxing on the sofa with a mug in hand. He was still smiling, but he cocked his head when he caught sight of her. "Everything alright? I've been worried about you, are you over this stomach bug thing?" With a slight smirk and a sideways glance, he blew over the top of his tea. "Or was Morgan playing nurse?"

She'd usually be happy to spar, but right now wasn't in the mood. "Yeah, I'm okay. How much did you raise on Wednesday? I'm sorry I wasn't much help, but it looked like you had enough of that from Emma."

His expression turned decidedly gooey now. "We raised nearly three hundred quid, so it was a massive success. And you're right about Emma." He bit his lip and then patted the cushion next to him, waiting until Adie had dropped onto it. "I take it Monica didn't tell you what happened last weekend?"

"Oh god, what?" The last thing she needed was her gran creating a third or fourth drama to deal with.

Morgan pulled out one of the folding chairs and shuffled forward on it, listening intently, and he hitched up his knee to get comfy. "Well, I invited Emma over on Saturday evening and Monica had agreed to clear out for us in exchange for a bottle of Hendricks." A pause for dramatic effect, and Adie could boot him. This had better be good. "We were getting on great and I had this really cheesy thing planned where I was going to ask her to be my girlfriend." He held up a hand to halt any teasing. "And before you say anything, don't. But your gran stormed in having a blazing row with Roy because he'd ambushed her and invited his granddaughter to dinner so they could meet."

Adie sucked her teeth and sunk back. Monica wouldn't have liked that one tiny bit. "No, she didn't give me details, she just said it had ended." She poked Josh's shoulder. "But let's not get hung up on that because my gran is entirely predictable. You asked Emma to be your girlfriend? How cheesy are we talking?"

"Very. I mean, fondue level cheese. I cooked a romantic meal, used a tablecloth, lit a candle." He frowned at Morgan as she laughed, but it would only be the parallel with their own night that had tickled her.

"So? Did you still pop the question and gross her out with how lame you are, or did Gran ruin it completely?"

"Weirdly she helped me out. I was really nervous because I wasn't sure if it was too full on, you know?" He stopped, as if waiting for someone to jump in and reassure him, but it wasn't happening. With a little shake of his head, he was off again and showing more enthusiasm than he had in months. "But we ended up in hysterics and I told her what I'd planned..."

This time the pause was more exaggerated, and Adie indulged him. "Please go on, I'm dying to know," she deadpanned.

"Turns out Emma thought she was already my girlfriend. Go figure."

Oh yes, what a surprise that the woman he'd been seeing for weeks had assumed they were an item. It was sweet, though, in a geeky sort of way. She waited to see how long it'd be before he turned the tables, but he wasn't biting. "Aren't you interested at all in my love life, or have I been unceremoniously dumped now you've got a girlfriend?"

"Not really, that's old news."

She pulled a cushion from behind her back and whacked him over the head with it, while he held out the mug of tea, trying not to slosh it everywhere. "I think it's time for you to leave now." It was a shame because his company had been cheering her up until twenty seconds ago. Usually, she liked seeing him so happy. He was even looking at places to rent, which was a minor miracle, but it didn't mean he could get away with that kind of cheek. "We'll talk in four to six months when we're both single again."

Morgan got off her chair and swiped the cushion, bashing Adie over the head with it this time. "Hey, don't be like that." With a smirk in Josh's direction, she did it again. "There's no reason to think Josh will be single again that quickly. You, on the other hand." She dropped the cushion and climbed onto Adie's lap, pinning her arms behind her head. "Need to be very careful what you say."

Josh stood and carried his mug to the kitchen. "And on that note, I'm going to sort details with Jenny. Do you guys fancy the pub later? Presuming you can tear yourselves away from the bed, that is."

"I think we can manage that." Morgan fell sideways into the now empty groove. "We should go on a double date some time, too. It'd be fun."

"Definitely. I can't do next weekend because we've got plans with Emma's friends. Week after?"

Adie cleared her throat, hating to interrupt when her girlfriend and best mate were so expertly planning her life, but she did think perhaps she should get a say. Not that it wouldn't be nice to get to know Emma better. "Excuse me."

Josh was flicking through his phone, presumably inviting Emma and putting it in his diary, and completely ignored her. "I'm busy at the moment, it's all this youth group business and trying to move..."

"Good, I'm glad we cleared that up. Thank you for listening." She might as well be talking to herself and slumped further into the sofa with her arms folded.

"So a fortnight? I'll book us a table somewhere, and see you in The Anchor at say eight?"

Before Adie could reply or protest, Morgan had covered her mouth and agreed. Then she pressed her lips against Adie's ear so Josh couldn't hear. "Sorry, but I thought you wanted to be bossed around." Josh said goodbye and she grabbed a wrist, dragging Adie off the sofa and heading towards the stairs. As the door slammed shut, she discarded her T-shirt on the balustrade, then hooked a thumb to start tugging down her shorts. "Come on pouty, I've got a little unfinished business."

22

After half an hour of fun they really were pushing it, and Morgan had evicted them both by rolling up the duvet and dumping it off the end of the bed. They'd dressed properly and had another cup of tea, then driven over and made it to Liz's for half one, just about within the right time frame for lunch. Adie popped open her door and climbed out, spotting a wheelbarrow down by the side gate and knowing that meant there was some form of gardening in progress. They'd be eating outside as usual, and she sometimes wondered why her mum didn't just pitch a tent on the lawn rather than bothering with a house that was surplus to requirements for most of the year.

Morgan frowned and fiddled with her seatbelt, seemingly unwilling to move. "Are you sure you want me here?"

Adie leant forward, her palms flush on the bonnet. "Of course I do." Although it was a bit bloody late now if she didn't. "I thought Mum invited you?"

"Yeah, she did, but if you want to talk to her in private..."

Morgan unclicked her belt and climbed out, taking Adie's hand as it was offered. They wandered past the wheelbarrow and, sure enough, Liz was in her old work jeans wrapping the cord back around the lawnmower handle. She'd just finished and there was sweat running down her cheeks, but she wore a wide smile when she spotted them.

"What time do you call this?" She tapped the watch on her wrist as she strode down the garden, jumping off the little step onto the patio.

Adie sucked in her cheeks, trying not to smile at the memory of their most recent activity. "Sorry, Josh showed up wanting to tour Jenny's annex. We didn't know he was coming." Although they had found all the messages on Morgan's phone, which had been discarded on the side of the bathroom sink and was now recovering from steam damage.

"Yes, she told me he was interested in the place. Good news, it'll help them both." Was there anything she didn't know? All of a sudden, Liz was the centre of all gossip. "Are you feeling better now?" She stared at Adie's stomach as if it might speak for itself, and as luck would have it, there was a grumble of hunger. They hadn't eaten anything since pizza the previous evening. "I'll take that as a yes. Let me pop inside for the sandwiches." Squinting through the patio door, Liz turned and lowered her voice. "If you come inside, make sure you don't let Charlie out."

Adie laughed, unsure why they were hiding this information from the cat. He was hardly going to mount a protest. She released Morgan's hand and sat on the edge of the lawn, leaning back with her eyes closed and wriggling to get comfy.

"This place is phenomenal." Morgan's footsteps sounded on the slabs, and then she was casting a shadow over Adie's face. "Your mum is wasted in a garden centre. I know tonnes of people who'd pay her for landscaping skills."

"Yeah, I keep telling her that, but she says it's just for fun. If she wanted to earn better money she'd go back to accountancy, but right now I think she's happy." Or relatively happy, given how wildly it could swing.

"Even so, she's incredibly talented."

When Adie opened her eyes, she smiled to find Morgan peering down at her. "She's one of those people who is good at everything. I know someone else a bit like that."

They were interrupted when the door swung open. Liz was faffing because she had her hands full and couldn't close it again, so Morgan saved her and took a plate of cakes. There weren't just sandwiches at all, she'd gone all out with scones, Victoria sponge and everything required to make a full afternoon tea.

"This looks amazing, I feel even more guilty that we were late." Morgan set them on the table, then sat and patiently waited.

Adie hauled herself off the grass and pulled out the chair next to her, practically salivating and showing less restraint. "Thanks, Mum." She grabbed a plate and tucked in, piling it high until she realised they were both staring at her. "What?"

"I know you didn't eat for a few days but steady on. I'm not listening to you throw up again tonight, that'd really kill the romance."

"Speaking of which," Liz interjected. She took a large bite of scone and leant back in her seat, not even bothering with the savoury first. When she'd finished, she wiped her fingers on her jeans and took a sip from her flask of water but didn't say any more.

"Speaking of which?" Adie repeated.

"We said we'd talk more about that, so why don't you tell me what happened on Wednesday?"

Resisting the urge to stall and reply with "you know what happened on Wednesday", Adie took a leaf out of Morgan's book and pulled up her big girl pants. She wasn't wearing the real ones given it was the weekend, but there was a metaphorical tug. "Okay." She munched down a few more bites of sandwich because she was still ravenous and then pushed back her plate. "What do you want to know?"

"All of it, but why don't you start by explaining why all the drama when you both so clearly felt the same way about each other. I've never seen you in such a state."

That was a big question with a long answer which even Adie hadn't completely worked her way through yet. It was like everything had suddenly come to a head, although with hindsight it wasn't all that sudden. "I think the easiest way to explain it is that I've been trying to dodge my feelings for weeks and I hit the point where I couldn't anymore."

"Try years," Morgan corrected.

"Yeah, okay. Years."

Liz only looked confused, which was understandable. "Had you known each other before, then?"

"No."

"Oh." She was frowning so much now that she was practically squinting. "Well then what do you mean by years?"

Here they were, going down the rabbit hole. Adie shuffled and tried to find the right words, her grip tightening around the arm of the chair. "Before I answer, did you know I was gay? Because Morgan seemed to think from what you told Jenny that you've known for a long time." And right now, it felt important. Whether Robert knew before the affair came out was also playing on her mind.

"I thought you were probably interested in women, yes.

As young as thirteen or fourteen when you were following around that girl from the football team, I had an inkling, but whether that made you gay, bisexual, or whatever, it didn't really matter. Why?"

"Did you never want to ask?" Adie was trying to keep an even tone, but there was a brewing anger that all of this could've been avoided. Directed at whom, or what, she wasn't sure.

"Not really. I guessed you'd meet someone eventually and want to introduce us, but you've always been so focussed on work and saving for the house or going out partying. People want to settle down at different times, I was quite happy you weren't rushing into anything. Lord knows, I wish I hadn't made that mistake..." She was rambling a little, seemingly lost in thought as she stared off down the garden, but then shook her head and shrugged. "Anyway, when I was chatting to Morgan at work, I got the impression from the way she spoke about you that perhaps she was a girlfriend or at least wanted to be. If she'd gushed any more, I'd have needed to call for a mop and bucket." Liz shot Morgan a quick smile and pushed the cakes across the table. She'd gone bright red and was hiding behind a palm, so perhaps she'd regret coming after all.

"But there was nothing going on with us then."

"Really?" Morgan rubbed her free hand on Adie's leg, peering out from behind the other. She didn't sound at all certain but pressed on anyway. "Because I thought we were attracted to each other from the start. If I hadn't recently split from Lou and you weren't so... tentative... I don't think we'd have been swapping numbers just so you could get a new kitchen."

Adie went to protest but knew she couldn't. Jenny had spotted it in an instant, and even Josh had called her out, despite being hopeless at working out when women were interested. "Yeah, I'll give you that one." She turned her attention back to Liz, who was now regarding them with a warm smile. "In any case, we weren't together, and I had no idea you knew about this."

She shrugged. "So, is that why you were so reluctant to tell me about this on Wednesday, and why you were fretting?"

"Yes, sort of." Adie's face scrunched and she shuffled again. "Look, I need to explain something, but it might not be very easy to hear." Morgan's hand slid into her own and she squeezed it for reassurance. "We've never openly talked about my sexuality for a reason. At first it was because everything you said was right and I didn't think it was a big deal, but four and a half years ago that changed. It became a very big deal for me, more so than I think I'd acknowledged until now, and that's why Morgan said it'd been years rather than weeks."

It was Liz's turn to look wholly uncomfortable and she leant forward, drumming the pads of her fingers on the table. "Well, we both know what happened four and a half years ago."

"Yes, but I don't think you know all of it. I never told you this either, but I was the one who found out Dad was having an affair and forced him to confess." Adie broke for a moment of silence to see how that had landed, but Liz hadn't moved. Her face was still set in the same expression and she continued to tap her fingers on the table. There was a rising swell of nerves which made Adie's heart beat faster, but she couldn't stop now. "I told him to come clean because I wouldn't lie to you." It was ironic, given what ensued. "He refused at first and tried to cover it up, but he's a terrible liar."

Liz stilled her fingers and lay her palm flat, giving a slight shrug. "That must have been a shock, but I don't see how it's related."

"Because it wasn't as big as the one that I got next. I was with my girlfriend when I spotted and confronted them, and he started raging at me about how I was a fine one to talk secrets when I was going around with some girl behind everyone's back." They'd just left the pub and spotted Robert coming out of Sarah's flat above the sandwich shop. Given it was gone eleven, it was suspicious, but then he'd stupidly stopped to kiss her at the door. At that point it went from a bit dodgy to undeniable, and she'd had the courage to march straight over there with the aid of the three pints already in her system. It got nasty, on both sides, but she didn't want Liz or Morgan to get a verbatim retelling. "At first, I thought he was just angry and lashing out where I'd caught him, but we spoke again a few days later and his opinion hadn't changed. He said as a parent his job wasn't to tell me what I wanted to hear but to stop me making mistakes that'd ruin my life."

Apparently, being gay was one of them, but he'd never been able to qualify that with a reason. Not any good one. It was either that she'd be lonely, or have a harder time, or some other bullshit. The sad irony was that it was him who'd contributed to her being lonely and miserable.

Liz was silent for a few moments, but when she finally spoke her voice was quieter and cracking at the edges. "I'm so sorry that happened, love. So very sorry."

"You don't need to be sorry, Mum. Honestly."

"I do, if the things he said are still affecting you now. I had absolutely no idea, I promise you. When he told me about the affair he made out as if his conscience had got the better of him; you never came into it. If I'd known, I'd never have let this go on." She became more flustered as she continued, her eyes welling with tears which were flicked away. "Everything was so stressful, I didn't have the slightest notion even that there was something wrong between the two of you, besides knowing you were very angry with him for what happened with Sarah, and—"

"I know you didn't," Adie soothed. She rubbed the back of her mum's hand, still laid flat on the table, flooded with relief that she wasn't angry. It was an odd sort of reaction when Liz was clearly so distressed, but then she'd worried for so long about holding back the truth. "I'm sorry too, because Dad asked me not to tell you I was gay. He said on top of everything else it'd be too much, push you over the edge, and I shouldn't have believed him because I knew deep down that you'd never have a problem with it."

Liz's eyes widened and she withdrew her hand. "He told you to do what?" That had apparently been the thing to tip her over the edge, from upset to angry. "How dare he?" She banged her fist on the table, then seemed to regret whacking a lump of solid iron and rubbed it along the front of her jeans. "Good grief, is there anything else you haven't told me?"

There was plenty, but none of it relevant. "No, don't think so."

"Well, I suppose I got my answer." She let out a loud huff which scared a bird out of the shrubs. "No wonder you didn't want to share anything with me on Wednesday night." Her lip twitched and her features softened. "And presumably when Morgan described you as tentative, this was the reason?" It seemed more of a rhetorical question, and she slumped back in the chair with a sigh. "Understandable." It was like she'd begun processing out loud, but then her expression changed, and she caught Adie's eye. "May I ask what happened with your girlfriend? The one you were with at the time?"

"I also wanted to ask..." Morgan raised the hand she was holding to press it against her lips. "Always presumed nothing good but you never talk about it."

She never talked about it with anyone because it was too damn frustrating going over all the mistakes she made. Not all of them she could blame on Robert and his tirade, because it could've been handled better. She'd been immature and shut down, not talking about it even when asked, until eventually the relationship withered and died.

"No, nothing good. I didn't behave well, I know that, and I didn't leave her much choice but to end it. I told myself she was better off without the hassle and it'd worked out best for everyone." Adie shrugged and picked crumbs from her Victoria sponge. "Then I guess I stayed in the same place. Josh had just started on T when this happened, so I focussed on him to take my mind off it. Then Mum, you needed a lot of support, and I wanted to buy the house, so I got stuck into that." It was amazing how much time could pass when you stuck your head down.

"But then you got the house, the goal was met, and it didn't fill the void..." Liz smiled, finally resuming her scone. "Makes a bit more sense of why you left it such a state for so long." She leant back and luxuriated in the taste of the cream, dabbing a smear of it from her lip. "It sounds like you were ready for a change, though. That's why you let Morgan in."

"Oh no, am I getting a full analysis?"

"Something like that." She laughed and nudged Adie with her foot. "It's good, love. Time for a fresh start, and I think you know that. How have you left things with your father?"

That was a good question. At one point he'd said he accepted it, but she'd never tested that theory and didn't really know what it meant. How could you accept something you still abhorred? "Honestly? It's shit. I avoid him, he gets upset that I don't want to spend time with him, I feel guilty, but we never talk about the root cause of it. I have absolutely no idea where he is with any of this."

"Then is it also time to find out?"

That was not a welcome prospect, and Adie crumpled back into her seat like a drinks carton that'd just had the life sucked out of it. "Probably. He's about to get married, though, and last time we spoke he was stressed about Gran..." These were all excuses and she knew it but needed a few straws to clutch at. "Perhaps if they could sort themselves out—"

"No. He'll always have a difficult relationship with Monica. Don't go prying, believe me, because it's a whole other can of worms." Liz pointed her finger, in about as stern a mode as she ever reached. "Promise me, Adrienne. Resolve your own issues and leave that well enough alone."

She relented and took a bite of her cake before it completely disintegrated where she was still picking at it. If the 'Adrienne' card was being played again, Liz meant business. "Fine. He has been asking to come see the house for weeks, so I guess I could invite him over. No idea what I'll actually say."

"Want me there with you?" Morgan and Liz both asked at the same time and then laughed.

"No, Mum, and I really don't want you there if he kicks off." She gripped Morgan's hand. Every word to Jenny earlier had been true.

"I'm not made of porcelain. What did I say to you yesterday?" Morgan squeezed Adie's chin and tilted it up so she couldn't just stare at cake crumbs. "Trust me to support you. I'm not going anywhere."

"That's not the point. I do believe you won't leave me over this, but it doesn't mean I don't want to protect you."

Morgan flexed her bicep. "Who's protecting whom, exactly?" She laughed again and stroked away a wisp of stray hair that lay across Adie's face. "I don't mean this to sound flippant, but your dad can't hurt me the way he can you. I have no emotional investment whatsoever, besides caring whether you're upset."

It still felt counterintuitive, but maybe that was the point. This was about doing things differently, even if they were uncomfortable, and Adie nodded. "Okay, then I'd like that. Perhaps I'll invite him over next weekend. We'll just be ourselves and see what happens."

23

Six days later Adie was clinging onto that sentiment. She'd pleased her dad by inviting him for a tour of the house on Friday night, but as she got in from work and stuck some beers in the fridge, she was beginning to waver on the idea. Sarah was away for the weekend on a hen trip to some big old cottage in Cornwall, and for once Adie wished her future stepmother could have been in attendance, because she'd at least have provided a buffer. Even Monica might have done that, but she'd succumbed to a last-minute deal on trains to Paris and decided to treat herself. It was funny how that had happened when she was asked about the real story with Roy.

Morgan had arrived with a small case, planning to stay for the weekend, and hopped in the shower to wash away a day's worth of work dust and sweat. All the while Adie tidied and cleaned, as if the house looking perfect would somehow help with everything else. It wouldn't and she knew that. Robert had no interest whatsoever in viewing the renovations, only in winning the invitation.

"Are you all set?" When Morgan came down in a fresh pair of jeans and a soft grey long sleeve top, she pulled a beer from the fridge and twisted off the cap, making herself right at home.

"I thought you said alcohol was a poor way to cope?"

"It is. I don't endorse this at all." She set the bottle on the work surface and tugged the bottom of Adie's T-shirt to draw her nearer. "What I do fully support is getting through this as painlessly as possible, and then I have a surprise upstairs."

"Do you indeed?"

"Mhm." Two fingers walked up Adie's stomach and then rubbed across her lip.

Adie pressed forward, sinking into a kiss. They hadn't seen each other in days, and this was starting to look like terrible planning when there was an empty house and far more pleasurable ways to spend the evening. "Maybe I should just call and cancel."

Morgan hooked her hands around Adie's neck, both thumbs running along her jawline. "Your decision."

"Really?" That wasn't the reaction she'd expected. "Because I love it when you do that. You always touch my face when we kiss."

"I remember something else you said you like, too."

Adie went in for another kiss to hide the embarrassment scorching across her cheeks, but then she was becoming far too aroused for the occasion and pulled away. "We can resume this later. Stop distracting me."

Morgan saluted and took a swig of the beer she'd just opened. "Shall we watch TV until he comes? Nothing cools you off quite like the six o'clock news."

They bundled onto the sofa and sprawled out, but

Morgan's warm torso laid on top of her own did nothing to cool Adie's desire. Cancelling was still tempting twenty minutes later when her phone began to ring and she shuffled to pull it from her pocket, muting the television with the remote.

"Hello, sweetheart." It was Robert, and there was a whooshing noise in the background. "Sorry to do this, but we need to reschedule. Sarah's broken down on the motorway and I'm out here now trying to get it sorted."

"Doesn't she have breakdown cover?"

"Yes of course, but I couldn't leave her on the side of the road alone." There were voices in the background and she clearly wasn't alone. Three or four other hens would've been in the car, but then Robert could never resist jumping in to rescue her.

"No, I don't suppose you could."

"I've got golf now for the rest of the weekend, how about next Saturday?"

He'd suddenly become very loud and Adie pulled the phone away from her ear. "I can't on Saturday, I've got plans with Josh." And she wasn't cancelling them. Despite not having technically agreed, they came way higher up the priority list than he did right now. "It'll have to be Sunday. Can you do that?"

"Sunday it is."

The line went dead, and Morgan flinched as the phone hit the floor with a thud. "Sorry. Are you okay?"

"Yeah." Just fuming. This always happened, and then he wondered why she never bothered making plans with him. It wasn't all about what had happened on that street four years ago, it was the repeated double standard of being sulked at when they didn't spend time together and then either insisting Sarah was there when they did, cancelling casually at the last minute, or making it an uncomfortable hell. "You know, before my dad got together with Sarah, we actually used to get on well. Played a bit of football together, hung out, had a laugh. Then it was like something flipped about six months before it all came out, and he wasn't interested anymore."

"That must have hurt."

It did. It was always easier to focus on the rest, but things had been screwy for a while. "I know I'm an adult and I shouldn't care, but—"

"Hold up, what's being an adult got to do with anything? It doesn't matter what age you are, that's tough. If you want it back and for you guys to have a better relationship, you should talk to him. If he doesn't know it bugs you, he can't do anything to fix it."

"I guess." Adie wriggled to get comfy and stroked her fingers along Morgan's back. "But at least we get to spend the evening alone. Are you hungry? Shall I treat us to a takeaway?"

"Yes, although this conversation is not over." Because nothing ever got past her.

Morgan rolled off the sofa and wandered back through to the kitchen with Adie trailing behind and reached into a drawer to pull out a wedge of takeaway menus. You could get them all online, but it always seemed a waste to throw so much into recycling, so now there were leaflets from every restaurant in a ten-mile radius. They'd discussed this when the refit was happening and decided the stash should stay.

She began setting out piles of different food types on the kitchen table. Then she came across one that didn't fit and held it up. "Football sessions?" She turned over the flyer and read the back. "Are you thinking of going?"

Adie shrugged. She'd gone to meet Josh from the gym during the week and seen a stack of them on the front desk. Perhaps Morgan was right, and it wouldn't hurt to pick up an old hobby. "Yeah, maybe. It bugged me that I couldn't remember why I stopped playing because I used to enjoy it. I'm sure I could use a hobby where I can socialise without having to get pie-eyed."

"You have met footballers, right? I've seen what they get up to on the weekend." Morgan laughed and stuck it under a magnet on the fridge. "Good for you, though, I think you'd be great."

"Does that mean you'll come and watch me play?"

"I'll bring you an entire cheer squad." She grasped the bottom of Adie's T-shirt again, but this time slid her hands underneath and stroked her sides. "You did look hot in that kit the other week. Would you get to wear it home?"

That'd be a fun conversation, checking out whether the kit could be used in sexual role play, and Adie laughed. "Expect so. Tell me more about this."

"I thought you wanted food?"

She did, but that could wait. The only thing currently going through Adie's mind was the promise of what lay waiting for them upstairs. They'd spent the best part of the previous weekend having frenzied sex, desperate to please each other as quickly as possible. Now, though, she wanted to take it slower and explore.

Hooking her two index fingers in the front of Morgan's jeans, she pulled her forward, and when she let go it was to flick open the button. She smoothed her hands over each hip to pull the jeans down slightly, their stomachs brushing together as Morgan continued to caress her sides. It lit the first spark of arousal, and Adie dipped her mouth to grip gently on Morgan's bottom lip, giving it a tug.

"I was thinking we could eat later. What do you reck-on?" Another light suck, and Morgan's lips remained parted, her eyes half closed as she nodded. Adie took her hand and led her upstairs, warm light flooding through the windows. The sheets had been put on fresh and lay plump, until Adie sat on the edge of them. She parted her legs, feet flat on the floor, and gestured Morgan forward to stand between them. Then she lifted the shirt and lay kisses across Morgan's stomach as fingertips trailed over her shoulders, up her neck, and into the wisps of loose hair. "Was that a yes?"

Peering down and holding Adie's head against her torso, Morgan had a shy smile. She stepped back, crossing both arms over her body and removing the top in one smooth motion. But then she insisted on folding it and laying it next to her case on the floor. She did the same with her jeans, and as her breasts swayed from side to side while she wrig-gled out of them, Adie was already losing patience.

"Is this a new technique you've developed to torture me?"

Morgan stopped altogether. "You bet it is. Working?" She could see it was and wore a little smirk now. "Do you want to find out what I brought with me?"

The answer to that was equally obvious, but Adie indulged her. "Yes please."

"In return for your clothes. Get them off." She crossed her arms and tapped a foot on the floor, watching as Adie made far less fuss of ripping off her jeans, T-shirt, and underwear, then hurling them at the wardrobe and returning to her place on the edge of the bed. Morgan laughed, then crouched to open her case. She produced a leather strap and flung it at Adie, who dangled it from a finger. There was a vital component missing, and she raised her eyebrows to enquire, but Morgan only bit her lip and diverted her gaze. "Okay?"

Why she looked so nervous was unclear, and she didn't seem to have taken the hint. "Yeah, but where's the rest of it? If you want me to wear this, you need to give me something to work with."

Morgan smiled, her cheeks colouring, and reached into the case again. She produced a black dildo and threw it across the bed, the impact causing Adie to flinch. "Better?"

"Much." But she wasn't ready to use it yet. As Morgan stood, she drew her forward again and ran her hands over the black silk underwear, trimmed at the top with lace. Her thumbs hooked into the waistband and she slowly lowered it, replacing the fabric with butterfly kisses which caused Morgan to let out a quiet gasp. "Your body blows my mind." She stood and swept the hair from Morgan's neck, her stomach clenching as she inhaled a waft of perfume and pressed her lips there. Then she grasped an elbow and raised a bicep to her mouth. "So sexy."

Morgan grazed her bottom lip up Adie's throat as her arm was dropped and her bra was unclasped. She was about to say something but faltered when their breasts pressed together, swallowing hard and then running her palms flat along Adie's back to keep her there. "I've been thinking about you all week."

Finally parting their bodies, Adie took a nipple into her mouth and inhaled sharply when Morgan released her bun, gripping handfuls of hair. Pulling her mouth away momentarily, she peered up with a devilish smile. "Spare no detail."

"I'd rather show you."

A step back and she was against the wall. Adie groaned when she pressed a hand between Morgan's legs and felt how wet she was. She dropped to her knees, fingers still trailing through her hair, and placed a hand under Morgan's knee to lift it over her shoulder. The teasing kisses up the inside of her thigh didn't last long before she wrapped her palm over Morgan's quad, the other parting her lips. Adie's heart pounded as she flicked her tongue over Morgan's clit and felt her tilt her pelvis forward. She went deeper this time, compelled to be less tentative by the hands guiding her head and the murmurs of pleasure, but it came to an abrupt stop when Morgan unhooked her leg from over Adie's shoulder.

"What's happening?" She squinted up in confusion, rasping and breathless. Morgan's response was to grab the dildo from the bed. She slotted it through the metal ring on the front and handed it to Adie, who stepped in and tightened the fastenings, then lay back on the bed with her hands clasped behind her head. Morgan stared throughout, the flush on her face now extending down her chest. Adie felt a certain sense of smug satisfaction, enjoying what the sight of her body sprawled on the bed had done to Morgan. "So, where do you want me now? Because I haven't had any details yet."

She tapped her fingertips lightly over her lips and then climbed onto the bed, relaxing on her side for a few moments before rolling onto her back. "You need to be on top of me."

"You're the boss." Adie sat up, taking her time as she manoeuvred herself between Morgan's legs and knelt. Again, she waited a few moments, noting the quickening rise and fall of her chest, and the glistening arousal at the top of her thighs. She ran a finger through it and Morgan moaned, then she repositioned herself to insert only the tip. "Have you got some lube?" It was a cruel game, but she couldn't resist. She withdrew and sat back on her heels. "We might need it."

"We don't."

Adie went to move, but then stopped again. "A bit more foreplay, then?" She leant forward onto all fours and dipped her tongue to flick across a nipple, but Morgan pushed her shoulders.

"No foreplay, I want you to fuck me. Now."

Adie looked up with another teasing smile. "Okay, you only had to ask."

She thrust as deep as she could this time and Morgan wound both legs tight around her back to hold her in position. The low guttural sound Morgan emitted sent out a thrill of excitement and Adie moaned with her, withdrawing so only the head remained and then thrusting again in a smooth, slow rhythm. A hand massaged Adie's breasts in turn, the other squeezing her buttock as it clenched, and the heat between her own legs rose with every touch.

She lost herself to the motion until sweat began to pool in the base of her back, and her hips ached under the strain. "Are we sticking to the fantasy?" It was a long time since she'd considered how they'd ended up like this, and she thought she'd better check. "Is this how you imagined it?"

Morgan reached both hands around her ass. "Uhuh." She gulped and then groaned and threw her head back as the pace picked up for a second. "But we need to move."

Adie withdrew, the dildo glistening in the light, and rested back on her heels while she waited. She smiled when Morgan positioned herself on all fours, taking a rough grasp of her hips to draw her back. Then she reached forward to massage both breasts. "Never be nervous to ask, I told you it's sexy when you let me know what you want."

Morgan tried to back into the dildo, but Adie only ran a

finger around her clit. "Don't tease," she pleaded. "I can't take it."

Adie grasped around the tops of her thighs to pull her legs a little wider and entered her again, watching the bounce of her breasts with each snap of their hips and imagining them swollen against her tongue again. Morgan groaned every time, the pitch ever higher, and when Adie pulled her cheeks apart to vary the angle it came closer to a scream.

"Tell me when you're close, I want to know," Adie commanded.

"Now, I'm close now," came the panted reply. "Don't stop."

She had no intention of stopping but needed some stability. She managed to keep balance enough on the firm mattress to maintain a slow thrust, entering Morgan as deep as possible while reaching around with one hand to rub against her clit. The other grasped her hip to pull them together, and she could see Morgan's legs shake. She cried out, and it turned to near convulsions as she rode the orgasm, Adie pressing into her and holding tight until it subsided. She took care as she withdrew, fumbling to undo the straps while Morgan lay flat with her face buried in the duvet.

When Adie was free, she laid on her back alongside. "I can't tell you enough times how sexy you are, and I'm starting to get the impression you like me taking you from behind."

Morgan laughed, her hand trembling as she stroked the hair from Adie's face. She propped herself on an elbow and circled a nipple with her index finger. Then she sunk into a kiss as she felt the ridge of each rib, continuing her journey until her middle finger slid down the side of Adie's clit. Adie bucked her hips and reached for handfuls of hair, rolling into the firm touch, but then she shuffled back.

Morgan stopped dead. "What's wrong?"

Adie glanced at the strap beside her. "Do you have anything a little smaller?"

"Oh." She raised her eyebrows and smiled suggestively. "How rude of me."

"Is that okay?"

"More than." Adie laughed as Morgan got up and reached into her case, pulling out a bag that looked like it contained a lot more than they had time to get into right now. "Is it the plumber in you that insists on travelling with a toolkit?"

"Quite possibly. Pick a size." She held up two dildos and Adie pointed to the slightly larger one in her right hand. "When I asked you to pick bathroom fittings, you were a lot happier to let me decide. Seems I've found what's important to you." Stepping into the harness and tightening it, she reached into the bag again and pulled out a tube of lube. "And I am not complaining."

Adie was done talking for now. She tugged on the strap, pulling Morgan closer, and kissed her instead. Her hands moved lower, gripping Morgan's strong quads, but she was well beyond any desire to draw this out. There was only one thing she needed, and she intended to get it. She waited as Morgan dabbed a little lube on the dildo and threw the tube on the floor, then knelt between Adie's legs and nudged them apart slightly with her knees.

Morgan got the idea about what she wanted as she slid in fully, pressing all of her weight down and pinning Adie to the bed. Then she slowly backed up and did the same thing again, a devilish glint in her eye as Adie cried out this time.

"More, I want you deeper."

She repositioned herself, drawing Adie's legs wider, tilting her hips and driving down. "Like that?"

"Just like that."

The motion was smooth and controlled, her ab muscles contracting as she moved in and out. Morgan held herself up on one arm and glanced the other over Adie's nipple, returning to roll it between her fingertips as she thrust harder, beginning to pick up the pace. "I get the impression this isn't going to last very long."

"It isn't, I was close before you started. Just keep going."

Adie gripped the sheets, twisting as her orgasm built. She let herself go, giving her body permission to call the shots. Every one of her pleasure receptors was screaming thank you and she was happy to vocalise.

"What are you going to do if I stop?" Morgan pressed hard inside and remained there, and Adie contracted against the shaft. Each time it sent out a pang of pleasure. She desperately tried to rock into it, but Morgan wouldn't let her.

"Don't make me beg."

"I'm just slowing you down a little." She clenched her buttocks, creating the slightest movement, and then released again. Repeating the action, she slowly built up, pulling out further and then thrusting a little more each time until Adie was being pounded so hard that she couldn't hold on any longer, the orgasm ripping through her and her whole body vibrating with pleasure. She wasn't sure when it stopped, or if it had stopped, the aftershocks still rolling even after Morgan had withdrawn and climbed out of the harness. She was soon back, draping herself over Adie's torso and kissing her chest. "That was fun."

"Fun?" Adie snorted with laughter. "The fair was fun, that was... hot." She ran her hands over the rough goose bumps which had risen on Morgan's bum, following them down the backs of her legs. "Now, are you going to show me what else is in that bag?"

Morgan raised her eyebrows. "You haven't had enough for one evening?"

"Hell no, we were only getting started."

24

The following week she was gearing up for round two with Robert but first, Josh had booked them into an Italian with plush red leather booths and big candles in the middle of the table, dripping wax onto the menus. It was romantic, she had to give him that, except the others were all late and it was difficult to get in the mood alone.

Josh had gone to meet Emma from her train, Morgan was behind after spending the day being pampered as part of a birthday gift which she'd booked for Jenny months ago, and Adie was staring into a glass of red. Everyone who walked past shot her a sympathetic look as if she'd been stood up, and it was starting to get old now. How was it that she had no say in this and yet was the only one to actually arrive on time?

"Sorry, sorry, sorry," Morgan pleaded.

Adie turned sharply at the voice coming from behind. "Bloody hell," she muttered. If this was the reward for Morgan being late, it was a small sacrifice. "You look gorgeous. Stunning. There are no words, and yet I continue to find them."

Auburn hair was flicked from the lapels of a black leather jacket. "Not too much of a change?"

"No. Good change, but why?"

The blonde tips were gone and her hair was poker straight, feathered around her face and layered down her back. The red dye had been stripped, too, leaving what must be her natural colour. "It was a lot of upkeep and I'm not going to have great facilities for home dying in a few weeks, so it was partly practical." Morgan removed her coat, chucking it on top of Adie's, and revealed a figure-hugging black dress. "Scoot over and give me a kiss."

Adie shuffled across the bench and stroked the side of Morgan's head. "It's so soft." Then she leant forward for a kiss and let out a low growl. "My god, you smell incredible too. This is torture, can we just go home?"

"No, we can't, and you're developing a one-track mind."

"Your fault." A woman from the football team Adie had tried out with on Thursday evening nodded from the other side of the room, and after a quick wave she continued. "If you're going to show off the holy trinity of tattoo, cleavage and arms, I don't know what you expect."

"Who was that?" Morgan was staring and being less than subtle about it.

"Oh, just someone I met the other night. You know, when I was out trawling for other women."

"Mm, if you weren't still looking at me like that, I might believe you. I take it she's from football. How did it go?" As Adie shrugged and picked up a menu, Morgan grasped her wrist and turned it. "And how in the world did you do that?"

She had a massive purple bruise extending from her elbow to her watch and shrugged it off. "It's possible I got a little competitive."

"A little? What did you do, clothesline someone?"

That wasn't far off, but she wouldn't admit to it. "In any case, they've asked me to play in a friendly next Sunday. I was actually thinking I might invite my dad to watch." Given it was something they used to bond over, perhaps it was an opportunity to reconnect properly. "What do you reckon?"

"So long as he shows this time. Otherwise I may pull out a few wrestling moves of my own." Morgan flexed her bicep and laughed as Adie's eyes widened. When kisses were peppered all over the top of her arm, she briefly protested but then submitted, until Josh cleared his throat and interrupted them.

"I bring you to a nice restaurant and you make it look like a cheap brothel."

He tutted and then laughed, releasing Emma's hand and letting her slip into the booth first. She looked gorgeous, in a pair of smart jeans and heels. Josh hadn't scrubbed up too badly either and Adie resisted the urge to ask whether he'd ironed his own shirt. "Wow, you guys look nice. Check us out being all grown-up on a Saturday night. Is this what adulthood feels like?"

"No, I think adulthood was spending the afternoon in Ikea picking out bed linen and crockery for my new place. Who knew there were so many options?"

"Lesbians everywhere."

Everyone laughed and seemed to relax, even Emma, who made Josh look like a social butterfly. "Have you told them about your queer coding thing yet?" She put her hand over Josh's and gave it a squeeze, then turned to Morgan. "He's been going on about your dad all day, I think he's got a new idol."

Morgan crossed her legs and leant forward. "No, what's this?"

"Joshy went to pick up the keys this morning so we could

start dropping off a few bits and they got chatting. By the time we finally got out of there I think they'd planned the entire project—a scheme to teach at risk LGBTQ kids to code."

Adie was still trying to hold back a laugh that Emma had called him Joshy, two fingers pressed over her lips and tears collecting at the corner of her eye. She cleared her throat and straightened her face. "You met him?" Even she hadn't met Morgan's dad yet. It'd been easier to stay at her own house while they were cleaning out the annex. "What's he like?"

"So clever," Josh enthused. "He told me all about how he started his company and when I told him my idea, he knew exactly what I needed to do. He's even talking about helping and funding it."

"Bloody hell, that's amazing. What is it exactly that he does?" She knew he had his own business and travelled a lot, but they'd never gone into specifics.

"He founded an internet security company, but he sold it last year and now he does talks and consultancy work." Josh had rattled this off before Morgan could get a word in edgeways, and she sunk back chuckling to herself.

"Yeah, Dad's always busy with something," she mused, replacing her drinks menu with a food one. "I don't understand most of it. My sister used to work with him, so I usually just let them geek out and chat to Tim about plumbing. We're very different people."

Adie frowned and rubbed a circle in the small of Morgan's back. "You get on, don't you?"

"Yeah, of course. We camp and hike and all sorts together, I just don't get very involved in his work stuff. It's great that he can help you." She smiled at Josh, who was clearly struggling to hold back from gushing again. "He doesn't usually give that much away, so you've obviously impressed him."

Josh's face was bright red now and Emma squeezed his chin. When she leant in for a kiss it was almost a beacon you could see from space, but then he relaxed and wrapped an arm across her shoulder. "He's looking forward to meeting you." A kick under the table, and Adie flinched. "But don't worry, if it goes badly you can always rely on me to sort it, since we get on so well."

"Terrific," she muttered, booting him back. "But I think I'll be okay. If he didn't object to Lou even though Jenny hates her, I'm quietly confident." Despite never having met Lou either, she'd been consigned to a short list of people Adie was happy to write off entirely now. She had been well and truly thrown under the metaphorical bus.

"Sorry to burst your bubble, but Dad never met her." Morgan sucked her teeth and then closed the menu, pushing it to one side.

"Never? How long were you together?"

"Nearly a year."

Adie's mouth hung open and Morgan had to nudge it shut. "But why? I was assuming you were delivering him an upgraded model." She wasn't quite sure when she'd gained the confidence to see herself as a Ferrari either, but it had been helping calm her nerves over meeting Morgan's dad. She knew how important it was that everyone got on. "What if he hates me?"

Morgan laughed. "He won't hate you, don't be ridiculous. And as for Lou, she only got to meet Mum a few times, I never let her get to know anyone else." She shot Josh and Emma a sideways glance and a little colour rose on her face. Leaning forward to whisper against Adie's ear, she'd turned bashful again. "And I never said I loved her." She pulled away wearing a wide grin, and stroked Adie's burning cheek. "Why are you so wound up about this?"

"Daddy issues," Josh interjected. It won him daggered looks from everyone else, and he shrugged. "What? She does have issues with her dad, of course she's worried about this. It makes perfect sense. Not everyone is Robert, though."

"What are you, a psychologist now?" Although Adie was far more interested in what Morgan had just said to her, and the fact she'd shuffled over, stroking higher up her leg.

"No, but I do meet kids in very similar positions. I know you're a very big kid with a job and a mortgage, but there isn't much difference. Perhaps I should take you in some time as the poster child for moving on from such adversity."

Moving on? That was a joke. Before he arrived, she'd been sat there debating whether to invite her dad to a stupid football game. At nearly thirty years old, she was so worried he might not turn up that she was seriously considering not putting herself through it. "That is some sad poster."

"Why? You're doing alright these days." He nudged her with a foot this time rather than sticking in the boot.

"I guess. Fresh start, fresh start, fresh start," she muttered, hoping if she repeated it enough times it might come true. "Hey, what are you doing next Sunday? I'm playing in a football game." And a few more supporters wouldn't hurt. It was similarly depressing that she would be one of the oldest on the pitch.

"I could be persuaded, if you'll help move boxes first and buy me a pint after."

They got through to their dessert course still chatting about Josh's coding club idea and caught up on how the youth group was fairing in a new venue. It'd moved on Thursday, to a plush hall where the doors weren't falling off

the toilet cubicles and you didn't have to worry about frost-
bite during the winter. In many ways the sale had been a
blessing because it'd forced them into a change. Now there
were even surplus funds to subsidise trips and offer travel
money to kids on low income.

When the waiter came over with the menu again over an
hour had passed, and everyone sunk back holding their
stomachs except for Morgan. "Will you share one?" she
pleaded. "I love profiteroles, but I can't eat them all."

"You want her to share food? Good luck," Josh quipped.
He was deftly kicked for about the tenth time and rubbed
his shin.

Adie placed their order and collected the menus,
handing them back to the waiter. Then she held up her ring
finger and smiled at Morgan. "It's okay this once because
we're technically cohabiting all weekend."

"What is this, some sort of in joke?"

She explained the story of the burger and Josh smirked,
leaning to whisper something in Emma's ear which made
them both laugh. She was about to ask what was so funny
when the waiter returned with a bowl of profiteroles
smothered in chocolate sauce and set it on the table in
front of her. Morgan quickly slid it away and grabbed the
spoon, delving for an entire ball of pastry and then setting
it down again. "Um, excuse me. What happened to
sharing?"

Morgan raised a palm to cover her bulging mouth. "Sorry." She dipped in the index finger of her free hand and held
it out.

"You know we're in a nice restaurant?" Adie took hold of
Morgan's wrist and sucked off the chocolate before it
dripped into her lap.

"Don't care." She raised her eyebrows a touch, her eyes

sparkling with pleasure. Dipping in her finger again, she speared an entire profiterole and held it up. "Go on, be bad."

Adie ripped it off with her teeth, taking care not to bite Morgan's hand, but then she almost choked when she realised she was being watched. A short guy with thinning grey hair and glasses had stopped at the table and was jiggling the loose change in his trouser pocket.

"I thought it was you." He smiled, but Adie was still trying to work out who the hell he was. A client? Someone her gran had briefly dated? No, he was far too sensible looking. "I played in the football match a few weeks back."

That was all very well and good, but it didn't make them best buddies. Adie quickly chewed through her mouthful and tried to remain polite. "I remember," she lied. "Good to see you again." Another lie. All she wanted to do was resume eating chocolate off her girlfriend.

"Your dad didn't mention you were in here, you could have joined us."

"My dad?" Adie spluttered, banging her chest where a flake of choux had become lodged in her throat.

"Yes, we're out the back."

"Oh, well I'm here with friends." Which he could see from the full table. "I haven't seen him for a few weeks, we need to catch up."

"Right you are. Come and say hello, though. I'll tell him you're here." He gave a casual wave and was off, smiling to another couple at a round table near the hallway setting apart the two dining rooms.

"Do you want to get the bill and leave?" Morgan picked up her spoon again and took another mouthful of dessert. "I'm almost finished."

Adie went to say yes. It'd be easier to text and issue an invite rather than trying to converse with Robert and his old golf club buddies, but she couldn't really. He'd only be offended that she hadn't made the time to check in. Besides which, she had no reason to run from him and had already decided that this tiptoeing around had to stop. "No, we should go and speak to him. Do you mind?"

"We?"

"Yes, we. I'm not playing games. It's just a casual hello and I'll find out if he can come to the match. You up for that?"

Morgan nodded and then dabbed her mouth on a napkin. "Are you sure? Isn't this a bit like what happened before, running into him and...?" She grasped Adie's hand under the table.

"Yeah, perhaps a little. All the more reason to tackle it head on, right?" She wasn't sure who needed convincing here, but her reasoning was sound. The two glasses of wine she'd consumed with dinner certainly weren't hurting her right now because she felt surprisingly calm.

Adie left Josh to explain everything to a confused Emma and followed Morgan out of the booth, adjusting her trousers and taking a deep breath. She took hold of Morgan's hand again and led her through the archway, spotting Robert with three other guys at a table on the far wall. They were laughing over something and still halfway through their main courses, which hopefully meant this would be quick.

"Hey, Dad." Adie went for casual and gave him a little wave. "We're heading off in a second but didn't want to miss you. Is Sarah not here?"

"No. Boys night."

"Right." She placed a hand in the small of Morgan's back. "You remember Morgan, don't you?"

"Of course, hello Morgan."

The guy opposite him was still creasing up, his face taking on a purple hue which made Adie concerned for his heart. "What's so funny?"

"Oh, nothing sweetheart." Robert wafted a hand and wiped his mouth on a napkin. "Just planning my stag do, but I think I'm too old for all that nonsense." And too drunk to be out unattended. There were several empty wine bottles on the table, and they were all blasted apart from the one who'd stopped to say hello.

"I bet that'll be a riot, what are you doing?"

"Booked a space at that nice wine bar at the end of town for next weekend. Come if you like? Unless you're too embarrassed of your old man."

She was, but that wasn't the reason she was about to decline. "I'd love to," she lied, for at least the third time that evening. "But I've already made plans with Morgan. I'm playing in a football match next Sunday, though. Do you fancy coming to watch? You could come to the house afterwards, instead of doing it tomorrow."

"Did everyone hear that?" He raised his hands to the sides of his head and laughed. "Quick, before she changes her mind, someone get it in writing."

"Yeah, very funny, but you were the one who cancelled last week."

"Sorry, I was only teasing. Text me the details. We'll try and make it along, but I'll definitely swing by for my tour."

"We," Adie muttered, and Morgan squeezed her hand. "Anyway, *we'll* leave you to it," she concluded through partially gritted teeth.

"Okay sweetheart, I'll let you get back to your friends. Who else are you here with?"

Adie was half turned to leave but swung back. "Josh and his girlfriend, Emma." She took another deep breath, a mixture of wine, mild irritation and a new something-or-other in the back of her mind telling her not to give a flying fuck deciding to push the boundaries a little. "We're on a double date. It's pretty romantic in here, you lot should bring your wives."

The guy from earlier glanced up with a warm smile before anyone else could speak. "My wife would like that, thank you for the suggestion. I'll tell her it came from you; she was very impressed with your performance the other week. My granddaughter's driving everyone up the wall begging to join a team."

"Who knew we were so influential?"

He shrugged. "Well you are. A real power couple."

Adie held back on the urge to give his shiny bald patch a big wet kiss and waved them goodbye. When they'd made it back through the archway, she slumped against the cool wall and let out the breath she'd been holding in. She hadn't realised before, but she was sweaty and shaking, her feet slipping in her socks where they were so damp.

"You okay?" Morgan whispered. She cupped Adie's cheek and dabbed a kiss on her lips.

"Was that a really shitty thing to do?" It wasn't exactly the open and honest conversation she'd planned to have. "He did already know we were spending time together, and he will have suspected. Perhaps it's good that I've confirmed it without us both having to sit through an awkward conversation..." She trailed off, trying to justify it to herself more than Morgan.

"He didn't seem too traumatised, I wouldn't panic."

Adie spotted Josh and Emma getting out of the booth and pushed off the exposed brick. "In that case, I'm quitting while I'm ahead."

25

True to her word she'd hauled boxes for Josh the following Sunday, but given he was moving from a tiny bedroom it hadn't amounted to much. Then it was time for him to provide far more support and stand on the side of a football pitch for ninety minutes, some of which she might spend playing. It was hard to know what to expect when she'd only taken part in two training sessions, and the realisation dawned that they might not use her at all. Given the cheer squad, she'd look like a right wally if that were the case.

As the team filtered into the changing rooms, she counted players. Twelve, which meant they were probably desperate but also that she should get on the pitch at some point, even if she didn't start. It was a relief. But then it wasn't, and she continued to swing from one the other for the entirety of the warm-up.

Morgan and Josh waved from the other side of the pitch, which was thoroughly embarrassing, and when one of the other players asked how many people were coming to watch, she had to answer honestly that she didn't know. Right now, inviting anyone was looking like a massive error of judgement, because she was struggling to feel her extremities, and it didn't help when the manager announced she was their new centre back.

"Fuck," she mumbled as she traipsed across the pitch and Morgan blew her a kiss. Then she spotted her dad getting out of his car and felt her insides clench. The only saving grace was that the opposition had less ball skills than a set of Subbuteo players, which made her look very competent indeed, and at half time they were seven goals up. Robert had stood himself by the bar and had a pint in hand, chatting to some of the other spectators and probably using it as a networking opportunity, but surprisingly there was no Sarah in tow.

Just as they'd switched ends, Adie feeling confident this would be another easy half, her insides clenched again and this time she felt the rush of bile. Her mum and gran had just pulled up, and she waved frantically to Morgan, pointing wildly and signalling as if she were slicing through her own throat. The whistle was blown before she got to see what happened next and she had to concentrate but prayed Morgan had got the right message. If not, then maybe Josh.

It was a good three years since her parents had seen each other, and this slightly dodgy idea had just become a catastrophic one. She'd only mentioned it to Liz on Tuesday and hadn't expected her to take that as an invitation. The rest of the match passed in a blur, but she was relieved to see Morgan was chatting with her on the side of the pitch.

When the final whistle blew Adie made a quick show of shaking hands and ran over, propping her arms on the metal barrier. "Mum, what are you doing here?"

"Oh, that's nice." Liz brushed a clump of mud from Adie's shoulder and frowned. She was only one step away from pulling out a hanky and spitting on it to wipe her face.

"It's just, Dad's here. I wasn't sure he'd come, but he's up by the bar."

"So?"

So? You didn't avoid someone for that length of time and then say, "so?" and Adie struggled to wipe the confused frown from her face. "Do you want to leave? We're probably heading in for a drink, but…"

"A drink sounds nice, doesn't it, Monica?"

"Oh yes. Gin and tonic. Lovely."

They linked arms and ambled up the path, and Adie watched them go, sure she'd once again entered a parallel universe. "What just happened? Can someone check I'm still alive?"

Morgan grabbed the neck of Adie's shirt and pulled her forward, planting a kiss on her lips which made her heart bang with a triumphant confirmation that yes, she was still living. Behind her there was a whooping noise, and she turned to find the entire team were staring at them. Another new experience.

"You smell like sweat and mud." Morgan still had hold of Adie's shirt, keeping her close. "We should hurry up so I can get you out of it, and into a nice warm bath."

Adie ducked under the barrier and held Morgan's hand as they wandered up to the clubhouse. She could already see her parents deftly ignoring each other as Monica and Liz reached the big blue double doors into the bar, so not all that much had changed. "Hate to disappoint you, but I have to leave the kit here."

"What? Surely not, let me speak to the manager." Morgan tugged on Adie's wrist but then relented and laughed. "Maybe we'll find you a clean one to wear." Josh had sped up, no doubt disgusted by the tone of the conversation, and Morgan stopped to let him go. "Are you okay? I chatted with Liz and I think it's fine. Something along the lines of moving on for your sake."

"Oh good, are mummy and daddy making it work for the kids?" Adie grunted out a laugh, but then sighed and started towards the top of the field again. "Suppose I can only leave them to it."

When they reached the changing rooms, Morgan caught up with Josh and took him inside while Adie grabbed her stuff and put on some warmer clothes. The temperature had dropped rapidly as they ploughed through September and gone were the days of running around in Jenny's back garden with a water pistol.

As she emerged in the crowded bar, there was a definite divide, and her dad sat alone at a dark wooden table nursing another drink while the others laughed and joked by the pool table. This was where it got tricky. So much for never having to think about which parent to spend Christmas with.

"What did you think?" She pulled out a chair next to Robert and dumped her bag.

"Very good. Couldn't tell you don't play regularly."

He smiled, which was encouraging, and she sat down. "We'll head to the house soon if you want?"

"Is Liz coming?"

"I wouldn't have thought so. She just sort of turned up, I didn't realise she'd be here. Why, is it a problem?"

A little shake of the head, but nothing concrete. Robert turned his pint glass on the mat, then took a sip. "When your mother chooses your ex-wife over you, something has gone wrong." It was a brief laugh this time, but not a convincing one. "Watch out for that, they're very friendly."

He was peering over as Morgan and Liz laughed about something, and Adie craned her neck to watch. "Oh. Yeah."

She shuffled and turned back to face him. "We had a good chat the other week, talked through some stuff. Mum's been really supportive." Picking up a stray mat and tapping it against the table, she tried to decide whether to broach this now. It couldn't hurt to have some witnesses if it went badly. "I've been thinking about what you said the other week, when you told me about the engagement, and you're right. We need to move on, get a fresh start. Now you're getting married, and Mum's happier, and I have... someone."

"What sort of fresh start?"

She hadn't expected that question and let out an odd low-pitched whine as she searched for the right response. "I don't know, one where we get on. One where we have fun again and don't resent each other all the time." When he didn't reply, she pressed on, finding a bit more rope to potentially hang herself on. "I've been pretty miserable, to be honest. You hurt me, a lot, and I know you're hurt when I don't want to spend time with you. I don't want that anymore." She shuffled, desperate for him to jump in and say something. Anything would do at this point. "So...?"

"I still want that too, but your mother won't forgive me. We're not going to become best friends, you know. I've already admitted I handled things badly and I can't do anything to change that." He held up his hands defensively, but he seemed to have missed the point.

"No, I know. But it would be helpful to me if you could at least be in the same space occasionally, and that's not really what I was getting at. It's not that which has made me miserable, Dad. You said some pretty awful things to me, too, or have you just forgotten that happened?"

It was his turn to squirm, folding his arms and scraping back the chair. "No, I know what I said." He cleared his throat and glanced around the bar. "And I also told you I wouldn't say any more about it, so let's not."

"That's not strictly true, you said you'd accepted it."

"Same difference."

"No, it's not actually." One entirely avoided the topic, the other implied some sort of effort might be made.

"I'm never going to be happy about it, Adie. I'm sorry, but I can't change that either. Of course I'd like you to settle down and get married, most parents wish that for their kids. A nice stable home life, someone who'll look after you and who makes you happy."

"Great, because I have someone who I honestly think I might want to marry someday, and she makes me very happy." That was massively jumping the gun, but for the sake of making a case she was prepared to go there.

"Good, just—" He shrugged again, hugging his arms tight.

"Just what?"

"I'm sorry, but I can't sit here and lie that I'm comfortable with it. I'm sure Morgan is very nice, and I have a lot of respect for her parents, it's just never going to be what I want for you."

And there it was, neatly wrapped up. Adie nodded, finding that through all this she'd felt an overwhelming sense of calm, like she'd been immersed in a relaxation capsule for four hours. It struck her as odd, but perhaps it was just that the removal of uncertainty had that effect. She stood and drummed a finger on the table. "That's a real shame, because there's a lot I didn't want for any of us, but I was willing to try and work through this. I'm not sure that's possible, though, if you still can't really accept who I am and want to be with."

"Oh, come on, Adie. I think you're being a bit melodramatic. Bring Morgan to the wedding if you want. Is that enough proof that I'm willing to compromise?"

"No. I'm not going to compromise myself anymore and I won't ask you to do that either." She hadn't imagined getting to this point, but now it seemed the only option to preserve her own sanity. "I think it's easier for both of us if I just don't come, then neither of us has to feel uncomfortable. It's your wedding, you should enjoy it, and I know I won't. I hope it goes well."

With that she left him, dodging around a group of lads who now blocked the path to the pool table. She was still floating in that pool of tranquillity as she squeezed Morgan's shoulder and bent to kneel next to her chair.

"Where's your dad going?" Morgan turned to watch him push through the double doors. "Is he meeting us at your house?"

"No, but I'll explain later." When the familiar touch of soft palms ran over her face, she smiled. "Thanks for coming today. Was I any good?"

"You were extraordinary." Morgan dabbed Adie's lips. "Sensational." Punctuated by another kiss. "Magnificent." This time she lingered a few inches from Adie's mouth. "But you still smell."

Monica and Liz left after one drink, but Morgan was encouraging Adie to hang around and get to know her new teammates better while she thrashed Josh at pool. For more than an hour, Adie sat and joked as if her dad had never been there. It was like it'd been locked in a vault somewhere, safely stored so she could return to it later, when she wasn't surrounded by people who wouldn't understand the enormity of her words.

It was only when Josh skulked over, clearly having been annihilated successively, that she figured they should make a move. He was spending his first night in the annex and planned to drive straight there, and Morgan had promised a bath. That would not usually have been particularly enticing, but there was always a chance she'd jump in too.

Adie wrapped her arms tight around Josh and felt him squirm. "You poor guy. Did she thrash you?"

"Yes, and now you're getting my favourite sweater all dirty. I hate you both."

She laughed and released him. "Good luck tonight. Remember, when you wake up in the morning and your mum isn't there to make you a cup of tea, you just fill that kettle thing in the kitchen with a bit of water." Ducking because he'd swiped at her, she tried her luck with Morgan instead. Cuddling in from behind as she neatly arranged the pool balls on the table, Adie hoped she'd got away with a stinky hug. "Are you ready to go?"

Morgan raised a hand to Adie's cheek and twisted for a quick kiss. "Yes, but don't think I've forgotten you're disgusting. Is the roof still down on the car? If not, it should be."

"Then it will be. We can have that bath when we get back, then I'll cook you something nice. Are you staying tonight?" she asked with a hint of pleading. If Morgan had an early start she might stay in her new room at Jenny's, but this was one time when Adie didn't want to be alone.

"I see. *We're* having a bath, are we? I'm staying with Tim all week and I planned to head down tonight, but I could be up for that first." When Adie's grip tightened, she twisted for another kiss but found herself in a constrictive bear hug.

"Hey, are you okay? Tell me what's going through your head."

There was nothing much going through her head, which was still blank and tranquil, but there was a definite emotional response which meant she wanted Morgan as close as possible. She loosened off and kissed Morgan's temple. "I'll explain in the car."

They said goodbye to everyone, then Adie filled in Morgan on her conversation with Robert as they drove the ten minutes back to her house. It didn't take long since not much had been said, but the further the story progressed, the firmer Morgan's hand squeezed Adie's leg.

"So, what does this mean? Are you not going to see your dad for the moment? At all?"

Adie shrugged. "I don't know, I hadn't thought that far. It's weird but I've had this overwhelming sense of calm since I sat down with him." She was trying to find the words to explain and switched off the stereo in the hope it'd help. "You know how sometimes you worry about going to the dentist and you're sat in the waiting room feeling nervous as hell, but then they call you in and check your teeth or get out the drill and you just go to this otherworldly place? Then when you come out you can't remember."

"Sort of. That's probably how I was on the plane. I just held your hand, closed my eyes, and went somewhere else for two hours."

They turned onto Adie's street and she was about to make a quip about how Morgan was probably fantasising about her underwear, but then she spotted Robert's car on the verge. She pulled up and unclicked her seatbelt, the calm shattering. "Shit. I wonder what he wants?"

Morgan frowned. "What who wants?"

"That's my dad's car." She pointed to the silver Porsche,

realising Morgan wouldn't have a clue what he drove. When they reached the front door there were raised voices, and Adie's heart thumped in her chest. Prizing it open and inching into the hallway, she slipped off her trainers and peered around the living room door. "What's going on?"

Monica and Robert had both stopped dead, one on each side of the room with their arms folded, and she was the first to speak again. "Nothing, and your father is just leaving."

"Like hell I am. Not until you tell me what you've said to poison my daughter against me." His face was red with anger, but the slight tremble of his lip had returned him to that little boy from the café.

"That was all your own doing, I can assure you. How I raised such a narrow-minded bigot of a son I'll never know."

She went to say something else, but he got there first, his voice lifting at least an octave. "Raised me? That's a joke. Palming me off on just about anyone else you could to make your own life easier is more like it, and I'm not a bigot. I'd just like a bit more for Adie than I ever had for myself."

"And what exactly does that look like? A miserable, closeted existence pretending to be someone she's not for everyone else's benefit? Open your eyes, Robert. That's not more of a life, it's significantly less." This time when he tried to talk over her, she held up her index finger and only became louder. "And I don't purport to be a perfect parent, far from it, but I gave you the best life I could in the circumstances. Have you any idea how difficult it was in the sixties to be eighteen, single, and pregnant? I did everything I could to keep us together, and I've always considered myself extremely lucky that my parents were such forgiving people. They loved you dearly, my boy. Don't you ever take that for granted."

He fixed her with an intent stare, his features set and sure. "I don't. Someone had to love me because you sure as hell didn't. I was just a millstone around your neck. The same as every other man who's tried to get close to you."

The resultant silence was heavier than any of their words, and Adie shuffled with discomfort, her hand rubbing circles on Morgan's lower back. She needed to clear it, somehow, but had no idea what to say. In the end, she just turned and walked up the stairs. This wasn't her battle, and Liz's warning to stay out of it sounded at the back of her mind. She knew there was more to the story, from the conversations she'd had with her gran, but there was always a point Monica wouldn't go past. Even if she did, it wouldn't alter anything for Adie.

She went straight through to the bathroom and turned on the shower, stepping under the jet and rinsing away the worst of the dirt. Then she put in the plug and turned on the taps, stealing some of her gran's luxury bubble bath from the shelf and pouring in a liberal glug. Stood naked in the middle of the tub, the water pouring in around her ankles, she let out a deep breath. "I am so over this. Honestly, I'm done. Mum was right, they need to work out their issues, but it doesn't change anything for me."

Morgan had shut the door and was sat on the toilet lid, pulling down her socks. "Hate to say it, but I agree." She stood and unbuttoned her jeans, then stood with them around her ankles. "Your dad is obviously very hurt, but it doesn't mean he can hurt you in return."

Adie reached over the side of the tub to tug away the sweater and T-shirt. "I know. I'd love to rebuild a relationship with him, but right now I need to focus on rebuilding my own life."

She strained to unfasten Morgan's bra and chucked it at

the radiator. Now fully disrobed, Morgan stepped into the bath and sat back so Adie could nestle in front of her. She swirled her fingers in the water, letting out a low humming noise until Adie twisted and frowned. "Sorry, I'm just creating the illusion of a whirlpool. Don't you wish you'd spent the extra?" Pressing her thumbs into Adie's neck and her lips to an ear, she let out a brief laugh. "We're good, though, aren't we? Even if you're not where you want to be with your family. You don't regret any of this?"

Finally, a question she could answer without hesitation.

26

When they'd emerged from the bathroom Robert was gone. There had been no more raised voices, but he and Monica had continued to talk. Quite what that meant Adie hadn't been able to ascertain because her gran was being uncharacteristically cagey, but she was at pains to say she'd promised to make more of an effort with Sarah. As for the rest, there wasn't enough surplus energy to ask. Adie had struggled to lift her head all week, shattered from the football game and everything that'd ensued after, and had spent almost every evening on the sofa. Even Liz had been cancelled because she didn't feel up to it.

"Are you planning on doing anything tonight?" Monica had on her shoes already, preparing to leave for dinner with a friend, and was tramping across the living room in them.

Adie wafted her towards the entrance hall with one flailing hand. The other was on the remote as she sprawled across a sofa, flicking through Thursday evening soaps. "Get off my new carpet." She grumbled when her gran continued to block the television, raising herself up slightly to peer around. "Haven't you got somewhere to be?" And the sooner

she could be there, the better. She'd been a constant annoyance all week, fussing over making meals or doing the
chores as if Adie were gravely ill, and the only break from it
had been going to work.

"Are you sure you won't come? Dinner is on me."

"No, I'm alright here."

Monica relented and held up her hands, making a move
for the door, and Adie shuffled back into a comfier groove.
Morgan had shown concern about how much running and
drinking she was doing, so why then did everyone seem
more worried now? Spending a few evenings relaxing on the
sofa was perfectly normal for half the British population.

She pulled the blanket over herself and rolled onto her
side, dropping the remote onto the carpet. It was a long time
since she'd really allowed herself to vegetate like this,
watching EastEnders and powering through mugs of tea,
while slipping in and out of sleep. Truth was, though, there
wasn't the energy for anything else, and she wasn't sure she
could run even if she tried. It'd been enough to get out to
work, which wasn't usually a struggle, but every muscle felt
weary and heavy. Perhaps they really had been over trained.

She'd just drifted off again when a loud knock jolted her
upright. Fumbling for her phone on the floor, she felt a
sudden pang of fear that it might be her dad spoiling for
another argument. It quickly dissipated at the flash of
auburn hair in the window.

"Morgan?" she muttered, ripping away the blanket and
half tripping as she tried to extricate herself. Bleary eyed,
she humped open the door.

"Surprise," was delivered with a lot less enthusiasm than
you might expect. Morgan was frowning, her hands stuffed
into the pockets of her leather jacket. "Miss me?"

Adie stepped aside to let her in. "Of course I've missed

you, but what are you doing here?" And why did it look like she was here to deliver bad news? "Is everything okay? This looks serious." So serious that it was causing a surge of tears and a tingling feeling in the fingers.

"Your gran called me, she said you weren't doing very well. I was a bit worried you'd be angry, but she only rang because she cares, so don't take it out on her."

"You drove all the way back here for that? I thought you were staying at Tim's and we weren't seeing each other until Saturday?"

Morgan shrugged, then took off the jacket and hooked it over a peg. "Yeah. You can tell me what's going on, but first." She held out her arms and Adie fell into them, not even caring how cold the hands were, pressing into her back. "Hello."

"This cuddle is great, although I can't help feeling it's a long way to travel for one if you've got to be up early for work in the morning. Traffic will be a nightmare unless you leave at the crack of dawn." The hand was still freezing as it slipped into her own, and she rubbed her other over the top of it to generate some heat.

"I'm taking a day off." Morgan slipped off her trainers and kicked them at the shoe rack, then her clothes quickly followed. "These are dirty," she clarified, bundling them into a pile at the foot of the stairs. She pulled Adie into the living room and surveyed the scene. "This looks comfy, are we getting in?" Without waiting for an answer, she climbed under the blanket and patted the space beside her.

Adie only stood with her hands on her hips, peering down at her nearly naked girlfriend and questioning her sanity as she asked the next question. "Are you sure you should be here?"

Morgan shuffled onto her side and patted the cushion

again. "Yes. We didn't have much on tomorrow and I want to
be with you. Now get on this sofa because I'm spoon-less."

"I'm so sorry, Gran shouldn't have asked you to do that."
Another wave of exhaustion crashed over her and she
couldn't do anything but submit to crawling under the
cover.

"No, you're right. You should have."

Adie peered over her shoulder, eyes wide, then rolled so
they were facing. "Excuse me?"

"Why didn't you tell me you were feeling so shit? When I
left you on Sunday, you were doing okay."

"I am okay."

"Oh, yes. Obviously. That's why you're hiding out on the
sofa in your pyjamas when you'd usually be up and about?
That's why you look like someone's died and can barely
keep your eyes open with exhaustion?"

There was no good way to answer that without lying, so
Adie only kept quiet and closed her eyes again. They were
heavy and sore as she pressed against Morgan's chest, wriggling forward and holding her tight. It didn't matter how
she'd ended up here, the scent of her T-shirt and the protec-
tion of her arms as she stroked across the top of Adie's head
was sending her to sleep.

"I'm just glad you're here," Adie mumbled. When the
side of a finger caressed her cheek, she smiled and tilted her
head enough to kiss Morgan's chin.

"Of course I'm here. I love you and I would've taken a
week off if I needed to."

Adie's stomach clenched and she buried her face in
Morgan's shoulder, taking a deep breath and trying to ride
out whatever emotion had just been unleashed. Her eyes
were suddenly swollen with tears again, which seeped into
the fabric and stung the skin on Adie's face, all the more

sensitive with a few days' worth of sleep deprivation. She exhaled slowly, her mouth now glued together with strands of crackling saliva.

What she wanted to say was that she loved Morgan too, because she felt it. Right now, though, the urge was being overtaken with a far stronger sense of foreboding. The word 'but' repeated in her mind like a taunt, echoing around a cavernous space. *I love you, but I don't like this. I love you, but I can't understand why. I love you, but I'd rather not know.*

The arms wound tighter and held her close, stroking reassuring circles on her back. She knew there was no 'but' coming from Morgan, which somehow made it all the harder. How did you deal with someone who wanted to love you without compromise or concession? The level of openness required felt almost too dangerous, and the desire to confirm turned into an urge to get up and run. Fighting against it was like going against the tide in a kayak, knowing that to get to the best bit of beach would take an extra effort.

Gentle kisses peppered her forehead and she willed her shoulders to relax, slumping deeper into the sofa cushion. She wrapped her legs around Morgan's as an anchor and tried to find the words to express what had just gone through her head. If she could let her have a glimmer, it would be a start.

"I just wish there wasn't always a but."

"I know."

Did she, though? Had any of her family ever asked her to just try and be a different person, because it would make their own lives a lot easier? Adie squirmed with discomfort at her own rising anger, knowing it was misdirected, and went in for another shot of honesty. "I can't work out how to feel better about this. I woke up on Monday morning feeling like I'd done ten rounds with Nicola Adams and it won't go away."

"Not sure there's a magic fix; sometimes to feel the high happy you have to also feel the low sad. Not to mention everything in between. Give it time." That was an unwelcome prospect, and suddenly the idea of running or drinking didn't seem so bad. It still felt as though her body had mounted a protest to stop her doing either, though. "If you're desperate to get off the sofa, weren't you supposed to be at a football training session tonight? There's still time if you want to go."

Adie craned to glance at the clock. It didn't start for another half an hour, but she was struggling to find any enthusiasm. "I'm not really in the mood tonight, but I said I'd play again on Sunday, so I'll stick to that. I promise I'm not actually marrying the sofa."

"Good job really, because I think I got in first." Morgan turned the ring on her finger, then held it against Adie's chin.

"I think it's partly exhaustion from years of carrying ten tonnes of shit. My body and mind are just resting for a bit."

"It's probably got something to do with why you feel this way, but don't discount being sad. You love your dad and standing up to him will have been tough."

"Yeah, I know." Adie smiled and traced the features of Morgan's face, then dabbed a kiss on her nose. It was still cold, and Morgan shivered, wrapping the blanket tighter around herself before wiping away the stray tears with the side of a finger. "I love you as well, though, and I won't deny that for anyone."

She stopped, her palm coming to rest on Adie's cheek. "You don't have to say it, you know, just because I did."

"I promise I wouldn't ever do that. It's probably way too soon but it's the truth." A little shrug, and they both smiled.

"We'll work on our own timescale. You can be with someone for months—years even—and not feel it. Or you can spend three months getting to know a person and find it slips out like the most natural thing in the world."

"Very profound, did you read that in a greetings card?" Adie laughed as Morgan tickled her sides, the blanket becoming tangled as she wriggled and squealed.

"You still need to be very careful what you say."

She pinned Adie to the sofa, straddling her hips, and gripped her hands to hold them either side of her head. They were both breathing hard, and she blew a chunk of hair off her face, then sunk forward and parted Adie's lips. Soft tongues massaged together, and Adie moaned against Morgan's mouth. Morgan pulled away slightly and released her grip, but whatever she was about to say was forgotten as Adie's arms wound around her back and pulled her closer.

They kissed again, and this time when Morgan moved it was to tug off Adie's pyjama bottoms, then her own under-wear, while Adie sat and wriggled to remove her T-shirt. As Adie sunk back into the sofa cushion, Morgan's left arm slid under her lower back, her right hand coming to rest on the inside of a thigh. She trailed her fingers there, leaning on her side and taking a nipple into her mouth.

Adie parted her legs, an overwhelming surge of arousal lighting up her weary body. She threw back her head as Morgan's fingertip rubbed her swelling clit. "I need you inside me. Please."

Morgan shuffled down slightly and circled Adie's open-ing, an involuntary buck of her hips causing her fingers to slip away before pressing inside. As they curled and twisted, Adie writhed, reaching to trace the curve of Morgan's breast and over a hardened nipple. Every thrust made her grunt with pleasure, and when Morgan's thumb splayed, she rolled into it, letting out an anguished cry mixed with a laugh.

The orgasm overtook her as quickly as the initial urge and flooded her body with warmth, then another wave of exhaustion which melted her limbs to the sofa. Morgan's fingers remained inside, and Adie felt pangs of pleasure as she pulsed around them, trying to relax her muscles and let it wash over her.

"That was unexpected," Morgan whispered, as she slowly withdrew. Adie twisted to release her trapped arm and then rolled over to let her cuddle in behind. "Feel any better now?"

"Put it this way, I don't feel any worse."

"Okay, well I've had better feedback, but I'll take it." Morgan laughed and kissed Adie's shoulder. "We should probably put on some clothes or go to bed. Not sure Monica needs to walk in on us like this later."

Adie grumbled, back to wondering whether letting her gran stay in the spare room so frequently was a good idea. She was never usually in it for this long, and it was starting to feel like her permanent home. There was another trip to Canada planned for after the wedding and perhaps when she got back, she could make other arrangements. "I might ask her to stay with mum next time, she's cramping my style for once instead of the other way around. One day, in the very distant future, I'd like us to have the option of living together without a rampant pensioner bringing home random men."

"Living together, huh? For someone who spent four years doing everything they could to avoid a relationship, you're certainly jumping in with both feet."

Was that a bad thing? Adie rolled over, the renewed colour draining from her face. "Yeah, I am all in. I thought you knew that?"

"Relax," Morgan soothed, her eyes crinkling as she smiled. "I'm only teasing you. It's a relief. I was always a bit worried you might go the other way and hold back. When I came over tonight, I panicked that you'd push me away."

"But I didn't?"

"No. You didn't."

27

A few weeks later Adie shoved through the doors of The Anchor, groaning to see the karaoke machine was already being put to use. Unfortunately, it was by a couple of tone-deaf teenagers. Morgan grabbed hold of her jacket before she could flee and flagged down a bartender to order them both a drink. She'd need it if this was their entertainment for the evening. Robert's wedding reception was starting to look like the better option, which was saying something.

They'd decided to head out rather than sit at home, stopping for pizza at the nice Italian on the corner before settling into the pub, given the weather was miserable. It was almost eight now and dark outside, rain lashing against the window. Adie rubbed her hands together to warm them and then reached under Morgan's sweater, laughing as she jumped and swiped them away.

"Get off me with those things."

"Careful, or I'll send you home to your mother."

Morgan turned to point. "This is a tough day for you so I'm letting a lot slide, but just wait until tomorrow. I will not make you breakfast."

"Is that really the best threat you can come up with?"

She smirked now, pausing to create some drama. "Might change my mind about your Christmas present." There was a little shrug as she paid and picked up her pint glass. "Think very carefully before you say anything else."

What was there to consider? Christmas was well over a month away, and a pair of socks wasn't much to worry about. "There's still a chance you will have dumped me by the end of December."

"True." Morgan reached into her coat pocket and pulled out her phone, flicking across the screen. "It's a shame, because I had hoped we'd be spending New Year's Eve on the beach."

"You haven't had enough of Spain?"

"California, but if you're not interested..." She shrugged and held up the screen to show a picture of the coastline, then began a slow wander to a booth.

Adie was rooted to the spot, slack jawed. She'd never been to America before, or anywhere outside of Europe. "Are you kidding me?"

"No, I'm deadly serious. I'm happy to find someone else, though, it shouldn't be a problem." She took off her coat and threw it into the booth, then turned and folded her arms. "What about Josh?"

"Don't you dare!" There was no point trying to hide her excitement. Adie lifted her arms, spilling lager all over her wrist and causing half the sad lot of punters to look around. For a Saturday night it was dead, which was either the shit singing or the fact it was nearly pay day. None of it bothered her right now if they were going to California.

Morgan tried to keep a straight face, but the glint in her eye gave her away. "I don't know, it's a long way to travel with someone who isn't into it."

"It's a long way to travel without kisses and cuddles."
Adie set down her drink and ran the flat of her tongue
around her hand, then removed her jacket and threw it on
top of Morgan's. "Not to mention all the other perks of
having me with you." She wrapped her arms low around
Morgan's waist and enthusiastically kissed her neck,
pushing her against the table so that she almost fell back,
giggling and making vague protests. "If this is your way of
cheering me up, by the way, it's worked."

Morgan straightened out her top and perched on the
edge of the table, slotting her hands in the back pockets of
Adie's jeans to draw her forward. "Not exactly, and I've
misled you a bit. It's my dad's sixtieth in January and he
wants to fly everyone out to visit my grandad, so technically
this isn't a present from me. Have I put you off yet?"

Was she kidding? After worrying he'd hate her, this was
a sure sign that wasn't the case. No matter how loaded you
were, you didn't fly your daughter's girlfriend to another
continent for your birthday without implying one hundred
percent approval. "Not even a tiny amount. Thank you. I can
make my gran and Josh legitimately jealous."

"Glad to be of service." Morgan leant forward and kissed
Adie's nose. "Now, tell me how you're doing."

"Great." How else could you feel when your girlfriend
had just sprung a surprise trip to California for New Year?
And besides all the other reasons it was such good news, it
also meant Morgan got to see her grandad. The woman Adie
had met in the summer wouldn't have got on a plane for
twelve hours, and she'd come a long way. "I'm proud of you.
Do you know that?"

"I'm kind of proud of me too. This feels good. I'm appre-
hensive, and you may have to hold my hand, but I'm quietly
confident." When was she ever quietly anything? She'd

vocalised every thought that'd crossed her mind since they met, and there was a risk she was about to do it again. "There's still time to head to your dad's reception for a bit, are you sure you don't want to go?"

Adie buried her head in Morgan's neck, inhaling deeply of the comforting scent. She did want to go. There was always a part of her that'd want to return to that old position. The one where she placated, hiding in return for acceptance. Wanting something and knowing it wasn't right, though, were two different things. If she capitulated now, he'd see it as an admission of wrongdoing. An apology, or a concession. "No, I'm not going."

"Okay, just checking." Morgan placed a hand on Adie's stomach and pushed her back towards the bar, picking up a folder covered in red plastic. "So, what are we singing?"

Adie leant in to whisper against Morgan's ear. "I love you."

"Who's that by?" She managed to keep her poker face for an impressively long time before her mouth twitched into a little smile. "How about some Janis Joplin?"

"How about no, I'm still not singing with you."

* * *

An hour later the pub had begun to fill, and Adie was getting into the spirit of the night. The karaoke didn't improve, but with another pint the shrill edges were knocked off, and she'd found herself joining in on more than one occasion. They'd also taken a virtual tour on Google Maps of the area where Morgan's cousins lived, and decided how to spend their week, when Monica came through the door and shook out a large golfing umbrella.

"Lord, find me a gin and tonic." She propped it by the

bar and ordered a round of drinks, then carried them to the table. "I hope you don't mind me joining you. I presume this is the official wedding reception refuge."

Adie laughed and lifted another pint from the tray. "No fun?" The widened eyes and slight shake of the head was enough response. "They didn't mind you leaving?"

"I had to; it was becoming a little uncomfortable. People kept asking where you were, and I didn't like to lie, so in the end it was best to just step away. I've no idea what he was saying, presumably not the truth." She seemed to catch some indication of the empathy, or sorrow, or something which had just risen in Adie. It was difficult to know quite what it was, but it caused her palms to sweat slightly. Monica rubbed the back of her hand. "For what it's worth, I had a little chat with Sarah."

"You spoke to Sarah?" Adie struggled to hide her incredulity.

"Surprised me too, but I said I'd make the effort and I'm sticking to that. Seems she had a word with Robert before the wedding and tried to make him see sense, but he's adamant he was happy for you both to be there and it's enough. I suppose it's some consolation that at least she can see your point of view. Perhaps he'll start to understand."

The thought caused a lava flow of anger, and Adie took a deep breath to cool it. She didn't want him to change his mind just because it might piss off his new wife. "What, so if Sarah thinks he's in the wrong he might do something about it? I'd love to see how he dealt with Jenny tonight, trying to explain why I'm not there in front of her." Everyone from work was invited, and he'd be desperate to present the right image. She knew exactly what was going on, and was bound to call bullshit on any lies, if that was the route he was taking.

"Wouldn't have had the chance, she didn't show."

Morgan leant forward and took a sip from her pint, her other hand firmly wrapped around Adie's leg. "Really? I saw her earlier and she was getting all dressed up for something."

"Well, it wasn't the reception." She clinked their glasses together. "Sounds like a show of solidarity."

"I don't need a show of solidarity." Adie rubbed a hand into her face. This wasn't what she'd intended at all, having everyone boycott the wedding. Now she was just as likely to get an earful for decimating his guest list.

"You don't know that's why she changed her mind. She may just have had a better offer. It wouldn't be particularly difficult."

"Even so..." It would look that way, and some sort of 'us against you' mentality would only create more of a divide. She didn't want a big gaping rift, that wasn't the point at all.

"Let it go." Monica's tone was soft. Pleading, almost, but gentle. She held onto Adie's hand on the table. "Let people support you. Let them be angry on your behalf if that's what they are. But most of all, let go of this notion that you can fix the situation if you bend enough. Some things are just out of your control. I learnt that a long time ago."

"But what if this is it?" Forever and always. Cards at Christmas if you were lucky. And what if Sarah did manage to have a baby? Would they see each other?

Monica shrugged. "Then you'll grieve, but life will go on. It always does. All we can do is live it, to the best and fullest of our ability."

"Sounds like a load of hippy bullshit to me, but if you say so."

Morgan let out a burst of laughter. "Says she who earlier

this evening was dancing around the room with happiness. Remind me the last time you did that?"

"Beach in Spain."

"Right, and before that?"

"This is a trap."

Both Monica and Morgan laughed this time. It felt awkward. Was she the only one in the room who didn't know what it felt like to be happy? Repeatedly happy? Happy to the point of dancing around a pub, without worrying who was looking? Perhaps happy wasn't even the right word because Morgan was right, you couldn't expect to be deliriously happy all the time. Free, unguarded, and honest. That was closer to the truth of it.

Morgan seemed to catch Adie's face drop and squeezed tighter around her leg. She leant in, kissing Adie's cheek and tousling the hair that'd shaken free of her bun. "Are you okay?"

"Just thinking." She was distracted, hearing something familiar. "Dangerous, I know, but occasionally I have a spark of inspiration." Peering around the side of the booth, she caught sight of Jenny and Liz up on the stage a few bars into 'Islands In The Stream' and shook her head. They really were in a parallel universe. "I should do more things I genuinely enjoy. I need to figure out what they are."

There was another ripple of laughter. "Um, yes. Have I not been telling you this for months?"

"I was listening, that's why I joined the football team, I'm just not sure I really understood. I don't know how to explain. I honestly thought everyone else was like me: apathetic most of the time but that's life. You get by, try to find ways to make it less of a shit shoot." There was a pause as she shrugged, trying to work out where this was going, but she was still distracted by Jenny's warbling. Morgan certainly didn't get her singing ability from that side of the family. "Help other people where you can, try to make it less of a shit shoot for them." The end destination was no clearer, but perhaps that was the point. "I don't know, I guess I had this vague notion that kept me going, where I might meet someone who I liked enough to spend the next thirty years of my life arguing with Dad. I never expected much of an upturn in things, though."

It seemed ludicrous now, but there it was.

"How much have you had to drink?" Morgan peered into the pint glass in front of them and squinted, but then smiled and squeezed Adie's chin, looking her dead in the eye. "Please tell me there's a happy ending to this story."

"God, I hope so."

On the outside, things weren't perfect. Morgan would be living back in London in a couple of weeks, Robert would remain in his current somewhat unresolved state indefinitely, and Adie had no clue what the New Year would bring besides a trip to California. Then of course Jenny was trying to hit a high note.

It wasn't a traditional happy ending, but perhaps it was a happy ending in every way that counted.

ACKNOWLEDGMENTS

Thank you to Kat Jackson for her stellar proofreading and for the number of times she simply commented "what in the world is that?!" (custard creams, coconut shy, tombola). After my first novel I will never again utter the words "of course I can proofread this myself..."

Thank you to Finlay Games for his consultation on the character of Josh. You can find out more about Finn at www.finlaygames.com

To Susan Fleming and Angie Craven for their beta reading skills. Susan in particular pulls me apart on every dumb-ass idea, and also stops me throwing my computer out the window when I'm frustrated and making no progress.

Finally to Spring Wise for the wonderful cover illustration. You can find more of Spring's artwork at www.facebook.com/springwiseart